THE
GONE
BOOK

HELENA CLOSE

THE GONE BOOK

Little Island

THE GONE BOOK

First published in 2020 by
Little Island Books
7 Kenilworth Park
Dublin 6w
Ireland

A British Library Cataloguing in Publication record for
this book is available from the British Library.

Cover illustration by Holly Pereira
Cover design by James Tuomey
Typeset by Tetragon, London
Copy edited by Emma Dunne
Proofread by Catherine Ann Cullen
Printed in Poland by Drukarnia Skleniarz

Print ISBN: 978-1-912417-44-5
Ebook (Kindle) ISBN: 978-1-912417-60-5
Ebook (other platforms) ISBN: 978-1-912417-61-2

Little Island has received funding to support this book from
the Arts Council of Ireland / An Chomhairle Ealaíon.

1

Dutch Gold tastes like piss. Especially when it's warm. It doesn't bother Mikey, though. He's slugged back four and is reaching for the last one. He grins at me, eyes disappearing in his fat head.

'Would you jump it?' he says, punching my arm.

'You're langers,' I say, flicking my can into the quarry below. I can hear it bouncing off the rocks.

Mikey pops the can. He's staring at Death Leap, a split in the bank with a sheer drop down. Lads jump it all the time, bellies full of beer and girls watching. Gowls.

'We should have left them where we found them,' I say.

'Bit late now, Matt. And anyway, if somebody's going to stash their cans in the quarry, they should do it right. Fuck sake – they were waiting to be robbed, like.'

The sun's lasering us, making sweat patterns on our T-shirts. I'm lying on the springy grass, using my skateboard as a pillow. A hard pillow. Mikey's still fixed on Death Leap.

'Did I tell you the one about –?'

'Fuck off,' I say, before he can launch into some stupid joke he just learned. Mikey fancies himself as a stand up comedian. 'Let's go – your mam said six o'clock.'

Mikey takes out a nobber and lights up. He blows the smoke in rings, a new trick. He's going nowhere.

'Come on, I'm starving,' I say. I get up and flip my board into my hands. I spin the wheels, brand new, just broken in. Mikey finishes his fag butt and flicks it into the quarry. He takes a huge slug from the can, crushes it and whacks it in after the fag. He lies back on the grass and closes his eyes. Bastard. He's snoring, or pretending to. I poke him with my board. He's a dead weight. I grab him by his sweat-wet T-shirt and shake the shit out of him. 'Get up, gowl.'

He opens his eyes, pushes me with a giant paw and I'm down on the grass again.

'Race ya,' he says and he's up and taking a run at Death Leap before I know what's happening. He's lumbering towards it, trying to gather speed and I don't want to look but I'm glued and fuck he's going to kill himself, he's going to die. He flips himself across the split and Mikey, big lumpy Mikey's floating over the quarry and he thumps onto the ridge at the other side. I'm screaming but I can't hear screams. I can't hear anything. All the summer sounds are gone – birds, dogs, children. I've dropped my board and it's rolling towards Death Leap following Mikey and that's what moves me, the stupid board. I grab it and run, circling Death Leap, the long way around.

He's dead. I'm sure of it. He's sprawled face down on the rocky ridge. I try to pull him towards me but maybe I shouldn't move him at all. I'm terrified he'll edge over so I put my arms under his armpits and haul him the few inches to safety. I try to turn him over onto his back and I'm thinking all the time I'm killing him more and I can't remember what you're supposed to do to check if someone's dead or alive. Pulse. That's it. I check his pulse but I might as well be combing his hair for all I know about pulse. There's blood on his forehead where he whacked a rock as he landed. It's coming from a deep cut in his head. I can see the blood spurting.

'Mikey, wake up. Fuck you, wake up, man. Why do you always have to be a gowl, you gowl?'

He's dead. The stupid mad bastard's dead and somehow it's my fault. Mrs Chung'll kill me and Mikey'll still be dead.

I hug him and I kiss him on the cheek and I'm swallowing a giant rock in my throat. Fuck. I have to get help. I take out my phone but it's dead too. I grab my board and run towards Mikey's house, skating once I hit the tarmac.

Mikey's house is unique. It's in a row of terraced houses. Right in the middle. It's beautiful. The garden is full of roses. Mikey's mam loves roses and sometimes when you pretend out of being polite that you like them she'll capture you and tell you the names of every single one of them.

Dainty Bess, Sexy Rexy, Knockout. And there's a fancy porch and these new white windows. Nobody else on the terrace has them. But that could be because nobody else has any windows at all. The other houses on each side are boarded up, some of them blackened where they've been burned out. So Mikey's house really stands out. We used to live beside them but Dad wanted to move and the Regeneration people put us in an apartment in town. Mikey's mam won't live in town. She's really fussy about where she lives. Here I am outside Mikey's house while he's dead, thinking about roses and houses. Mrs Chung's car's in the drive, all shiny and clean. There's a lone football in the garden, belonging to Mikey's two little brothers. The United Colours of Benetton. That's what his mam calls the boys. I'm telling myself to go in and I force my legs to move and I'm halfway up the path when I see him, the fucker, running across the green.

'Fooled ya, Matt,' he says. 'That was the best laugh. I wished I could've seen your face but I was "dead", like.'

He's in front of me now, blood drying on his forehead, big grin on his dumb face, sweat pumping from him. I want to thump him right into his split head. I push past him and jump on my board.

'Where are you going? What about the lasagne?' he says.

'Fuck the lasagne,' I say and skate down the path and head for home.

Dad. Bastard. I haven't been out since the quarry. I got landed minding Conor while Dad did an Ironman in Kerry. Three whole days locked up here.

Our apartment has a view of the river. Dad says you'd pay through the nose if it was in New York with a view of the Hudson. But it's in Limerick with a view of the Shannon so that's that. We're here eighteen months. Me, Dad, my older brother, Jamie, and my kid brother, Conor. We moved in the Christmas before last, when I was as fat as Mikey and Jamie was sound. He bought me a skateboard and I laughed out loud. Did you ever see a fat skateboarder? But out of boredom I started to go to the skate park by the quay and watch the skaters. And then on New Year's Day I brought my board and it changed me. It really did. The fat melted and I made all these friends and now I'm, like, one of the best skaters in Limerick. And that's how I met Anna. She's the same age as me, fifteen. And she's Polish. Well, she's not really, because she doesn't want to be. She wants to be Irish so she talks in this Limerick accent. She's a good skater. Good, but not great like me. They still call me Fat Matt.

But another thing happened when the fat melted. I started to look like a girl. I swear. Prettier than any fuck-ing girl I know. But the skaters didn't care. So I grew my hair longer and now I even tie it up in a ponytail, especially when I'm skating. Fuck them all, including Dad. He has a thing about ponytails on fellas. And man buns.

So that's what I'm doing now. Putting my hair up in a ponytail. I'm still awkward at doing it. Girls can do it and

11

you don't even notice. It's like breathing to them. But I have to stand in front of the mirror and fiddle with it for ages. The hard bit is trying to hold all the hair together while putting on the go-go. That's tough. But it's done now and I admire my work. Jesus I'm very fucking pretty all right. I wink at myself and go look for my skateboard.

The apartment is dead quiet. Jamie's out as usual and Dad is at the pool with Conor. Dad is determined that one of his children will be an athlete. Jamie was the star until he turned into a horrible person. I was too fat so poor Conor is the chosen one now. The fat was handy for that kind of thing. For not getting noticed by Dad. He's obsessed with his 'training'. You'd swear he was getting paid for it – like a real job or something. Jamie says it's because he was fired from the army but I don't see the connection. I blame it on AA. The Twelve Steps. I know them better than nursery rhymes. And the stupid prayer. This silence in the apartment sometimes makes me want to scream.

2

Anna's waiting for me at the skate park. She's wearing her new Vans and a baseball cap. If I look like a girl, then she looks like a boy. She sees me coming and does an ollie off the high ramp. Show-off.

'Hey.'

'How's it going?'

'Grand.'

A couple of the regular street drinkers have gathered already for their evening session and they laugh at Anna as she tries to wrestle me.

'You show him, love,' says Black, a man you couldn't put an age on, with creases in his face worse than Gordon Ramsay. Black was the first friend I made in the skate park. A cranky drunk but dead sound when he's sober.

He's waving a can of Bavaria in the air. Hal is with him. Beanie hat stolen from one of the skateboarders, denim jacket, even deeper creases in the face. Except Hal is a woman. You wouldn't guess it looking at her. You'd have to know her.

Mikey won't come skating with us even though he knows that's how I lost all the weight. He says we should patent the diet and sell it to his mother's Weight Watchers group in the community centre. Bring all the women skating. Mikey says fat makes you funny and that it'll help his career as a stand up comedian. I haven't seen him since the quarry. Fucker.

But he always shows up for the burgers afterwards. And there he is, the big lump stuffing his face in the window of McDonald's. He gives us a wave, his face covered in mayo.

We order takeaway and eat in Arthur's Quay Park. This used to be a scumbag park but they cut down all the trees and took off the railings, so now it's OK until night. Then the scumbags come out of the woodwork to reclaim it. Like the Living Dead. I wish Mikey'd fuck off home. I'm still mad at him. He knows it too – that's why he hasn't told Anna about how he made a gowl out of me. We sit in silence for a few minutes, watching three kids play hurling. It's still warm but the sun's almost gone and there's a haze over the river that you only see in good weather. I can see the river from my bedroom and I've learned to tell what way the weather is by just looking at it. I lean back on the bench and close my eyes, my feet resting on my skateboard.

'Fuck,' says Mikey. 'It's them.'

I can feel Anna stiffen beside me. I don't move.

'And there's more of them. The cunts are multiplying,' Mikey whispers.

I can hear their voices as they draw near. And then the usual salute.

'Fat Matt Lynch and Chubby Chung. Fucking gay picnic going on here.'

I open my eyes and smile. There's five of them. Three are the usual scum. Our cross to bear, as Mikey calls them. They've stolen our phones, our boards, our shoes once – but they threw them into the river because they weren't Nike. Mikey says they won't stop until they steal our virginity. I hope that's a joke.

'Well, lads, how's it going?' I say.

'Lookin' for your brother, Fat Matt.' A guy of about sixteen stands right in front of me. He's wearing an Adidas tracksuit with the bottoms tucked into his socks. His head is shaved and it has a terrific collection of scars. A tiny diamond twinkles in his ear. Hammer Hayes. Bane of our lives. A guy stands at each side of him – the muscle men, one dumber looking than the other.

'Is that right?' I examine the new people. One is a girl, hair in a tight ponytail dyed a dirty yellow. She's wearing huge hoops in her ears and I'm praying Mikey doesn't make a stupid joke about them. Anna feels tiny beside me, like she's able to shrink herself when danger comes.

'Lookin' for the bastard. He owes me.'

My stomach does a flip then, like when you're almost

to the top of a half pipe and you don't think you'll make it. 'Don't know where he is.'

'He's acting the bollocks lately, d'you know that?'

I shrug. 'Not my problem.'

Hammer kicks the skateboard from under my feet. I can't believe it. Not another skateboard wasted in the Shannon. 'I'll make it your fuckin' problem, Lynch.'

'Lynch?' The girl looks at me, her eyes a turquoise blue. Lovely eyes, except for the too-bright matching blue eye-shadow over them.

I nod, watching Hammer as he flips my beautiful board with his big Nike-clad foot.

'Matt Lynch?'

Another nod from me.

'Do you live in Woodbine Park? Near the railway?'

'Used to.' I'm barely listening. I'm way more interested in what Hammer's going to do to my board.

'You're my cousin.'

Mikey laughs, a loud, deep one, right from the bottom of his belly.

I look at her, stunned. Even Hammer stops the board-flipping, all ears now.

She grins, knowing she has a captive audience. I say nothing but my stomach is somersaulting.

'Your mother is my aunt but we don't talk to her.' She examines my face for a reaction. I want her to shut up but I know she won't. 'Is it true? Is it true she just like walked out years ago and ye never saw her since?'

I shrug but my eyes are watering and my leg keeps jumping and I can't stop it.

Hammer's phone rings and he drops my board. It drifts off like it has a mind of its own, towards the river. It stops at the railing, nose hanging over the water.

'Gotta go,' says Hammer, walking away. His disciples follow him.

The girl turns around as she's walking away. 'She's back, you know. Lives in Park View. Near the college.' She smiles at me as if she's given me something nice. Sweets or a slice of cake. And then she's gone.

The apartment is silent. I take out my book. My Gone Book. I don't want to but I have to. Dad and Conor are in bed. Jamie's out with the Living Dead. His new horrible friends. Up here on the fifth floor, you can barely hear the traffic. I do what I always do when I open the book. I read the very first page. Written in a ten-year-old's shaky barely joined-up writing.

Monday nite on 29 May 2014. The Gone Book.

The day you left I was home from school cos I had a pain in my head and the runs and I herd you and daddy shouting and then everyting went green. Jamie came home from school and he punched the wall over and over and said bitch hoor bitch hoor bitch til his hand was bleeding and dad burnt oven chips and trew them at the wall too. I was crying then but in my bed. I cant remember where conor was cos it was four days ago since you went. Theres alot of washing on the floor in the kitchen. Conor peed into it tonight. I cant believe your gone.

And it goes on like that. Five years of it. All the things she missed. My confirmation. Me getting fat and then thin. Conor winning the swimming galas. Me being a great skateboarder. Jamie being ... well ... being a really cool brother and now being a shit. All of it. Well, not all of it. Sometimes I wouldn't bother. I take out my pen, a Munster Rugby Supporters one that Mikey gave me, and I write in a new page.

Tuesday 30 June 2019

Today I met my cousin that I never knew existed. She told me where you live. I know youll hate me. I just know you will. But I can't help it. I'm going to find you.

3

20 September 2014

Conor wet the bed and Dad slapped him and I cried under the covers. I hate Dad more than Manchester United and Mr Delaney and Burkes dog Bruno. Mrs Chung came with our dinner. Sheperds pie. It was ~~delicos~~ lovely and I ate it all and so did Conor but Jamie said he wanted nuggetts and Dad got mad again and then Dad cried. Jamie nearly found the Gone Book so Ive a new hiding place now.I slip it under the carpet.I hate sharing a room with Jamie. Hes so nosey. My birthday is tomorrow. In one hour and thirty two seconds Ill be eleven. I got a Skullduggery book from Dad. The newest one. I'm sparing it.

Mrs Chung is making chicken casserole for Tony down the road. She says that we're growing up faster than Paul O'Connell and call her Terry because Mrs Chung makes her sound old. Mikey's upstairs doing his stupid hair and

I'm sitting mortified while Mrs Chung pulls meat from a cooked chicken. She has the best smile though. Her face kind of shines when she smiles, just like Mikey. She beams at me now.

'How's your dad keeping? I haven't seen him for a while.' She wipes her hands on a tea towel that says Eat Pray Cook.

'He's grand. Training for the marathon.' I check my phone for messages even though it hasn't beeped. Mrs Chung rolls her eyes.

'Another one? I suppose he could be doing worse. How's Conor? Did he get his braces yet?'

Troy, Mikey's little brother, comes in then, wearing just a T-shirt. Mrs Chung scoops him up into her arms and kisses his fat brown cheek.

'Conor's grand. He's at level five now in swimming. They go every day, sometimes at six in the morning.'

I can hear Mikey upstairs whistling. I wish the fucker would hurry up. It's a long walk to the college and it'll be night before he's ready.

'Jesus, six in the morning. That's early. That's the middle of the night.' She smiles again and the boy laughs up at her and nuzzles her neck. 'Jamie?'

I knew it was coming, the Jamie questions. Fuck Mikey anyway. I shrug. 'He's grand too.'

She nods. 'Did you ask your dad about coming to Lahinch for the week?'

I nod even though it's a lie. The best thing to do with Dad when you're asking for something is to wait until the very last minute and then kind of spring it on him when you catch him after a good run or if Conor won a race. Loads of time yet for that.

Mikey finally appears and I glare at him. Not that the fucker notices.

'What's got twenty faces and three teeth?' he asks, his face creased from smile and fat.

'No idea. So tell us,' I say.

He grins. 'An episode of *Jeremy Kyle*.'

Mrs Chung laughs. I don't. It's not that funny and I've warned him already about those handy one-liners. I mean, he fucked up the Colm's Talent Show in May with those thick gags. There I was, sitting in the audience waiting for Mikey to come on. Sitting through shit. I never knew there were so many piano players in our school and rugby players that wanted to be Ed Sheeran. And all Mikey had to do was what we'd fucking practised. And he came out and delivered these one-liners and nobody laughed and he was booed off the stage still fucking ranting the jokes that everybody knew from Facebook and a contortionist from third year won.

'I was reading in the paper the other day about this dwarf that got pickpocketed. How could anyone stoop so low?' Mikey laughs and his mother joins in and so does Troy.

'Let's go,' I say, grabbing my skateboard from under the table.

'Hang on just one minute, you two,' says Mrs Chung. 'I want you back, Mikey, for seven. I've my Weight Watchers in the community centre.'

Mikey nods and we walk out the door.

We're walking along the Dublin Road. Mikey's sweating even though it's not that warm. I'm carrying my board so he can keep up with me.

'Where's Anna? Thought she was coming.'

I wheel my skateboard onto the ground and do a perfect ollie off the kerb. 'Her mother's sick or something.'

Mikey shakes his head. 'She's always sick. No wonder – she doesn't go outside the door and she looks like a vampire.'

'She goes to Mass like every day.'

'She could be a vampire though – they're from somewhere near Transylvania.'

'They're from Wroclaw, Mikey. It's in Poland and your geography is shit.'

The university is cool. I love skating there, with the trees and the river and the fountains. The buildings seem to grow by the day. Every time I go out there's a new one. We're on the bridge and it's shaking something awful and I'm wondering is Mikey too heavy for it. The river is in high tide and we spit down into it, watching the spit swirl and then disappear.

'So where does your mam live again?' Mikey coughs up a huge gob of spit and aims it towards the river. I like that about Mikey. Not the big spits – the straightness of him. He'll say the stuff out. No matter what it is. Whether you want him to or not.

I shrug. 'Dunno. I just know the name of the estate. Park View.'

'That'll be easy so. We'll find her no problem. Can you remember what she looks like?'

I kick my skateboard and watch as it rolls towards the seat near us. Do I remember what she looks like? I don't know. I don't know what's real and what's a dream and sometimes I find photos of her and she's a stranger, her features not remarkable at all. Like a face in a crowded supermarket. If I saw her I'd know if I remember her.

'Course I do. Let's go.'

But it isn't easy to find her because Park View is massive. I mean massive like a small town. Mikey and I wander up and down cul-de-sacs that all look exactly the same and finally we give up and sit on a kerb. The sun is belting down now, hot on our necks, burning us. My stomach is talking to me I'm so hungry and Mikey has ire between his legs. It's all he can talk about, the fucking ire. I don't know what I expected. A big sign saying *Matt I love you and this is my house*? Sweat drips down my back from my too-tight ponytail. I stand up and flip my board. 'Let's go home. This is stupid.'

The flat smells of burn and when I go into the kitchen, I can barely see Jamie through the smoke. He's standing at the cooker, watching a pot of beans bubble over.

'Jesus, open a window, Jamie, or Dad'll go crazy.'

He doesn't even look up from his burnt-bean stirring. His face is pale, as pale as Anna's mother's and he has cold sores on his lips, like small join-the-dot pimples.

'Hammer Hayes was looking for you the other night.'

Still no response. He slaps two pieces of bread into the toaster.

'Did you know Mam is home?'

Jamie freeze-frames on the spot, his hand hovering over the pot, spoon in mid-air, dripping bean juice onto the sizzling hob. I could kick myself now for opening my big stupid mouth. But sometimes when Jamie is in moron mode, I just want a reaction out of him, any kind of reaction is better than none.

He turns around, his eyes creased in a trademark frown, a Jamie special developed over the last six months.

'I don't have a mother so she couldn't be home. My mother's dead,' he says, holding the spoon out towards me like a weapon. The bean juice is now dripping onto Dad's clean white tiles.

'Believe whatever you want, Jamie,' I say, shrugging my shoulders and walking into the living room. Then suddenly I'm on the floor and he's on top of me like a fucking lunatic.

24

He's sitting on me and trying to choke me and my face is hurting from being rubbed into the carpet. And now he has my head by the ponytail and he's banging it off the floor and he's crying. Jamie's crying.

I smile up at him and this makes him madder and he starts screaming into my face, 'She's only a bitch, a fucking whore is all she is!' and then thank God there's Dad above Jamie pulling him off me, and Conor's little pinched rabbit face, hair still wet from swimming.

'What are you doing? You're like a madman,' Dad shouts as he pushes Jamie up against the wall. I stand up, my legs shaking. I check to see if my ponytail is still attached to me and not lying on the carpet somewhere. My cheek feels like it's on fire. Conor has disappeared into his bedroom.

'I said what's going on? I told you already you're on a last chance. I'm not having any son of mine turning into a scumbag. What's going on here?'

Jamie gives Dad the frown and I'm willing him not to. Dad is fine if you just play along with him and don't confront him all the time.

'Why don't you ask your daughter?' Jamie says in his sneer voice. Dad hates the sneer voice and he really hates me being called a girl.

Dad's hand tightens around Jamie's neck and he's flexing his other hand like he's gearing up for a punch. Then Dad just lets go and Jamie's rubbing his neck and glaring and then he storms out of the room, the air tingling with anger after him. Dad looks at me, all guilty and I want to say to him it's grand – the little shit deserves a punch – it might even sort him out, it might be what he needs.

I need to get out of here.

So we're in the skate park, Anna and me with like the best skater in the world, who's doing aerials and backslides and kickflips right in front of us. We're sitting on the benches watching, totally mesmerised by Smart. That's his name, not actually his state of mind, and he's sponsored and all by Element and he's won everything there is to win and I know one day I could be as good as him if I really work at it. I mean he had a head start didn't he? He had no fat to lose first.

'I love him,' says Anna, never taking her eyes from him.

'That's a bit of an over-reaction, Anna.'

'No it's not. I love him. I want to marry him and have lots of skateboarder babies with him,' she says, eyes still glued to Smart.

'Me too,' I say, laughing.

She gives me a quick grin and then it's back to admiring Smart. It's early morning, my favourite time of day here. The sun is warm and watery and not too hot. The Living Dead are all still asleep in their beds. Well, not exactly beds, in their doorways and skips and hostels, if they're lucky.

It's the best time, early morning, when the day stretches out ahead of you, long and lazy and mysterious. And I love the soundtrack of morning. The rumble of traffic and river and the rhythm of an ace skater.

'Will you come with me today? I feel lucky,' I say, flipping my board up and down with my foot.

'Sure, but I think we're being thick, going out to that giant estate just trying to guess where she lives. We should have a plan, a system or something.'

'What do you mean?'

She pulls her baseball cap down on her head and looks straight at me. Her eyes are dark brown with gold flecks.

'You should find out more information.'

'How? I can't ask my dad – it's like the Unmentionable in our house. Same with Jamie.'

'I was thinking more about that blonde girl – Hammer's groupie – we should find her and ask her for your mother's actual address.'

'Come on. Let's go out there now. We can skate in UL first if you like.'

Anna doesn't hear me. She hears her phone, though, when it rings. She's talking urgently in Polish and I can hear the garbled voice at the other end, high and distressed.

She hangs up and flips her board up into her hand with her foot. 'Gotta go. Mam is sick, very sick according to Dad. I've to go to the stupid hospital.'

She walks away and there's something about her small baseball-capped frame as she picks her way through the park that makes me feel sad. She's like a dog being told to go home.

'Hey, wait up.' I skate after her and crunch to a stop right in front of her. She's crying.

'You OK?'

She shrugs. 'Same old story – you know – hanging around that hospital.'

'I'll come with you'.'

'Seriously?'

I nod. 'No problem.'

The Novaks are both tiny, just like Anna. We wait in A&E, the mother doubled over groaning and the dad spouting high-speed Polish at Anna. A nurse arrives and Anna speaks to her and then translates to her parents. A&E is packed even though it's early morning. There's a whole family at one end, laughing and joking and taking turns going in and out for smokes. I can't make out exactly which one of them is sick. Maybe the dad with the sweaty face and a heart tattoo on his arm. Then there's a boy right across from us in a football strip. His ankle looks bad, kind of wonky and his mother is talking rapidly into her phone, giving someone the low-down on his injury. Another family, Indians or Romanians or something like that, sit cross-legged on the floor, having a picnic. There's rice in plastic cartons and flat bread and something yellow that looks like snot. Smells great, though.

'Go home, Matt. Looks like we'll be here all day,' says Anna when the nurse disappears yet again.

'No, it's grand. This is better than daytime TV.'

And before I have it said a fight breaks out between two guys with the smoking family. They seem drunk and are rolling around the floor in a tangle of arms and legs and Nike trainers. Security arrive and pull them apart. Mrs Novak groans loudly and her husband spouts Polish at her.

It's evening when I get home. The sun is a ball of fire, low on the river, and the air is warm and still. There are a few stragglers in the skate park and Black and Hal are having a drunken fight that involves waving cans of Bavaria in the air and trying to punch each other but missing by a mile. They stop when they see me and Black puts an arm over my shoulder.

'How ya, Matt,' he says. He smells of piss and fags. 'You're my old buddy, aren't you? Come on, have a can – she's no company, her. Always moaning.'

That starts Hal off again and they're back to fighting. They don't notice when I walk away and their voices carry through the night.

The apartment is stifling. Dad never opens the windows. He says the traffic fumes get in if you open them but that's a lot better than stale hot air. Conor's watching telly and

Dad is doing weights in his bedroom. I can hear him groaning and the thud of the weights as he drops them onto the floor. I'm thinking about Anna. I'm thinking about how you could tell a girl of fifteen that her mother has cancer. That she might die.

10 *March 2015*

Today in school we made Mothers Day cards and they all looked at me when Mr. Delaney said mother. Johnny Tolan even laughed and I stared at the blackbord so hard so that I ~~woolnt~~ wood not cry. They never looked at Tara Hayes and her Mam is dead. So it's ok to be dead is it? Dead is better than gone? Jamie punched me hard in the belly at tea time cos I ate all the twix bars and he told Dad but he wasn't mad at all cos he bought a tent and were going camping. Conor has to stop sucking his thumb cos dad says his teeth are sticking out and hell need a brace. Jamie said Im a fat greedy basterd and Ill get a heart attack and die.

PS (we learnt PS in school last Friday it means post script) I made you a card anyway with a heart and roses your faverit. I put it in this book a t the back.

PPS I miss you and I want you to come home. Mrs Chung wants you to come home too. And Granda. The Chungs got a lovely pup but dad says he's a lab mix and his shits will be big.

4

Mikey's sitting on the kerb just down from his house, sucking on a fag like it's air that he needs to breathe.

'They'll kill you, Mikey.'

'My mother will kill me first if she finds out. So what's the plan?'

I shrug. 'I was thinking of going out to UL.'

'No fucking way, Matt. Not again. Where's Anna?'

'Her mother's sick.'

Anna doesn't want people to know how sick. She's kind of private like that. Mrs Chung comes out to the front door, scanning the road for Mikey.

'Fuck,' says Mikey, stubbing the fag out with his tackie. 'Do I stink of fags?'

He stands up and waves at his mother. She walks out of the house and climbs into her little red Fiesta and reverses out of the drive.

'Get in,' she says as she pulls up near us. 'You too, Matt. I'm going to Castletroy to pick up the lads from soccer camp. I need ye to do a few messages for me.'

We get in. We've nothing else to do and I might sneak a skate in the UL campus. A sudden shower of rain crashes noisily on the roof of the car and Mrs Chung flicks on her wipers. We turn into Park View – there's a shortcut to soccer camp, according to Google. Mrs Chung loves her satnav. There's a woman pushing a buggy ahead of us. She's thin, very thin in white skinny jeans and a pink vest top. Her hair is in a messy bun, a honey colour. It's her walk that I recognise. Back very straight, long strides, head slightly to the side. It's her. I'm positive it's her.

My mother. My breathing is so loud that I think Mikey'll hear it except he's fallen asleep in the front seat. Mrs Chung doesn't notice anything. I'm trying to decide what to do if we pass her. Should I duck down or just let her see me? I can't decide but she decides for me. She steers the buggy into the driveway of a brand-new semi-detached house with a bright red door and flower baskets on each side.

I don't realise I've been holding my breath until we're well past the house and turning into a long road towards the playing fields. The lads aren't finished training yet and Mikey's roaring at me to come for a kick-around. He's holding a rugby ball into my face. I can't move. I sit in the car and I can't move.

We do the messages in Dunnes for Mrs Chung and I want to go skating but Mikey forces me to go to the Chopstick with him. He says he wants to see his father. He's the head chef there. What Mikey really wants is a big dirty free portion of Singapore noodles. Anyway, it beats going home. I know if I go home I'll want to blurt it all out. I really want to tell Dad. I want him to make it disappear. Make her disappear. Make her gone again, not living in a house in Castletroy with a baby and hanging baskets full of flowers.

My phone rings. Dad. I step outside so that I can hear him.

'Matt, have you seen Jamie? I've been out all evening looking for him ... I ... tell him ...' Dad goes silent and I don't fill in the blanks for him like I used to when I was fat. This is what Dad is really saying: *Find Jamie and bring him home and tell him I'm not mad with him over the fight the other day or if he stays out all night. I'm worried, so you sort it out, Matt.*

The phone crackles and I watch a cab pull up outside the Chinese and spill more hungry people onto the footpath. They must have all heard about Mr Chung's Singapore noodles. It's hardly Mikey's jokes that they're coming for.

'Find your brother. I'm putting on spaghetti bolognese.'

Silence on my end.

'Find him, Matt. I'm worried.'

Dad hangs up. Now I'm worried too because Dad never says he's worried out loud.

The noodles don't last long. Not that we eat them or anything – Hammer Hayes and his pals do that for us. We hand them over like we're two toddlers. Here, have our noodles – would ye like anything else with that?

These are the risks you have to take when you go looking for Jamie. In the twilight parks and alleys, under Sarsfield Bridge where all the suicides hang out, down by the boat-house or at the back of the Clayton. And that's where we meet Hammer. He's wound-up, high on something, and I can sense Mikey's fear as we get nearer.

'Did you see Jamie?' I say, trying to keep my voice steady.

Hammer looks at me, his eyes glassy. 'I'm looking for that little prick myself – I want my money and he has it, slimy fucker.'

Mikey farts loudly – one of his specials.

Hammer laughs. 'Gimme that bag, what's in it?'

Mikey hands over the bag and smiles at Hammer.

'Fuck sake, I hate them noodle things. I thought it was Supermac's,' Hammer says and his pals laugh like it's the funniest joke ever. But he takes out the silver container and the plastic fork and starts to shovel noodles into his mouth. Then he spits them out and glares at Mikey. 'What the fuck is in 'em? You fuckin' did that on purpose, you fuckin' fat bollocks you.'

'Chilli peppers,' says Mikey. 'Chilli peppers. Prawns. Chicken. Noodles. Singapore noodles ...'

'Singapore, my hole,' says Hammer.

My stomach does a flip, like when I do an ollie on my board and I don't think I'll make it, don't think I'll stay on my feet. I wish Mikey'd just shut up. If he says nothing and lets Hammer do the talking then we'll be grand.

Hammer's buddies are cracking up now and Hammer's loving it, playing to the crowd. 'OK, Chung, answer us one question and we'll give you back your noodles,' Hammer says. 'Are you riding him? Are you riding little ponytail man?'

Mikey looks at me and grins. Fucking eejit. My legs are doing the jittering thing. Hammer high-fives the small burly guy next to him.

'Two little gay-boys – why don't ye have a ride right now and show us how it's done?'

The air is still and all the night sounds have stopped. My ears are ringing and I can't get air into my lungs. 'Look, have you seen Jamie? That's all we asked –'

'Shut the fuck up, you,' Hammer says, circling behind Mikey. 'Bend down.' Hammer's voice has changed. The laugh is gone out of it. He's dead serious. 'Kneel, you fucking gay-boy, kneel down on the ground.' Hammer kicks Mikey into the small of his back and Mikey half-falls, half-kneels on all fours.

I can feel a fat tear running down my cheek. Mikey has his eyes closed, like he's just waiting for the worst to happen. Hammer looks straight at me and sticks his fingers down the sides of his tracksuit. I can see his boxers, grey in the dim light. My phone is in my hand in my pocket and I think about ringing it. Pressing the button for the last caller. Dad.

'Stop,' I say.

'Stop,' says Hammer in a high-pitched voice. The others laugh.

'So, fatso, you like it up the arse, don't you?' Hammer's eyes are mad-looking and I know if I try to do anything, I'll only make it worse. He's coked up – definitely.

He kicks Mikey up the arse. 'Say it, gay-boy. Say it, you bastard.'

'I ... I ...' Mikey's crying. There's a string of snot running down his nose.

Hammer kicks him again. 'Say, it fatso. I. Like. It. Up. The. Arse.'

'I ... like ... it ... up ... the arse,' Mikey stammers.

Hammer pulls down his tracksuit bottom and grins at his pals. 'Will I make his night? Will I give him one?'

The pals are like one person now, all watching Hammer, hanging on his word, all answering him together. 'Do him, Hammer, that'll teach them ...'

Then Jamie's there, coming out of nowhere, screaming at Hammer. 'What are you fucking doing?' he shouts.

Hammer pulls up his trousers and puts a hand out towards Jamie. Jamie drops a wad of notes into it. 'Nice wan,' says Hammer, flicking through the notes. Jamie pulls Mikey up from the ground.

'Just having a laugh, that's all. Take it easy, Jamie,' says Hammer, smiling at everyone. 'Money talks, that's for sure.'

The pals laugh and Mikey smiles too. Hammer flicks Jamie a small bag. 'Bonus,' he says and walks off, the pals forming a circle around him.

Jamie grins at me.

'That was a piece of luck,' he says.

Mikey laughs, his voice high. 'I thought I was a goner.'

I don't talk to Mikey. Can't even look at him as we walk up Henry Street. He's all excited, adrenaline pumping through the fat cells. I know I'm being stupid, blaming Mikey for Hammer's madness, but he could have done something, anything except get down on all fours like that. I barely say goodbye when he heads for the bus. Jamie's all adrenaline too, but I know it's the little bag in his pocket that's fuelling his.

'Lucky I turned up,' he says. 'Mikey's a retard – you know that, don't you?'

Jamie walks faster. I nearly have to run to keep up with him.

'Fuck off, Jamie. Hammer's the retard.'

'Hammer's all bluff. Mikey should have stood up to him. Easy.'

We're passing the skate park. I've a mad urge to go for a night skate.

'Easy? Hammer's a lunatic. You can't stand up to lunatics. What did he give you anyway?'

Jamie laughs. 'What did he give you anyway?' he repeats in a high-pitched voice. 'What do you think? Jellies?'

'I ... Dad has the dinner ready and he's worried cos you stayed out all night and ...'

Jamie stops dead and looks at me. Then he laughs. A car whips by, blaring country music.

'It's spaghetti bolognese.' My voice is low, almost a whisper. I know that spaghetti bolognese can never compete with the bag in Jamie's pocket.

He laughs again. Louder this time.

And that's when my stupid mouth lets me down big time.

'I know where she lives,' I say. 'I know where she lives. I saw her today.'

There's no laugh now. He stares at me, and I think he's going to belt me. But he doesn't. Instead he just runs.

Saturday night 21 November 2015

I am sorry about the phone call. Granda gave out to Jamie for throwing the phone off the hall table and chipping it. The table that is. Conor cried and told dad you rang Granda's house and he shouted and said who talked to her and Jamie never told on me even when Dad banged the wall with his fist. Your voice sounded funny and far away. You said hello Mattie three times. That was all I heard before stupid Jamie grabbed the phone. Dad says Jamie could win the county meet if he keeps up the swimming I hate swimming and so does Conor. Dad said yesterday all I like is eating and if I don't stop I will burst. I laughed but Jamie said that it was lousey and that if I came training with him the fat would be gone. He showed me how to do press ups but it was too hard. My new Liverpool jersey the away white one turned pink in the wash and I cried I couldn't help it and Dad tried to get the pink out all day and Mrs Chung came with Vanish and fixed it. Dad hugged her. Vanish is great. Why don't you go on facebook? Then we could talk. Even Mrs Chung is on it.

I got an A in English in my summer tests. 5 As, 3 Bs, 2 Cs and a D (Irish I hate it) Jamie is done second year and he got 9 As imagine that.

5

I wake in a sweat and sit bolt upright. My T-shirt is moulded to me and the sheets feel wet. The room is pitch black, my breathing the only sound. Then I hear it, the noise that was in my dream. Somebody puking. I climb out of bed and pad into the kitchen. Jamie's vomiting into the bin but he's missing it so clumps of orange vomit are spraying onto the white tiles.

'Jesus, get your aim right,' I whisper, taking the bucket and mop out of the cupboard.

Jamie grins at me, his eyes wide and glassy. 'Bad burger,' he says, wiping his mouth with a tea towel. 'Never trust Sombrero – I should have gone to Chicken Hut.'

'Yeah, sure,' I say, wiping the floor. 'Keep down your voice or you'll wake Dad.'

Jamie laughs. 'So? I'll wake Dad – big deal.' He takes out a pack of cigarettes and searches in his pockets for a lighter.

'Don't, Jamie, you know what he's –'

'I'm not scared of him. He's a pussy. Thinks he's so fucking great, so perfect. Thinks he's the big man,' he says, lighting a fag and pulling hard on it. He's leaning against the kitchen table, head cocked to one side, watching me. 'That ponytail needs to go. Everyone's laughing at it.'

'Who's everyone? Hammer Hayes and his dumb friends?' I put the mop away and change the stinking bin liner. Jamie sucks on the fag. I flick on the cooker hood to get rid of the smoke.

'He taught you well.'

'Who?' I'm spraying bleach onto a dishcloth. The smoke and vomit smells are mingling together.

'Him. Daddy. Our Father who art in Heaven. Dickface. Boss Man. Fucking Marathon Man.'

'He does his best. He tries.'

'You're just like him. Neat-freak, fucking obsessed with shit.'

'Me? Obsessed? With what?'

'Your stupid skating, off with all the weirdos.'

I laugh. Jamie death-glares me.

'So let me get this straight – Hammer's not a weirdo? Cool.'

Jamie stumbles a little, spraying ash everywhere.

'Go to bed,' I say, dropping the dishcloth into the sink. 'Fucking eejit.'

'Yeah, I know. Go to bed.'

He stubs the fag out on the lid of the bin. He's so close I can smell taco burgers and beer. He leans into me, pressing his mouth to my ear.

'I don't want to see her. If she asks about me, tell her nothing. Tell her I'm dead. Tell her I walked out and never looked back.' Jamie's voice whisper-crackles and I think he's going to cry. I bend my head, pretending to wipe the lid of the bin. 'You shouldn't see her either, Matt. Fuck her – how long is she back and she didn't even call us?'

I squeeze the dishcloth, watching dirty water dribble down my hand.

'Dad's right, she's a whore, a selfish fucking bitch who ...' Jamie's voice trails off. I look up and Dad is standing in the doorway. Jamie stares him down, a stupid smirk on his face.

Fuck. Fuck all of it.

'Dad, we were ... it's OK, I ...' I stutter. I'm waiting for all hell to break loose and I don't know if Dad heard the bit about her being back. I can hear the muffled sound of a siren on the street way below and the ticking of the cuckoo clock that Granda gave us one Christmas.

Dad walks out and Jamie and I gape at each other in shock. He staggers a little and then starts laughing – fits of laughing that only drunks can do, like Black and Hal after a Bavaria party.

'His face ... his face was priceless, Matt. See it?' says Jamie, still laughing.

Then the door bursts open and Dad comes back in with an Ireland hold-all that's spilling clothes along the floor. Jamie's clothes. 'I want you out. This is it. Finito. Party over,' says Dad, throwing the bag at Jamie's feet.

'Dad, it's the middle of the night,' I say. 'Look, go back to bed and –'

Dad walks right up to Jamie and prods his chest with a finger. 'Out of my house. You were on a last chance, sonny, and you won't do whatever you like and come and go whenever you please, spoilt little shit.'

'Big man talk – I've been listening to that all my life.'

'Shut up and get out,' Dad says, his voice angry and tight.

'All my life – no wonder she left you – no wonder she walked out – couldn't get away fast enough.'

Dad raises his hand and it's like a slo-mo clip. The hand swings back in a high arc, then forwards and, my Jesus, the sound when it finds Jamie's cheek, and then the cuckoo comes out because it's on the hour.

Dad drops his hand and I feel sorry for him when I see his eyes. Eyes like Anna. And Jamie's are bright now with tears but he won't let them out and he has a deep pink handprint – like a cartoon one – on his face.

'I want you out,' Dad says, his voice a whisper. He leaves and then Jamie lets the tears come. He stands there against the kitchen table, tears running down his face, snot hanging from his nose.

'Jamie ...' He doesn't even hear me, he's crying so hard. 'Jamie, look ...'

His shoulders are shaking from bawling. I take his arm and walk him towards our bedroom. He staggers and weaves as I sit him down on his bed. Snot and tears drop on my head as I take off his runners and his socks. Then I get him to stand up and take off his jeans, stinking from vomit. Then his hoodie and his T-shirt. I pull back his quilt and he lies down on the bed, dry-sobbing now, like all the tears are used up.

'Sorry, Matt ... sorry,' he says.

'It's grand, Jamie, it's grand.'

'You're not a weirdo, Matt, not really,' he murmurs, already falling asleep.

'Good to know,' I say to the Steven Gerrard poster over my bed. I go and check on Conor in his room. Asleep or pretending to be. Then I go back into the kitchen and get the gear bag and the clothes so Dad won't see them in the morning.

I hear Dad's key in the front door. I'm glad he had a run. I hope it was a long one – the longer the run the better his mood.

He's doing his stretches against the wall when I come in. I watch him as he does them, knowing the exact sequence. I like the stretching routine. It makes everything normal. He finishes and flicks on the kettle.

'Tea?' he says, sweat still running down his face. His running top has dark, wet blotches on the back.

'Yeah. Please.'

'Green tea. Better for you,' he says.

He makes the tea and both of us take it out to the balcony. There's no room to sit, so we lean over the railing.

'Like it?' He smiles at me. Poor old Dad.

I sip the watery green tea. It tastes and looks like Shrek's piss. 'Lovely. Really good.'

'That's my favourite, although I like to break out the jasmine tea on special occasions.'

'Oh. Sounds nice.'

'I'm joking, Matt.'

'Good run?'

Dad smiles and takes a sip of tea. 'Brilliant. Five miles – three seven minutes and two at six. Good going.'

'Very good.'

The sun hovers over the river, as if it's trying to decide whether to climb any further up the sky or not.

'Do you like it here, Matt?'

'Limerick?'

'No. This place. This flat. Would you prefer it to Woodbine Avenue or maybe one of the new estates out Dooradoyle way?'

I think about the question. It's a hard one. I miss Mrs Chung being near us, knowing what was going on. I miss green fields sometimes. I miss home. I don't say any of this to Dad, though. I have a job to do today with Dad.

'The skate park's great – it's like my own private park.'

'That's it?'

'The view. I love the view, feeling like you're looking down on everyone. I love that.'

Dad takes a long drink of tea. 'I love the view too. It's like Lego City down there and you own it all.'

I grin at him. 'Exactly how I feel. Especially at this time of the morning.'

Dad finishes his tea. 'A hot shower is in order.'

'Dad –' I try to think of the right words to say. 'About Jamie ...'

His face hardens, goes all tight at the mention of the name.

'He was sorry last night, he told me he was sorry and –'

Dad is shaking his head and the more he shakes it the more desperate my pleading becomes.

'Just let him stay, Dad. You can't throw him out. He'll have nowhere to go and ... he won't do it again.'

Dad looks at me. 'He was trouble before he was even born.' He picks up his cup and walks away. I watch as the morning traffic thickens below me. I think, it's OK. He didn't say no and that's good.

Anna and I are first into the park and I take off by myself, loving the early morning feel of the place. I just lose myself in the skating, letting it blur everything for me. The street is a blur as I skate by and the river is a long silver blur and everything begins to stop in my head. Jamie, Dad, Mikey on all fours last night and Mam and how young she looked. And how happy – not a care in the world.

I skate harder, grinding with such force that a chip flies off my board but I don't care. I go faster and faster and now I think I feel what Dad feels when he runs, a calmness very deep inside me, a lovely calmness with no questions, not even one.

There must be something in the air this morning. The park is filling up so fast with skaters it's actually annoying. I'm there just doing a lovely clean run, hitting the rails, really concentrating hard and there's a bunch of newbies in my way, struggling to get on their boards, let alone use the rails and jumps. I take a seat and watch as Anna shows the newbies how it's done. Smart arrives and Anna ups her game, nosesliding and popping, then throwing in a beautiful tailslide. She's ace. Finally she stops at my feet, flips her board up, and sits down beside me.

'Show-off,' I say, grinning at her. She smiles at me and pushes her baseball cap back further on her head. Then she watches Smart as he tries to find a clean run in the now crowded park. I root in my bag for my water bottle and offer some to Anna first. She grabs it without taking her eyes from Smart and pushes it back into my hand when she's finished drinking.

'You're welcome,' I say, taking a long slug of the warm water. Smart glides up on his board, hand outstretched for water. Fuck sake. I hand him the bottle.

'You can skate,' he says to Anna. 'Green room skating.'

I have no idea what he means and I'm not going to ask him.

'What's that?' says Anna.

'It's the zen of surfing – when you're in the barrel of a wave and the light's perfect. Everything's perfect. Same with skating.'

'You surf?' Anna says.

Of fucking course Smart surfs too and probably plays ice hockey for Canada in his spare time.

'Yeah. It's the coolest. Want to go for a skate out by UL? It's shit here,' he says.

'Gotta go home,' Anna says. 'See ye.' She flips her board into her hand and walks away. I'm staring after her, knowing she's pissed at me. Fuck it – it's not my fault she can't come.

'Run,' says Smart. 'Bus.'

We get off the bus to buy rolls in the Spar near the college entrance and Smart insists on paying and I'm very impressed with his Element wallet.

'Sponsored,' he says, flicking the wallet closed as we leave the shop and head into the college. That's the first time he does something not cool – telling me he's sponsored by Element. Everyone who skates knows that. Knows he's the only person in Limerick sponsored by them.

'So you've never surfed?' he says as we walk up the long road towards the science building.

I laugh to myself. Imagine me surfing last summer, squeezing the fat into a wetsuit, looking like a giant sausage trying to stand up on a surfboard without it sinking.

'I'm going to Lahinch for a week soon so I might try it then.'

'Lahinch – yeah – getting a bit like the skate park now though – the water's jammed at times.' He takes off and does a grind down five steps and lands it perfectly.

Smart is some skater. He does the hard tricks like they're just everyday, ordinary skating. Beautiful carves and tailslides and top guns all running into each other like Dad's stretching sequences. A glorious caballerial, followed by a fakie backside 360 ollie that I love and cannot do. So I do a stupid thing. I try a half-cab, just to show off. And I do it off the Rocky steps, over by the sports building. Which would be grand if it was a first attempt but I nearly broke my neck the last time I tried it and Mikey had to call his mother to collect us and she made me go to A&E because of the vomiting and the duck-egg on my forehead. Smart goes first. Aw man – beautifully executed, he takes off at the top of the steps and sails, beautiful full turn halfway down and then lands like a dream and even the students passing stop and clap. Amazing. He looks at me and nods at the steps.

'Your turn.'

Before I can change my mind I'm at the top, looking down and Jesus it looks way worse from up here and my belly is flipping already but I take a deep breath and launch myself into the air and straight away I know I've made a total balls of it, the balance is all wrong and I don't have that right feeling like I had this morning in the park and I whack off the edge of the railings and manage to roll in a ball before meeting the ground which seems to be rising up towards me in a huge arc. I open my eyes and see trees and then Smart's worried face.

'Man, what did you do that for? I was only joking with you. It took me a year to master that one. Man, that's the White Knuckle – only three of us have ever landed it. Are you OK? Why are you laughing?'

'Dunno. Felt like Superman ...' I laugh again and my head starts to hurt and now Smart laughs too and we're like two lunatics on the ground laughing our heads off. He pulls me up then by the arm and I'm a bit woozy and I've a golf ball on my forehead this time. We walk towards a bench under some trees and Smart sits me down, then gets our bags and boards, and dumps them beside us. He pulls out my roll and my water and hands them to me, and then starts munching on his – a giant breakfast roll with cheese. I take a bite of roll but I can't taste it. I feel weird, sort of high and excited and alive – like I have super powers.

'I haven't seen my mother for four years,' I say, surprising myself. Where the fuck had that come from?

Smart looks at me and nods like this is perfectly normal.

'So I'm in Arthurs Quay the other night and this wan comes up to me and says "I'm your cousin and your mother is back"...'

'Was she a looker?'

'Who? My mother? Jesus, how would I know ...'

'No, you ape – the new cuz.'

'Naw – she was a Fanta Face.'

Smart bursts out laughing at this. 'Fanta face – brilliant – know them well – covered in orange make-up – brilliant.'

It was Mikey's word but I smile, accepting the praise for Mikey's brilliance.

'So then we were driving through Park View – you know it? Just down the road? And there's my mother pushing a buggy and she goes into one of the houses.'

Smart takes an unreal bite from his roll, like half the roll and chews noisily. I feel calmer now, back to normal and glad I told someone at last. Even if that someone is the last person I'd have chosen.

'And then what happened?' says Smart, his mouth full of breakfast roll.

'Nothing. I hadn't the guts to do anything.' I slug back the last of my warm water. The lump on my forehead is throbbing like it has its own little lump heart.

'Fuck me,' says Smart. He pushes the last of his roll into his mouth and chews hard. 'Do you want to see her?' he says eventually.

I shrug. 'Think so. I just want to ask ... just want to know why ...'

'Why she left or why she left you?'

Smart hits the nail on the head. Maybe he's the right person to tell after all. The person that's not involved in it in any way.

'Me. Us. Why she left us.' My eyes fill up and I look away and blink them until the tears go back.

Smart takes a noisy drink of water and smiles at two girls passing nearby, their arms full of books. They giggle and smile back at him.

'When you're surfing, you know, when you're out there and you look out towards the horizon and there's like this wave ...' He stops talking and grins at me. 'The wave you've been waiting for all day, no, all week and you feel it inside yourself, exactly like skating except a million times better, you start to ride the wave and your heart is like all over the place and it starts to tunnel around you and you feel so ... I don't know ... so right ...' His voice trails off and he looks back towards the college.

'Yeah, I know that feeling from skating, when every-thing is right.'

He smiles. 'The green room. Best place in the whole world.' He stands up, stretching lazily before picking up his board and his rucksack.

'Gotta go,' he says.

I gather my stuff and follow him. We skate as soon as we hit the footpath, a nice easy skate, an end-of-day one.

'You should go see her,' he says, as we stop outside his house. 'You should go see her and make her pay.'

He keys in a code to open the huge electronic gates.

'That's some gaff,' I say.

He shrugs. 'Wanna come in? The parents are at work like 24/7.'

'Naw, you're grand,' I say and watch as the gates close behind him. Like magic.

My calves hurt. Four hours of skating does damage. My head feels better, though. Clearer. It's evening now and my stomach is rumbling again. I'm strolling past Park View, thinking about curry chips, and I turn in, like my legs have a mind of their own.

I find a spot down the hill a bit and watch her house. People pass and give me strange looks. I know I look suspicious, like I'm casing the joint, and I know I should just walk up to the red front door and knock.

I make my legs move towards the house. They feel paralysed but I force them to walk. The red door is straight in front of me now. There's a doorbell with a name under it. Wilson. My finger shakes as I press the bell. It chimes so loud I jump. I want to run but I stand there, waiting for the door to open. Willing it to open and willing it not to. It doesn't open and it feels like she's done it on purpose. Made sure she isn't home when I finally call.

There's a bubble of anger inside me and I take a swing at one of the hanging baskets. It vomits earth and leaves and flowers onto the doorstep.

The door swings back. She's standing there, blonde ponytail, Jamie's brown eyes, fat crying toddler on her hip. She glances down at the mess on her doorstep. Then she raises her head slowly, stares straight into my face. She has tiny wrinkles at the edge of her mouth. Her lips are blood red, matching her tight red T-shirt that says 'Diva' right across her boobs. The toddler buries her head into my mother's neck, sobbing loudly.

Then I see it creeping across her face. She knows who I am. For a split second I can't remember where my board is and then I feel its weight in my hands. I drop it to the ground, jump on awkwardly and skate over the bumpy cobbled path. I hear her voice and can feel stupid tears spilling down my face.

'My flowers.'

I barely make out the words with the crying kid and my own breath loud in my head and the roll of the board wheels flying down the path. My flowers. My fucking flowers.

I force myself to think about the green room all the way home.

23 April 2016

I thought youd be there. Hiding in the church maybe so Dad wouldn't see you. I looked at every face though and the confirmation mass was so long I had loads of time. Mrs Chung was there sitting next to Dad and Granda. Poor Granda – he's losing it a bit Dad says and he talks out loud and he farts when he stands up and he forgets to turn off the cooker. I made420 euro. Mikey made nearly a grand but that's because of the Chinese take-away. He just went behind the counter with his badge for an hour and all the drunks coughed up. When we came out of the church I looked up and down the road just in case you were there. We went to the Texas Steakeout. It was nice I had a steak and so did Jamie. Granda had the chicken and he said you were always a bolter and that I was getting as fat as a pig and dad made him say sorry. About the fat not about the bolter. He bought me a book in O Mahoneys after. Endgame. Gibbons new one. I love his books.

Conors teeth are gone very bad. He looks like a rabbit now and Dad says its from your side the buck teeth. He's getting train tracks. Jamie has a girlfriend Lisa Crowley shes really pretty and she lives in a big house on the ennis road. I bought your favourite with my money. A giant Toblerone it was lovely. I got jumped coming home from school on Monday. Jamie was with his girlfriend and it was only me cos Mikey was off in Dublin spending his money. They were sure I'd have my money on me but I'm not thick. I rolled in a ball and let them kick me and after a while I didn't even feel it. At least the fat is good for something.

I thought you'd come. I was so sure I even said it to Jamie but he laughed and said not on your life. Maybe you were there but you just hid. Granda said he told you it was on.

Mrs Chung is having another baby but its not Mr. Chung's Mikey says. I miss you.

6

'Come on into Penneys, I've to buy socks.' I elbow past the crowds of smokers and buggy pushers outside the shop, Mikey trailing behind me.

'Where's your new pal today?' Mikey says, as we're going upstairs to the men's.

'What're you on about?'

'Your new pal, Smart, the rich kid.'

'Cop on, Mikey, we went skating like.'

'You could have asked me.'

'Yeah but you don't fucking skate so what was the point?' I'm beelining for the socks.

'I don't like him. Smarmy bollocks,' he says.

'He's pure sound when you hang out with him, you should try it.'

I'm rooting through the socks, trying to find cheap ones that won't rip on the skateboard, when Mikey starts poking me in the back.

'Stop, you eejit,' I say without looking up. I find a value pack of socks, five pairs for three euro, and am dead pleased with myself. Mikey pokes me again and this time I do look up. Straight into her face.

'Matt,' she says, her voice soft. 'Mattie.'

Mattie. Nobody called me that since she left. I know I'm smiling and I see faces behind me going up and down the escalator and the moving people make me dizzy. I look at her eyes instead and she's crying, small neat little tears – a couple under each eye, like someone placed them there.

'Mattie,' she says again but not out loud. She just mouths it, her pale pink lips forming the word. Soft like a kiss or a hug.

And then I run. Past the socks and the boxers, past a couple with a baby in a buggy, past a group of girls, almost knocking one of them over, past the security guard on the door and out into the street, my legs pumping as hard as possible, my lungs bursting for air. I don't stop until I reach the river and then hang over the railing, gulping in oxygen.

My whole body is shaking and I feel tears on my face. Fucking bitch making me cry. I kick the railings so hard I think my toe is bust. Why did I even bother knocking on her door last week? And why the fuck did I run away? This is way worse. Fucking Penneys of all places. All the times I had that first conversation in my head. What I'd say. How I'd make her feel so sorry that she left. I'd make her raging with herself for leaving such a great kid. I'd make her suffer. All I did was mess up her stupid flowers – and now this. I kick the railing again, with my other foot this time. Then I notice that I still have the socks in my hand.

My phone vibrates in my pocket. I pull it out, hand shaking all over the place like Black before his first can. It's Mikey.

'Where the fuck did you go?'

I say nothing.

'Fucking bastard leaving me there with her, sure I didn't know what to say.' Mikey's whispering and I can barely hear him. 'Look, I'm here in The Buttery with her and she wants to talk to you, just for a few minutes. Matt, fuck sake, hurry on. I'm mortified, like.'

Mikey hangs up before I can say anything, the cute bastard. I want to go home to Dad. Watch him coming in from a run, doing his stretches, making his tea, drinking it out on the balcony with me. I want to sit and watch telly with Conor. Dumb stuff. *The Simpsons* and *Britain's Got Talent* and the ads. Conor loves a good ad. I want to be in Mikey's house on a Saturday night when Mrs Chung has the smallies just out of the bath and the living room smells like Chinese food and coconut shampoo and Mikey's telling a new joke and nobody's listening.

Or a good skate. That's what I'd love to be doing now, skating. Early in the morning, sun beaming down, the board heavy in my hands, the wheels oiled. I can hear the noise in my head as the board slaps on to the ground, then my feet as they land on it, feeling for the right foothold so my weight is even. Then slowly building up speed until I'm in that place where the world is a blur. That green room place that Smart loves so much.

But it's like a magnet, knowing she's so near. I go instead to the cafe and stand outside watching them through the window. She's chatting away to Mikey and he doesn't look a bit mortified, tucking into the biggest slice of carrot cake I've ever seen. She's so pretty and young-looking. I'd forgotten that – how pretty she was and how everybody smiled when she arrived places like the supermarket or even the school. Well, not everyone – mostly the men. She's wearing a tight pink T-shirt and blue jeans and dangly earrings that swing when she moves her head.

My heart does a little ollie in my chest and I have a terrible urge to piss. I go in before I change my mind. Walking to the table seems to take for ever even though it's really only a few steps.

She stands up as I reach her and I take a step back, just in case she's planning to hug me or anything.

'Mattie,' she says in that soft teasing voice, like my name is the most special thing in the world.

'Matt,' I say as I sit down opposite her. Mikey's itching to leave but he can't drag himself away from the carrot cake. I realise I'm still holding the stolen socks and I put them on the table. A waitress comes with her notebook.

'What would you like, Mattie – cake? A sandwich? How about chips? You do chips and burgers, don't you?' My mother smiles at the waitress and then at me. She looks so young, way younger than Dad, and her hair is the nicest colour, kind of two colours, beige and gold, and her eyes are exactly the same as Jamie's. She smiles at me and I can feel my face going bright red.

'Am ... thanks for the cake ... Mrs ... am ... thanks ...' says Mikey, jumping up and almost knocking the waitress as he backs out the door.

'Coke. I'll have a Coke,' I say to the waitress. She smiles and walks away and I want to call her back and tell her to sit down and have a chat with us.

'You're so tall and so handsome,' my mother says, stretching out her hand towards mine on the table. I pull my hand away and look out the window. I can feel her eyes on me, examining my face. I want to do exactly the same thing to her. Examine every bit of her face, remember the tiny lines at each side of her mouth, the way her eyes pierce you and make you tell the truth, the way they shine sometimes when she kisses and hugs you.

'You look so different but the same too. Do you know what I mean?' She smiles again and does that thing with her eyes that most girls except Anna do when they're trying to get you to like them.

'It's so good to see you ... it's ... you have no idea ...' Her eyes fill up with tears and she looks away, sniffing. She bends down, roots in her handbag and comes up with a tissue. She dabs her eyes with the corner of the tissue, gently, just a bare touch. 'I know this is hard, Mattie – Matt – I know there's a lot to talk about.'

The waitress comes with the Coke and I'm glad because now I have something to do with my hands, something to look at and fiddle with.

'Last week, Mattie – Matt – that was you, wasn't it? That was you at my door.'

I shrug. The ice clinks in the glass.

'I ... you were gone before I could say anything ...'

I watch Coke bubbles rise and burst. She did say something. She did. She said *my flowers*.

'How's Conor? I miss him so –' she looks away again, does the eye-dabbing thing again.

I say nothing because I'm afraid I'll forgive her. Just like that, I'll give in and forget all the years without her just so she'll hug me. Just so she'll like me.

'Matt ... look ... I know it's been hard for you, for all three of you, but I promise you I'm going to make it right. I talked it all out with Rod last night –'

'Who's Rod?'

She smiles at me and shakes her head, like I should know who the fuck Rod is. 'Rod is my ... he's my partner. And you have a baby sister. Taylor. She's gorgeous, you'll love her. She's walking now and she's trying to say little words, you know – she says *mama* and *dada* and *doggy* and *hot*. She points at the fireplace and says *hot* and it's so cute ...'

I keep staring into my Coke, watch the ice swirl around. They give you so much ice it must make the Coke very watery once it melts.

'Rod and I agree that we want to do things properly. We want it sorted now, seeing as we've moved back ... Matt, are you listening to me? I mean if you don't want to see me, if Jamie and Conor and you choose not to see me, then that's fine ...'

She catches me unawares this time and her hand flies out and grabs mine and I'm kind of mortified but thrilled all at the same time. The touch of her is lovely. Soft like a cushion.

'Today was meant to be, Matt. It's fate. We were meant to bump into each other in that shop,' she says, patting my hand like a real mother would. I pull away from her then, from the softness of her and the hugs and the cuddles and the constant comforting chatter of her, all the bits of her that are real now in front of me and the bits that are memories and imaginings mixed up together.

'I thought about you a lot since you knocked on the door. All the time, actually. You see? It's fate.'

'No, it's not fate. Nothing is fate. You had a choice,' I say, my voice shaky. 'You had a choice too and you left us. Why?'

I force myself not to cry.

She pulls back from me like I just slapped her hard on the face and I think I remember that about her – the way she had of making you feel guilty or bad, just by looking at you.

'Things were very complicated, Matt. I know your dad has poisoned you all against me –'

'No, he hasn't – what gave you that idea?'

'Look, Matt, you're upset and maybe now isn't the time to go into all of this.'

'Grand. We'll wait another five years so – how's that?'

She picks up her coffee cup and takes a sip, eyeing me over the rim. 'I was sure now that you're older ... that, you know ... we might be able to chat about it like adults.' She fiddles with her spoon, turning it over and over in her hand. I feel guilty, like I'm acting the maggot, being childish or bratty. I'm just about to say something to her, something to make her feel better when the flower baskets pop into my head. Big beautiful baskets with all sorts of greenery, kind of colour matched, one on each side of a bright red door.

'How's Jamie doing? I heard ... he's a bit wild?'

I glare at her. The fucking cheek of her talking to me about Jamie like he's my son and it's my fault that he's gone off the rails. I take a deep breath so that I won't shout at her. And so that I won't cry. 'You heard – he's your child and you heard like it's gossip or something?'

'Matt ... look ... things have been difficult and –'

I raise my hand to stop her watery excuses. 'Jamie's great, he's fine. He's flying it. And Conor is, like, the best swimmer ever – Dad says he'll be in the Olympics he's so good – and Dad ran four marathons already this year and he got placed in the Cork one and he was up against all the younger guys and the Ethiopians. They're complete speed merchants the Ethiopians, they're just born with it like red hair or something ...'

My voice trails off and my great ad for my family takes a huge dive and she notices it but I hold her stare this time and smile at her like I don't give a shit. My phone beeps a text and I could kiss it for the great timing. It's from Mikey, telling me he's waiting outside and am I alive?

'That's my dad – our dinner is ready, I have to go,' I say to her, standing up and knocking the last of my Coke over the clean white tablecloth. 'See you around,' I say, pushing my way out of the cafe. I can't get the stupid door open, I'm pushing it instead of pulling it, and then she's behind me, hugging me and kissing my head. I'm trying to push her away, fucking bitch, and finally the door opens and I stumble outside into the white-bright street. She's right behind me and she grabs me again and I can't resist. I fall into her arms like a big baby and she holds me so tight and I think this is the safest place in the world but I know it's not.

'I missed you and I wrote all the time and you never even fucking rang and I missed you ... All of us missed you and I hate you for it ...' I bury my head in her chest, tears and snot rubbing off on her lovely T-shirt.

She's crying too – I can feel her shoulders shaking as she murmurs into my hair. 'It's OK Mattie, it's OK now. I'm back and I love you and I've missed you too and I wrote and I rang and your father ... well, he ... Anyway I'm back to stay and that's the important thing.'

I pull away and wipe my nose with my sleeve. I'm mortified now, standing in the street being hugged like a two-year-old. I can see Mikey at the corner, kicking the footpath with his heel, pretending he hasn't seen us. 'I've to go, Mikey's waiting for me,' I say, without looking at her face.

'Can I have your phone number, Matt? I want you to meet your sister and ... and I want to see Jamie and Conor.' She smiles at me, her tears gone now. She takes out her phone and keys in my number. 'I'll text you mine – no, better still I'll ring you later and we can have another chat, OK?'

I nod agreement. She hugs me to her again and kisses my head. Then she holds my face in both her hands and looks at me with those piercing eyes. 'This is a new beginning, Matt, a new start for all of us, and I'm so happy about seeing my boys again, so, so happy.'

She smiles at me and walks away, glancing back and doing a fluttery wave with her fingers before turning the corner. Mikey's beside me straight away.

'Your mother's a MILF – imagine that and I never noticed before,' he says, grinning at me.

'You never noticed before because you were a kid,' I say. We're walking towards the Dock Road and home.

'What did she say?' Mikey asks as we wait for traffic to pass before crossing the road.

I shrug. 'Not much really.'

'Did she say why she left and never came back?'

Another shrug from me.

'Did she say she'd give you all the presents and money she owes you?' He grins at me and both of us burst out laughing. 'You should send her an invoice – itemised with interest added. She says she's calling out to see Mam – I'll be missing in action for that one.'

'Why?' I say. We're across the road now and heading towards the skate park.

'You're joking, Matt, aren't you? My mother'll go for her and then she'll rant for Ireland about it.'

'Yeah, well, it's none of your mother's business, is it? We don't know everything that went on so it's none of her fucking business.' I walk faster, knowing Mikey'll have trouble keeping up with me.

'Hey, wait up dickhead. I'm sorry I opened my fucking mouth,' he says, his breathing all raggy.

But I don't wait up, I go faster, almost running now. I reach the park, leap the railings, and sit on one of the seats, watching a couple of skaters ollie badly off the low rails.

'Bollocks,' says Mikey as he plonks down beside me. I swear the concrete seat moves with his weight.

'Big bollocks,' I say.

'Thanks.' Mikey takes out his fags and lights one up. The smell is sickening but nice as well. 'Want one?' he asks when he sees me sniffing the air.

'Nope.'

'Is she back for good?'

'Yeah – like the ancient Take That song.'

Mikey grins and takes a long drag of his cigarette. I feel bad now that I was mad at him. And he's actually right, what he said about Mrs Chung and my mother – you could sell tickets for that meeting.

A young kid takes a hopper near us and an older lad helps him up. There's blood on his elbow but he gets back on the board. We watch as he skates, he's pretending he's not hurt.

'I'm glad she's back, Mikey. She's my mother, like.'

Mikey lets out one of his specials – a long slow fart that'd knock out an elephant.

'Aww,' I scream, jumping up.

Mikey laughs. 'Come on, I've got to go home. I need to take a dump first in your place if the lift is working. I'm not walking up that fucking stairs. It's going to kill someone someday.'

They're all at home for once, even Jamie. Dad is stirring a pot of pasta in the kitchen and Conor and Jamie are slumped in front of the TV. Mikey goes to the toilet and I hover in the hallway.

'Doing anything tonight?' he says, when he finally comes out.

'Naw, don't think so.'

'See you tomorrow, so,' he says as we walk to the door.

'Want to stay for some grub, Mikey?' says Dad from the kitchen. I'm willing Mikey to say no – things can get out of hand in a second at our place and having someone else here only adds to the stress.

'I'd love to but I'll have to ring my mother,' Mikey calls in through the open door.

'Terry won't mind – here, use my phone,' says Dad, tossing it to Mikey. 'It's ready now and I've a ton of garlic bread in the oven.'

We all sit down around the table and Dad fills plates with pasta and carbonara sauce and chunks of garlic bread. I hand them out. There's silence as everybody eats, except for the slurping of pasta and chewing of bread. It's kind of nice. My phone rings on the table.

'Answer your phone, loser,' Jamie says.

'It's Anna, she'll ring back,' I say and reach for the phone. He's faster than me and grabs it and grins at me. It's stopped ringing and I pray in my head that it is Anna.

'Mattie has a woman – a woman he wants to keep secret. Imagine that, Dad?' says Jamie, looking at the phone. It rings again and he laughs as he answers it. 'Hello?' he says into the phone.

My face is red hot now. Burning red. 'Give me my fucking phone,' I say.

'Stop swearing,' says Dad.

'What do you get when you cross a cement mixer with a chicken?' says Mikey.

'Whoa,' says Jamie into the phone. 'No fucking way.'

Jamie's staring at me, holding the phone to his ear and just staring and I can hear her voice, like a cartoon voice.

'A bricklayer,' says Mikey, not even bothering to laugh himself now. 'How do you know that Indians were the first people in North America?'

Jamie's face is sickly pale and there are tears in his eyes. Dad and Conor are staring at him but he doesn't seem to notice. He just keeps shaking his head over and over and over.

'They had reservations,' says Mikey.

I glare at him to shut up. I consider doing a runner. Just getting up and walking out.

'You fucking bastard,' Jamie says to me, still holding the phone. 'You stupid fucking thick fool, running after her, that fucking slut ...' Then he screams down the phone, 'Do you hear me slut? I'm not like my stupid brother – I don't give a fuck if I ever see you again, do you hear me? You're not my mother, my mother is dead, do you hear that?' He roars the last bit so loud poor Conor jumps and Dad tries to grab the phone from him. 'We don't need you, you're only a bitch, so fuck off and don't come near us or I'll kill you, I'll fucking kill you –' Jamie throws the phone onto the table and a glass crashes to the floor. He pushes back his chair, tears streaming down his face. I stand up. He's towering over me.

'Jamie –'

And then he headbutts me right into the nose and there's a sudden bolt of pain and an explosion of bright red blood. I fall to my knees, holding my nose and the blood sprays through my hands onto the snow-white tiles. I can hear the front door banging as Jamie leaves and Conor's crying and blinking. When did he start that fucking blinking habit?

Dad lifts me up and holds a tea towel to my face. 'Here, hold your head forward – everybody thinks you should hold your head back but that only makes the blood run back down your nasal passage,' he says.

'Dad ...'

'An ice pack will help – I'll just see if I have one in the freezer.' He goes over to the fridge and I sit shakily down on a chair. I feel sick.

'I ... I think I'll go home,' says Mikey.

I nod and Mikey leaves.

'OK, here's some ice – is that better?' Dad says.

I feel guilty now. He's being so nice and he must know that was Mam on the phone. He has to know. And poor Conor, I can't even look at Conor's blinking eyes. He knows too that it was Mam. My nose begins to throb in a steady rhythm of pain and I'm glad. I deserve it after giving her my number just like that.

'Dad, I didn't mean –'

'Stop talking, it's making your nose bleed again. Hold your head forward, go on. Don't worry about the blood – I'll clean it up in a while. That's it,' he says.

'No, seriously, Dad, I –'

'Jamie's not getting away with this – we were having a lovely meal and all, and then all of this ...' Dad is kneeling in front of me. The front of his sweatshirt has a bloody handprint on it. A perfect one. Five fingers with lovely swirly fingerprints that *CSI* would be proud of.

'It's not Jamie's fault, Dad, it's mine.'

Dad pulls up a chair and sits down next to me. He's still holding the bloody tea towel up to my nose. 'No, it isn't. It's her fault. It's all her fault,' he says.

I don't say anything. I've learned my lesson when he brings Mam up.

'Waltzes back and already she's causing havoc. Hasn't the decency to ring or to meet up face to face, just strolls back into our lives like the last five years never happened ...'

He clenches and unclenches his fist and I can feel his body tensing beside me.

The blood has stopped. I lift up my head. Conor's sitting at the kitchen table now, still doing the rapid-blinking thing. His face is white and drawn. Poor Conor.

'Do ye understand now, lads, why I kept her away from ye? I knew she'd do this. I didn't think she'd have the cheek to come back after what she ... after all that happened.'

Dad gets up and goes for the mop. I know the dirty floor is annoying him. I walk into the living room, my eyes swelling now.

Conor follows me in.

'Are you OK, Matt?'

I grin at him. 'I'm fine – I won't be doing any modelling for a while but I'm grand. We'll watch a movie. Do you want popcorn?'

Conor nods. I go back to the kitchen. The floor is bleach clean. I can hear Dad in the shower. I dump a bag of popcorn into the microwave. My phone beeps on the table.

Sorry about earlier. Should have hung up when Jamie answered. Gr8 to see you today – will be in touch. Love Mam xxxxxx

'No, you won't,' I say out loud and I delete her number. The microwave pings and I get a bowl and dump the popcorn in. Then I find two cartons of juice and head back into the sitting room with them.

Conor smiles at me as I put the stuff down on the coffee table. He copies me by putting his feet on the table, next to mine. The movie hasn't started yet and we watch his new favourite ad, a mushy Cadbury one of a kid buying her mother a gift with buttons.

'What's she like?' he says, never taking his eyes from the telly. I've put the bowl of popcorn between us and he's shoving handfuls into his mouth.

Fuck. Why did I ever give her my number? That was dumb. Why did I go to the cafe to meet her? That was even dumber.

'She's the same.'

'I don't remember what the same was – what did she say?'

I take a fistful of popcorn. What did she say? Good question. What *did* she say?

'Did she ask about me?' He's still looking at the telly but I can see the blinking thing going on.

'She never stopped talking about you. How much she missed you and stuff,' I say. All lies.

'Which ad do you like the best?' He's still staring at the telly.

'This one – this one's the best.'

'Will you bring me skating some time?'

'Course I will. We'll have to get you a board – I think Anna's got an old one.'

'And will you bring me out to Mrs Chung's? I miss her.'

'Sure.'

The *Rocky* theme tune comes on. I can see Conor smiling at the screen. We watch the beginning of the film in silence, except for the popcorn munching and the juice slurping. Then there's an ad break already because it's RTÉ.

'Will you bring me to see Mam?'

I steal a look at Conor. He's rapid-blinking.

'I miss her, but don't tell Dad. Or Jamie, don't tell Jamie either.' He looks at me, straight at me, with his little buck teeth and his skinny face.

'I will. I'll bring you.'

'Promise?'

'Promise. Scout's honour.'

'You never joined the scouts.'

10 May 2016

Granda died. You never came.

7

We're outside the dole office, waiting for Anna. I'm skating up and down the footpath and Mikey's sitting on the kerb smoking. A queue of people snakes all the way from the doors right around the corner. Anna's waiting in line with her dad. I flip my board up into my hand and sit next to Mikey. The queue shuffles and coughs and chatters and smokes. Guys in smart suits, scumbags in trademark uniform of tracksuit bottoms tucked into snow-white socks, women dressed up like they're going out somewhere posh, an old guy at the back hawking up snot and expertly spitting it out of the corner of his mouth in long thin streaks.

And there's the pyjama girls. They are a howl. Fanta faces all covered in make-up and fake eyelashes, hair brushed and straightened. And after taking all that trouble to get ready they go out in their pyjamas. Weird.

Right behind the pyjama girls are Black and Hal, both working on breakfast cans of Bavaria, just sipping them.

It's a bit early for anything else. I wish Anna'd hurry on. The skating competition is today and I'm psyched. My face is a mess though. My nose is red and twice its normal size and my two eyes are slitty, but I can skate grand.

Mikey takes out another cigarette. He turns his back on the queue while he's lighting it in case Hal and Black spot him – that'd be the end of his fags.

'I'm going to sue you for passive smoking – Dad asked me last night was I smoking cos my clothes stank.'

'I'm going to charge you for all the free nicotine. What's Anna doing in that place anyway? She's a bit young to be signing on, isn't she?'

'She has to translate for her dad – they cut off his dole or something.'

A white Honda Civic comes careering around the corner and pulls up right next to us. Hammer Hayes is in the driver's seat. Jamie's sitting beside him. Hip-hop thumps from the car stereo and all eyes in the queue turn to look. Hammer jumps out of the car and swaggers up towards the front of the queue, which is now moving quickly through the doors.

'Hammer got himself a car *and* a bitch,' says Mikey under his breath.

'Shut up,' I say. Jamie motions at me to sit into the driver's seat. I stand up and flip my board into my hands. We haven't really spoken since the headbutt.

'Don't go near him, Matt. Fuck him – look what he did to your face,' Mikey says.

But I go anyway, and slide into the fur-lined seat. It's like a scumbag's cliché car, complete with furry dice and a St Christopher holy medal. It smells of Lynx – the one on offer in Tesco, two for the price of one. Tropics or Africa or some stupid name like that.

'Hi,' Jamie says. He's looking at his nails, examining them like they're the most interesting thing in the world.

'What do you want?' I say.

He shrugs and looks at me with our mother's eyes. 'Your fucking face ...'

'Yeah, nice job, thanks.'

'Look ...' he goes back to doing a recce on his nails. 'I'm sorry ... I'm not sorry for what I said to her – or to you either – but I'm sorry for hitting you. I don't know what happened to me. Her voice ... her fucking voice ...'

I don't say anything.

'You should tell her to fuck off, Matt.' He looks at me again. His ear is freshly pierced – twice – Dad's going to love that. His clothes are different, new, flashy Superdry hoodie, matching T-shirt and trackies. He has an iPhone on his lap. Latest model. I'd love a fucking iPhone. He shoves his hand into his pocket and takes out a wad of notes. Then he flicks off a couple and stuffs them into my hands.

'What's this for?'

Jamie shrugs. 'Buy yourself something – a new board ...' He looks over my shoulder and I follow his gaze. Hammer is strutting his stuff with the pyjama girls in tow. 'See ya,' says Jamie.

I get out of the car just as Hammer and the girls arrive.

'Fucking state of him with his ponytail. Fucking gay-boy,' he says. The orange-faced girls laugh and it's on the tip of my tongue to tell them to fuck off with their Oompa Loompa heads. But I respect madness and Hammer is mad.

'Little skater boy. You weren't half as gay when you were fat ...'

'Shut up Hammer,' Jamie says. 'Come on, let's go.'

Hammer and the girls climb into the car and it pulls off, the wheels burning rubber after them. You can smell it in the air.

'Apes,' says Mikey.

I look at my fist and realise that he's given me two hundred euro. Two fucking hundred euro.

'Jesus, did he give you that? 'Twas worth the header in the face. Ask him if he wants to headbutt me,' says Mikey.

I'm there like a fool looking at the notes. 'I can't take this – it's drug money or robbed or something.'

'Shut up, you gowl. Of course you can. Now, what'll we buy with it? You could bring me to Volcano Wings – I love their lava wings.'

'We'll be late for the skating competition if Anna doesn't hurry up – I'm going in to get her,' I say, dropping my board at Mikey's feet. 'Mind that with your life.'

After the dole office, I call in to my place for Conor – I'd promised him he could come to the competition. Dad's doing his stretches in the kitchen, his face slick with sweat. Conor's ready and waiting in the living room, a huge grin on his face.

'I thought you'd forget,' he says. 'Jamie said you'd forget me.'

'Nope, I didn't forget. And we're going to Mrs Chung's later for food – she invited us.'

'Yes, yes, yes,' says Conor, pulling his T-shirt over his head and doing a victory run around the couch.

Dad arrives in, his arm behind his head, other hand pressing against it, doing one of his many stretches. 'What's up?'

'I'm taking Conor to the skating competition and then out to Chungs'.'

'Oh right, yeah – Terry rang about it. She said she'd drop you home later.'

Conor is out the door in a flash and I follow, laughing at him.

'Matt?' Dad calls, just as I'm about to go out the door. Conor's at the lift, pressing the button over and over to make it come faster.

'Yeah?'

'I ... listen.' He looks down at his running shoes and then back at me. I'm halfway out the door, anxious now to get going. 'Thanks.' He winks at me.

'For what?'

'You're a sound lad. Good luck today.' He walks back into the kitchen and I stand there rooted to the floor with shock. Dad never says things like that. Not unless you win gold at a sporting event. And he thinks skating is for outcasts and weirdos – definitely not up there with the great sports of our time.

I walk out into the hallway. Conor is keeping the lift doors open and I go in. The smell of piss is overpowering. A young couple with a tiny black-haired baby get in on the third floor. The woman almost gags with the smell and shakes her head in disbelief.

Outside on the street I gulp in pissless air and Conor grins at me. Hot sun beams down on us as we walk the short distance to the park. We can hear the pulse of music and the sound of an MC talking. My heart's belting and I'm clenching and unclenching my fists. I love competitions. But I feel like I'm missing something. I check my pocket for my phone and keys and then I remember. My board – where the fuck is my board? I stop dead.

'What's up?' says Conor, jumping from foot to foot.

I close my eyes. Mikey has it. I can't believe my dumbness. I left my board with Mikey. I run the last few feet, Conor at my heels. The place is packed already and I push my way through gaggles of skaters and there's Mikey right at the very back, sitting on my board.

'Get off – you'll bust it.' I push him and he wobbles.

Mikey grins. 'That's nice – here I am minding the stupid thing for you and I get shit for thanks.'

I pick up my board and examine it. Feel the weight of it in my hands, spin the wheels, check it for damage. Mikey's no lightweight.

'Fucking marry it,' says Mikey. 'Did you bring food? Hey, Conor, man, sit down next to me and don't mind your dickhead brother.'

I kneel down beside them and watch for a while. A small group of scumbags has gathered on the river side of the park but the guards are there too, eyeing them up. The place is buzzing now, kids, teens, grown-up skaters, sponsors, DJs. Hal and Black are in party mood and have got themselves a slab of cans. They're sitting on the ground, the slab between them like a pet dog. Hal even strokes it now and again. They call the under 16s. I'm tingling. More than ready. Dying for it.

I'm skating unbelievable, best ever, and it's just me, Anna and a kid called Jake or Zac or some posh name like that in the final. Jake/Zac is up first and he wobbles on the rails, thumps the side of the low wall, and tries to pretend it's a grind but we all see the bits of board he's left behind, including the judges. Smart is a judge and he's all business, pretending he doesn't know us and flashing an identity necklace and looking serious.

Anna's fucking brilliant, even though I'm boiling inside with jealousy. Light as a feather on her board, smiling, loving every minute, pulling off every trick. When she finishes everyone claps, even Black and Hal. She beams at Smart and he winks at her.

Conor tugs at the sleeve of my hoodie. 'You'll win, you'll beat her, I know you will. Dad says you must believe you'll win.' He grins at me and runs over to stand on the wall for a better view.

My heart is bubbling in my chest and I can feel the blood pushing through my veins. I'm ready for this. The judge gives me a wave and I'm off. I can feel the sun lasering my head. The crowds blur so that there's just the board, the skating and me. I do a triple ollie and straight into a grind, keeping my speed. I'm flying around the park, the board is like another limb and I'm grinning to myself. I skimp up the half pipe and back down, and all I can hear is the board, whooshing and flying and grinding. I'm halfway through and the park is mine, it's just one of those days when everything fits, and that's when I look up and see her.

Time stops. I'm in mid-air, frozen, watching her as she nears. She's holding the hand of a young guy – not much older than Jamie. He's pushing a buggy and looking down into her upturned face. Everything around them is a blur – all the faces in the crowd are long streaks, like when a YouTube video loads all funny. She hasn't seen Conor yet but she's walking straight towards him. Fucking lousy. I don't realise I've fallen until I see the blood.

12 May 2016

Today I vomited at Granda's ~~funerel~~ funeral not cos I was sad well I was sad but it was over the sausage rolls. I ate 13 cos I counted and Jamie was drunk and he vomited too right next to mine out the back in Jerry O Dea's. Just near the used barrels. He cried under the duvet later cos he missed Granda the most Dad said cos he went like every day after school and weekends when he didn't even have to. We all were sure you'd come for the funeral. Your sisters came and they shook their heads and whispered with dad and then they rolled their eyes and Jamie stole their beer before they even knew and he drank it out the back and kicked the wall and screamed at me fuck off fatty when I came out and I only wanted to puke. Granda was pale in the coffin. Its the first time I saw a dead person and Mikey said he looked great but he didn't he looked dead. And every time I think of him I get a pain in my heart like the pain when you left and I knew after nine days waiting that you were really gone. You can't ring now cos Granda's gone but don't even bother. Jamie hates you. I hate you too.

8

I think I fainted or something because suddenly I open my eyes and the medics are around me. I sit up and see the blood all over my arm.

'It's fine. Just a scrape, they bleed like hell,' says one of the medics, a lanky guy with white skin, a shaved head and ginger eyebrows.

'I'm fine,' I say, standing up. The crowd claps. I search their faces for my mother's. I can see Conor, trying to push his way through the bodies around me but no sign of her. Maybe I dreamed it? My legs are jittery and Mikey pushes a bottle into my hand. I slug back the lukewarm water, scanning the area. At least Conor missed the happy-family scenario. And the teenage boyfriend.

'You OK, Matt?' says Anna, dragging me by the arm to sit on a low wall at the back of the skate park. The competition resumes, the music blaring and the MC calling up the next age group. 'You were brilliant,' she says.

I grin at her and notice she's wearing eye make-up. Gold stuff on her lids that makes her eyes shine and black liner and pink on her lips.

'What are you staring at – is something wrong? Is my face dirty?' She roots in her rucksack and pulls out a small mirror with diamonds on the back. She checks her face, angling her head.

'You ... you're lovely,' I say and suddenly my face flushes bright red. I look away. Fuck. I'm so thick sometimes.

She nudges me. 'Really? Does it suit me? It's, like, really hard to put on. My God, how girls do this every day is a miracle.'

I smile at her. 'Makes you way older – you look twelve now!'

She thumps me on my good arm. 'Fucker – I'm fifteen and you know it. Look – your man-crush is skating. Fuck, he's good.'

She stands on the wall for a better view and I climb up too, wobbling like a fucking eejit. She reaches out and takes my hand, steadying me, never taking her eyes from Smart's skating. And forgetting to take her hand away. Her hand tightens on mine. She turns and grins at me and my stomach does a flip and a grind all of its own. I'm trying to figure out why I feel like this about Anna. Fuck sake, just because she put on a bit of make-up. She's still the same old Anna, same old one of the lads. Maybe I have concussion.

So Anna beats me in the competition and I actually only mind a small bit, and when she hears her name she throws her arms around my neck and kisses me hard on the mouth and then runs off to collect her prize – vouchers for Skate Shop and a hundred euro too. I'm grinning like an ape and Mikey looks at me like I've just developed some highly contagious disease. He shakes his head in disgust.

'What?' I say, flipping my board up and searching for Conor. I see him at the edge of the crowd sitting alone, face as long as a poker. He's kicking the wall with his heels and he looks up at me and does the rapid-blinking thing.

'Sick,' says Mikey, walking away quickly, his thighs rubbing together with the effort.

'Wait up, asshole,' I shout. 'We're going to your house.'

Mikey rolls his eyes at me and for the first time ever I see his mother in that scrunched-up face of his.

'What's wrong, Mikey? Jesus, sorry for losing the competition. I thought you'd be glad I lost it to Anna.'

'Fuck off you wanker,' he says and starts to storm off again.

I grab him by his arm. 'What's eating you?' I say. Just then, Anna comes tearing over, all breathless. 'We're all going to Subway. I'm so thrilled – not because you lost, Matt – you know that ...'

She grabs my arm and does the flirty thing with her eyes that I thought I'd never see her do. Right up into my face. I like it. I grin at her, she smiles back, and for the second time today the world stops, but only for her. Everything else is blurry and voices mix with other sounds to make a loud buzz in my head. Like a huge swarm of flies.

'Are you ready, Anna?' Smart is butting into the picture, grinning at me with his lazy special. 'You coming for food, man?'

I shake my head and watch as she retreats, leaning into Smart as they walk away. The park is almost empty except for Hal and Black, who's calling me over to sit down for one of his drunken chats. I'm in no mood for Black. Mikey's grinning at me.

'Are you on your period? Talk about a mood swing,' I say, suddenly angry with the world. I beckon to Conor and he slinks over, his mood the opposite of earlier in the day. 'You on your period too?' I say, kicking the skateboard towards him so that he nearly trips over it. His eyes fill with tears and I'm furious with him and sorry for him all at the same time. What the fuck happened that made everybody so moody?

'He's a gowl,' says Mikey.

'Who?'

'Smart. He's like an ad – too good to be true.'

I shrug. 'Great skater though.'

'Still a gowl,' says Mikey.

We walk to the bus stop at Dunnes, Mikey whistling now, Conor with his head down examining the footpath and me full of an anger I can't explain.

Mrs Chung has our dinner ready. Conor's favourite – roast chicken, gravy, real stuffing and steeped peas. She hugs him to her when she sees him as if he's a lost child or something. Tony Howlin, the old man from down the road, is there too.

I know Mikey's over his sulk when the jokes begin.

'OK – I've a brilliant one. A faith healer was in Southill and he asked for people with special needs to come forward to be prayed for ...'

One of the United Colours of Benetton – the youngest one, Troy – spits peas onto their other brother, Leon's plate, making him cry, and Mrs Chung manages to silence the two of them with a look.

Mikey resumes his joke telling. 'Anyway, Antony steps forward and says, "Can you help me with my hearing?" The faith healer smiles and says, "Certainly, my son." He puts his hands over Antony's ears and he and everybody starts praying. "Has that helped?" says the healer. "Dunno," says Antony, "My hearing isn't till next Tuesday."'

Mikey guffaws and so do Tony Howlin and Mrs Chung, and the smallies giggle too even though they haven't a clue. Conor eats his peas, face glued to his plate.

'What's wrong, Matt? Lost your sense of humour?' Mikey says, stuffing a huge forkful of spuds and gravy into his mouth.

'You should use a different name,' I say.

'I like my name, it has stage presence: Michael Chung.'

'No. I mean Antony. They're always called Antony.'

Mikey glares at me as he chews his food, his cheeks bulging like a hamster. 'There's always something with you, isn't there? It's never fucking good enough, Mr Fucking Perfect, Mr Fucking Know it All Super Duper Fucking Perfect –'

'I won't have language like that at my table, Michael,' says Mrs Chung, her voice tight and low. Everybody seems to respond to the tone, even old Tony.

'I just meant ... I ... there are other names, that's all.' I say.

'And there are other girls you fucking big-headed prick-faced fucker –'

'Leave the table now, Michael,' says Mrs Chung, dropping her fork and knife. Mikey stands up, pushing his chair back so it crashes to the ground and walks backwards out the door never taking his eyes away from me. He bangs the door so that the glasses on the table shake.

'Prick-face,' says Troy.

'It looks like rain out there,' says old Tony.

'It's promised good until Monday,' says Mrs Chung. 'Conor, more chicken?'

Conor shakes his head. I stare at Mikey's barely touched dinner. He'll never forgive me for that. Him having to leave a full plate of dinner.

Then Mikey does yet another massive mood swing. He comes sauntering into the kitchen while I'm loading up the dishwasher as if nothing happened at all and winks at me.

'You giving your Weight Watchers class tonight, Mam?' he says to his mother's back. She's scrubbing pots at the sink.

'Yeah, I was wondering if you and Matt'd give me a hand setting up the hall? I'm starting an exercise class with them. Some of them I swear, they think the seats are magic – if they come and plonk down for the night, they'll lose a half stone.'

We all laugh and the tension seems to go out of the air.

'Put on the kettle there Matt, we'll have a quick coffee before we face the fatties,' Mrs Chung says and we all laugh again as if Mikey isn't fat at all.

She makes coffee and we both sit at the kitchen table. Old Tony is in the living room, supposedly to watch the news but one of the United Colours has changed the channel to *The Simpsons*. He doesn't seem to mind. Conor's glued to the TV. Mikey's gone to have a shower. That's the worst thing I remember about the fat. The sweat constantly dripping off me. And the smell of it.

'So, she's home.' Mrs Chung cuts me a huge slice of marble cake. Home-made. It wouldn't go down well in Weight Watchers – or maybe it would.

I shrug and stir sugar into my coffee and break off a piece of cake. A pink piece with a small swirl of yellow.

'She rang here. I barely spoke to her. She'd no right ... Anyway, Matt, if you need to talk ...'

I can feel her eyes on me and my face pinking up.

'She's going to a solicitor – wants her "rights" if you don't mind. Don't let her ...' She stops and again her eyes bore into me. I look away, watch the cat on the window-sill clawing to get in. I can't remember the cat's name. Blackie?

'Look, I don't want ye to be hurt again. I know her. Swanning back here and everything's great for five minutes and the second there's a hint of trouble or work or hard slog she's off again.'

My body tenses and I can feel that no-name anger like a hot, hard ball inside me. The cat climbs the window and slips back down. He does this over and over. Stupid fucking cat. Dubh. That's his name. I was close with Blackie.

'Matt?'

I break off another piece of cake. I can't taste it and I have to gulp to swallow it.

'Look, I know more than anyone how horrible this must be and I'm only trying to protect you, honestly. OK?' She pats my hand. 'You know that, don't you?'

I shrug.

'What's up with Conor? He's very quiet in himself.'

I shrug again. 'I think he's disappointed in me. I didn't win today and he was counting on me.'

'Your Dad needs to sit him down and explain all this stuff about your mother. Jamie too. All of you. She can't be let waltz around upsetting everyone.'

'She is ... she's our m-mother,' I say.

'Not for the past five years – ups and leaves her kids without a backward glance ... running off with ...' Mrs Chung stops when she sees my face. 'Hey, Mattie, I'm sorry, hon. Hey, it's OK ...' She leans across the table and hugs me to her and that makes the lump in my throat double in size. Just feeling her arms around me tight and sure.

'With who?' I whisper into her chest. 'Running off with who?'

'Nothing, Matt, nobody. It's over and done with now.'

'I want to know. I want to know what happened.' I pull back from Mrs Chung and wipe my eyes with the sleeve of my hoodie.

She shakes her head. 'It's none of my business, Matt. Not really.'

'Yes, it is. You were her friend – her best friend – just like me and Mikey, so it is your business.'

She smiles at me. 'It's complicated. People are complicated. More cake?'

I shake my head. I know she wants to change the subject and part of me is glad. Maybe I don't want to know what happened. Not really.

Mrs Chung takes another slice of cake for herself. A fine big slice. She obviously doesn't practise what she preaches down at Weight Watchers.

Mikey and I load up the car with Mrs Chung's aerobic stuff. Mats and skipping ropes and foam weights. Fuck sake, foam weights? Mikey's sniggering to himself all the time.

'What's so funny?' I ask.

'You'll see, all in good time,' he says, grinning at me. He chucks a weight at my head. And misses.

We set up the hall. Mrs Chung has changed into her exercise clothes. Lycra, same as Dad's running gear. She looks great – you'd never think she had a belly full of marble cake. Mikey's still sniggering away to himself. I wonder if he has a mental illness. I read up online about those things when Jamie turned into a ratbag after Christmas. How they can develop once the teenage hormones kick in. There are loads of them – bipolar, schizophrenia. He's fucking manic today – that's for sure. The class wander in, all shapes and sizes.

Mikey and I hang out at the back of the hall, inflating the giant balance balls and organising the dumbbells for Mrs Chung. The class line up to be weighed.

'I was so good this week, Terry, I'll go first,' a blonde woman says, beaming at the rest of the class. Her sweatshirt is so tight it looks like somebody pumped her into it and she's wearing lycra leggings that outline the rolls of leg fat perfectly. I watch her body wobble as she climbs on the scales.

'So, let's see, Jen, what you've lost this week,' says Mrs Chung. 'Wait, that can't be right. You've put on four pounds.'

Jen's face drops and her eyes fill up with tears. 'I was so good, never even had a drink ... I just don't believe it.'

Mrs Chung checks the scale again. 'It's probably just water retention.'

Jen climbs off the scales. 'Four pounds of water retention? I must have a whole fucking reservoir inside me.'

A man steps onto the scales and Mrs Chung leans down to take a closer look at the dial. Mikey snorts with laughter beside me.

'This is weird. You're four pounds over since last week.'

'I weighed everything that went past my lips – the wife said I was like a drug dealer with the weighing scales out all the time. Four pounds?'

A skinny woman with a protruding belly and boobs is next.

'Five pounds up, Angie, on last week,' Mrs Chung says, shaking her head.

'You're joking me, Terry? I'm after losing four stone, I write every crumb I eat down, every bite that passes my lips. My body forgets what full feels like.'

Mikey sniggers.

Mrs Chung looks down at us and her eyes narrow. 'Come off the scale a sec there Ang, I want to check something.'

'Run,' says Mikey, grabbing me by the arm, and the two of us race outside. We collapse onto the grass laughing.

'The reservoir woman ... fuck me pink,' says Mikey.

'How did you do it? You shove a coin into the dial or something, is that it?'

Mikey nods. 'More or less. There's a knack – so that the scale reads proper like before you step on it but it adds then once there's weight – brilliant trick.'

'Not if you're reservoir woman!'

We crack up again, rolling around on the grass.

'Come on, let's go – *FIFA* calls,' says Mikey, groaning as he gets up. 'Jesus, I could do with going to the fat class myself,' he says as we head towards his house.

'I told you what do – skate. It's your only man to melt the fat.' I grin at him.

'Naw, skating's boring. Going around in circles on a bit of wood with little wheels? Boring. Maybe if I just cut out Chinese grub altogether?'

I glance at Mikey. For as long as I've known him, he's never wanted to lose weight. This is new. 'So, what's brought this weight shit on?' I ask, studying his face.

'Nothing. Summer – the heat, that kind of shit.'

'Liar,' I say. 'You like someone, don't you?'

'No.'

'Let's see ... Mia Togher? Naw, she's a douche. Amm – Leah Curran? You always sit with her at break time but she's a lesbo ...'

'How do you know she's a lesbo?'

'That's easy, bud. The Docs, the combats and the lezzer haircut.'

Mikey rolls his eyes. 'You can't talk – the girl's face, the ponytail, hanging out with the older skater boys ...'

I dig him in the side. 'And I forgot, black lezzer lipstick.'

'Isn't that emo – you know, the crowd that wear black and dream of suicide?' Mikey says with a grin.

'So who's the girl you want to get killer abs for? Go on, tell me – I can keep a secret.'

'Well, fuck me sideways,' says Mikey.

'Nope, I'll pass,' I say.

'No, you fool, look ahead – it's your brother and Hammer Hayes flying around in that car. Too late – they've seen us,' says Mikey.

I can hear it then in his voice. The fear, the thing that the Hammer Hayeses of the world thrive on. The thing that pisses me off about Mikey. Absolute cowardice.

'Fuck them,' I say, pretending I don't see them as they slow down and kerb crawl next to us.

Mikey slows down too and beams at them like they're nice people looking for directions. The car thumps with rap music, so loud I wonder how they manage to talk to each other. Jamie leans out of the window. I glance at him from the corner of my eye but I keep walking. He's smiling at me but he can't see. Stoned or drunk or both.

'Get in,' he says, and Hammer stops the car.

'Fuck off,' I say, walking faster. But Mikey stops and smiles at them and if he had a tail he'd be wagging it as well.

'Run, Mikey,' I shout, increasing my pace. I look back over my shoulder and there's Mikey climbing into the back of the fucking car, the douche. I run back but the car speeds off. I watch as it careers dangerously around the corner. I take out my phone and ring him. No answer. Then I ring Jamie. No answer, so I leave a message. Should I tell Mrs Chung? What if they hurt him?

I walk around the estate for a while trying to spot the car but there's no sign anywhere. I end up in the field where we found the bag of cans. It's busy tonight because it's Saturday and they're all out bush drinking. I can hear little knots of them, laughing, talking loud and playing music on their phones. The sun's setting over Keeper Hill, gold against green. A gang of lads are playing hurling at the far end of the field, and the clash of the sticks reminds of being up here as a kid, watching Jamie play soccer, Dad screaming from the sideline. *Go on, Jamie, go yourself, that's it, go on, there's nobody on you, go on, Jamie, go on ... yes!* My arm is aching where I fell on it earlier and my head is splitting now. I'm glad of the headache. It makes me stop thinking about Mikey.

It's almost dark by the time I go back to Mikey's. I have to get Conor – otherwise I'd just go home. The last person I want to see is Mrs Chung but she's all chat when she answers the door.

'I'll drive ye home in a few minutes – go on up there to Mikey, he's not feeling too good,' she says, wiping her hands on a tea towel. I can hear old Tony in the sitting room playing with the smallies. The hall smells of coconut shampoo. I love that smell. I run upstairs to Mikey's bedroom. He's lying on the bed watching his favourite DVD – Lenny Bruce live somewhere in America.

'Man, why the fuck did you get in? Why didn't you run like I said?'

Mikey says nothing, just turns up the TV.

'What the fuck did they want you for anyway?'

He turns then and looks at me and then I see it. The fear that was in his voice is in his eyes.

'What did they want you for?' I ask again, almost shouting it this time.

'Nothing. I can handle myself you know – I don't need you babysitting me all the time. Breathing down my neck.'

'They want you to do jobs for them, don't they? Well don't, Mikey. Just don't.'

He goes back to watching Lenny Bruce. I stand there like a gowl for a minute and then I march out, banging the door behind me. Fuck him and his moods.

There's a note on the kettle when we get home.

Pizza there if you want some. Gone to a meeting. Will be late. Dad.

Conor goes straight in to the sitting room and flicks on the TV. It fills the room with an eerie light.

'Do you want pizza?' I ask, sitting down beside him on the sofa.

He shakes his head, eyes transfixed on the screen.

An old episode of *Father Ted* comes on – the one where they're in the Aillwee Caves. I'm laughing away at it and Conor's staring, blinking and pulling at his hair.

'I saw her,' he says, keeping his eyes fixed on the screen.

'Who?' I say, my concentration still on *Father Ted*.

'Mam. I saw Mam with her new child. I saw her and she saw me.'

I look at his blinking profile. He's staring at the TV, concentrating so hard that his face seems twisted. I want to hug him, make it OK, tell him it'll work out fine. But I can't because it's all lies. I don't know what to say. I go into the kitchen and make toast.

1/2 (cos its midnight) July 2016

Jamie's girlfriend finished with him. Her parents called and Dad said come in sit down would you like tea? They shook their heads and stood at the door even though it was flogging out. They banned Jamie from their house and their girl. Said he hit her. Dad said no way. Mikey's Mam is having another baby and Mikey says soon he'll have to put a tent in the front garden for himself. We got a new computer and Dad is learning to use it and I googled your name but nobody came up except a girl in Texas with a dodgy photo. You have to be famous to get found on google. Sometimes I make up email addresses for you and I send you these pages. I scanned them all into the computer but I still like writing them first with a pen. Just to see the words written down in front of me. And holding the Gone Book in my hands. You can't do that with the computer.

9

Jamie's moving out. All his stuff is piled in the hallway. There are white patches on the wall in our bedroom where he's taken down his posters. Stevie Gerrard and Mo Salah and the National. I'll miss them. They were like pals, watching over me at night when I read or wrote in my book.

I don't want him to go even though he's a fucking pig lately. I still don't want him to go and live in a stupid apartment with all those wasters, pretending he's grown up. Dad talked to him last night, begged him to stay and Jamie laughed in his face and said, 'You spent months throwing me out and now you're begging me to stay? Fuck you.'

Conor slinks into the kitchen, his face pinched and white, and sits beside me on a stool, watching Jamie pile up the last few bits and pieces. Dad's gone running again even though he went already this morning. I remind myself to ask him about Lahinch with Mrs Chung. She's going on Friday and I still haven't said a word.

Jamie comes out of our bedroom, carrying his *Simpsons* talking alarm clock and whistling a Stormzy song. He stops when he sees the two of us watching him. 'Cheer up lads, nobody's dead,' he says, grinning at us.

'What if you forget about us?' Conor says, his voice small.

My stomach does a kickflip and in my head I'm begging Jamie to be kind to Conor. He's only a kid. Jamie rolls his eyes and walks out into the tiny hallway. *Fucking bastard*, I say to myself, staring at his back. He turns around then, like he heard me, and comes back in, clock still in his hand.

'This is for you,' he says to Conor, placing the clock on the breakfast-strewn worktop. 'And I want you to do me a favour. I want you to mind my bed in case I need to come back. Can you do that for me?'

Conor smiles, a tiny, barely noticeable one but a smile all the same.

'It's a hard job, Conor, minding that bed. Loads of things could go wrong – Matt could move a woman in there ...'

Conor giggles at this.

'Or he could get fat again and need two beds to sleep in.'

Conor laughs and so do I in spite of myself.

'I'll call all the time. And I'll bring you down to the new pad – we have a jacuzzi bath and surround sound and a fifty-inch plasma that Hammer bought yesterday. Now, could you give me a hand bringing this stuff down to the car and I'll give you a tenner – how's that?'

Conor jumps down off the stool and runs into the hallway, gathering up duvets and pillows in his skinny little arms.

When Dad comes back, Jamie's gone. All traces of him, including his favourite mug – a giant *Star Wars* one that Mrs Chung got him last Christmas over him loving a mug of tea. Dad says nothing. Does his stretches in the kitchen, his body dripping sweat for the second time in one day. I'm supposed to meet the lads at the skate park ages ago but I don't want to leave Conor on his own – not today. I take the Lahinch plunge.

'Am ... Mrs Chung is taking me to Lahinch on Friday. She's got a mobile home there for a week, a loan from her friend. So is that OK?'

Dad does a hamstring stretch followed by a calf stretch. Then he repeats it on the other leg.

'What about Conor?' he says between stretches.

Conor's in the sitting room blinking at the TV. I can hear Judge Judy's voice giving out to someone. Dad continues his stretches, going into the floor series now. I have a mad terrible urge to kick him. Kick him so hard that he doubles up in pain, that he never runs again, that he never even walks.

'What about Conor? What's it got to do with him?'

He stops his exercises and looks up at me from the spotless white-tiled floor. 'I've a lot on for the next week.

There's a half-marathon in Connemara. Someone will need to stay with Conor.'

'How about you sort that out? He's your child.'

He's up on his feet in a flash 'He's your brother,' he says, his voice low.

His spit lands on my face and I can smell his sweat. I can see it, popping on his forehead like raindrops.

'So I can't go – is that what you're saying?'

'Are you starting now too? Are you going to end up like the other fella? I don't know what I reared – one a waster and you running around with a bloody skateboard and girl's hair.'

'I could be you – just running around with no board and no hair.' I smirk at him, very pleased with my reply.

His eyes gleam with anger and he raises his hand and curls it into a fist. Still I don't flinch.

'Go on, hit me. You see where it got Jamie. So hit me now and then start on Conor and soon you'll have the whole flat to yourself. Soon you'll be all alone running in circles around the town.'

He drops his hand and stares at me and I know I've hurt him by the look on his face but I don't care. Fuck him. I can't even go on holidays. He walks out of the kitchen, his shoulders drooping. I throw bread in the toaster but when it pops, I don't feel like eating it any more.

It's evening by the time I get to the skate park. There's no sign of the lads and they're not answering their phones. I jump on my board and bang around, not enjoying it at all. I stumble on a stupid easy little grind and kick my board so hard against the railing a piece of the deck chips off. I leap over the railing and sit on the grass facing the river. Two swans with necks like question marks glide up and down, coming near the riverbank when they see me. They do a recce of me for bread and when they realise I don't have any they glide off again, their silhouettes mirrored in the dark still water.

'Fuckin' bitch,' a voice says from the ground.

I look around me and see a heap of crumpled rags thrown down beside the rubbish bin. The rags move and a face appears, eyes swollen from sleep.

'Black? Is that you?' I say.

'Hal is a fuckin' bitch. She stole my slab while I was asleep,' he says, staggering to his feet. He walks unsteadily towards me and slides onto the grass beside me. The smell off him is unreal. Stale piss, beer, and vomit.

'You've a face like a slapped arse – what's up with you?' he says, taking a battered nobber of a fag from an inside pocket. He sticks the fag in his mouth and then pats himself down looking for a light.

'Nothing.'

Black laughs, a deep rich laugh that you'd never think belonged to him.

'Did somebody steal your slab too?' Black grins at me,

his mouth like something from a horror film, teeth missing or else rotten.

I shrug. Black starts the search for a match all over again. He finally finds a lighter in his shoe. It says *I heart Limerick* along the side. Then he lights his fag butt, pulling the smoke deep into his lungs.

'My mother left us.' It's out of my mouth before I even realise.

'She'll be back,' says Black, looking at the water. 'We all need to fuck off every now and again.'

'It was five years ago.' I kick my board so it rolls against the railings.

'She's taking her time. She must be really needing a break.' He takes another drag and the butt is right down to his brown dirty fingers.

'A break from what?' I say, my voice quivery. Fuck sake; am I turning soft or something with all this whinging?

Black does the lovely deep laugh again. 'From life, kid. From life and all its miseries and worries. The human condition. This mortal coil. Call it anything you want and it's still miserable.'

I nod, pretending I understand what he's talking about. 'She came back a few weeks ago,' I say but his eyes are glazing over, like he's forgotten I'm there next to him.

'I was a boxer once.' He grins at me, that mad horror movie grin.

'No way,' I say.

He nods at the water. 'Damn good one as well. Boxed all over Europe.'

He crushes the fag out with the heel of his ancient boot.

'A wife and children and a mortgage - the king of Suburbia – that was me – I had the lot. Even the fucking lawnmower.'

The swans glide towards us again, still hoping for crumbs. The sun is setting low in the sky and the evening has a pink glow. Traffic hums around us, on the road and on the bridge. Lights in the Clayton Hotel flicker on, spraying tiny spotlights on the dark river. The birds are singing their hearts out, not realising the day is over. We sit like that for a while and it's almost enjoyable.

'I haven't gone back yet,' he says after an age. 'Don't have the guts.'

Black's in another world now, eyes glassy, looking at the navy and pink striped sky. Just when I'm thinking to myself that he's actually back there in his head, playing football in the garden with his kids, waving at his wife, who's standing by the window watching him, he farts loudly, follows it with a belch and a demand for money.

'Few bob, kid? Give it back tomorrow – I swear.'

I search my pockets and find a fiver and Black greed-ily snatches it from me, and is up and on his feet like an athlete.

'Bavaria here I come, see you later,' he says, and disap-pears, leaping over the railings like a young fella. I stay there, king of the skate park, listening to the night city.

It's black-dark by the time Mikey and Anna arrive.

'Where were ye? I rang and texted – sneaky bastards,' I say, feeling my rotten mood return at the sight of the two of them all giggles and jokes. Anna has the make-up on again; I can see it, even in the dark. Mikey's grinning from ear to ear. The cat that got the cream.

'We went to the movies – wait up – I have a movie joke. What do you call security guards working outside Samsung Shops? Guardians of the Galaxy.'

Mikey grins at me and Anna laughs. Then he looks at her with big adoring eyes and it dawns on me that she's the one that he likes. It's Anna. For no reason, I want to hurt him, just because I can.

'I'm not going to Lahinch.'

Mikey grins at me. 'Heard all about it – Mam is ringing your dad, she's trying to sort it out. We'll be down in Lahinch this time next week like two surfer dudes.'

I shake my head at him. 'It's not because of my dad – it's because I don't want to. It'll be boring with just you and me. I'll be bored out of my tree.' I watch as he digests what I'm saying, and it's like watching a punch or a kick land in the right place. The place that hurts the most.

'I ... we'll ... we'll have a great time ... swimming and surfing and stuff ...' he stutters. Anna's glaring at me, her hand on her hip.

'Swimming, surfing? You? Seriously Mikey, seriously. Get real for yourself.' I walk away, my board under my arm.

Black moods are like grey skies. Sometimes it takes ages for them to blow off somewhere else. I wake the next morning to Dad shouting into his phone. Conor has moved into my bedroom and Woody from *Toy Story* stares down at me instead of good old familiar Steven Gerrard. I feel like I'm six again. I glance over at Conor as Dad's voice rises – *You walked out and now you want to waltz back in as if nothing happened? I told you this is exactly how it'd pan out once you got sick of your little toy boy or he got sick of you I told you that. Bitch, fucking bitch hanging up on me …*

Conor's pretending to be asleep. I know he's pretending because of the blinking. He blinks now even with his eyes closed. It's as if he knows I'm watching him so he whips the duvet up over his head.

I don't want to get up but I make myself. I wander into the bathroom and brush my teeth, my eyes still bleary from sleep. The place feels different without Jamie. I splash water on my face and stare at myself in the mirror. I look so different without the fat that every now and then I get a shock when I see this skinny little face with cheek-bones and no double chin staring back at me. I miss the fat. It was like protection around me. Things didn't change so much when the fat was there. Jamie was still here, Mam was still gone and I never fought with Mikey. I was never mean to him. Not that I can remember anyway. And Dad was bearable and Conor wasn't blinking all the time. The fat days were the best. Mikey shouldn't bother his arse trying to get thin.

Dad's already in his running gear when I go into the kitchen. I pour myself a bowl of cornflakes but the sight of them swimming around in the milk makes me feel sick. Dad's edging around the kitchen and I know he has something to say but I don't want to hear it. It'll only make the black cloud worse.

'That was her,' he says eventually.

I swirl the soggy cornflakes around in the bowl.

'She wants to see the three of you. Suggests I drop you "somewhere neutral" and she'd take ye off for a few hours. The absolute cheek of her. Thinks she can drop her kids like … like knitting and come back when she feels like it.'

I've hunched my shoulders without realising and Dad notices too.

'I … look … I'm only doing what I think is best for ye. Do you want to see her?'

The question is like a slap. I've tried not to think about her at all since that accidental meeting in town. Mikey says she's a can of worms, she's the shit ready to hit the fan, and he's right. If I open the can or turn on the fan, then I know what'll happen and then it's all going to be my fault. All of it.

'No.'

Dad stares at me until I look up from my cornflakes. 'Are you sure? Because I told her that ye mightn't want to see her at this late stage in the game and she said if you all say no then she'll accept that.'

'No.'

He smiles at me. 'Well, that's that, then. I'll –'

'I want to see her.' Conor's standing at the door in Munster pyjamas, his eyes swollen from sleep.

Dad looks at him and then at me like I have the answer to something. I shrug. Dad examines his runners. 'I don't know if that's a ...'

'I want to see my mammy.' Conor's eyes are blinking rapidly, squeezing out tears with every blink.

'Stop crying, Conor,' Dad says.

Conor blinks away his tears but some have escaped already and run down his cheeks.

'Your mammy walked out and left us and never even called to see if we were alive or dead. Remember that, Conor, when you're crying over her. Just remember that.' Dad stares at Conor, his hand on the door handle.

'I ... I just want to see her. That's all.' Conor's voice is tiny. I'm willing Dad to be nice to him. It works. Dad runs his hand over his head, as if he still has hair. The little bit he has he shaves off.

'We'll talk about it when I get back – OK?' he says. He goes over to Conor and is about to hug him but just pats his head instead. 'See you in a bit.' Then he leaves.

Conor stands there staring at me as I play with my cereal. 'You promised me.'

'Promised you what?'

'You promised me you'd take me to see her and now you won't just cos you can't be bothered cos you saw her already and I didn't ...' He runs from the kitchen back into the bedroom, almost taking the door off the hinges he shuts it so hard. Something clatters to the ground in the room. My reading lamp. Conor has taken up the door-banging where Jamie stopped and my lamp always suffers.

I slam around the kitchen for a while, black anger knotting inside me. Conor reappears, with his T-shirt back to front, and I feel a desperate sadness for him. Like he's a prisoner up here on the fifth floor and this is his entire world. These four walls, that telly and the constant swimming practice. At least I can go out by myself, have another life. He pours himself cereal and spills the milk as he fills the bowl to the very top. Then he looks at me angrily and carries the bowl into the sitting room, leaving a trail of milk after him.

So I end up taking Conor skating with me. First, we stop off in Tubes Skate Shop and he picks out a board – I push him towards the cheaper ones. Pointless getting an expensive board if you mightn't even stick with it. Then we wander down Henry Street, Conor admiring his new board. The skate park is empty except for a couple of newbies with shit boards. Gowls. You can't skate on shit boards. There's no sign of Mikey or Anna and there's no way I'm texting them. Fuck them. They can sneak off to the cinema again for all I care.

I'm still teaching Conor the basics when Smart arrives with a new crowd of skaters. I'm glad to see them because Conor might be a great swimmer but he'll never be a skater. I know by just watching him stand on the board, without ever pushing off. No sense of balance at all.

'We're heading up to Tait's Clock,' Smart says, then wheels away and does a huge ollie off the low wall. That's how you skate. Fluid, lazy, easy, like running.

We tag along up to Tait's Clock with them but Conor's annoying the fuck out of me with his sulking. He's sitting on the footpath, big dejected head on him, throwing me guilt glares. He finally finds a stray dog with a scabby back and plays with him while we skate. The others leave one by one until it's just me, Smart, Conor and Scabby Back. Smart shows me tricks and shortcuts and I practice until I'm perfect.

'I'm done in,' Smart says. 'Gotta go.'

My stomach is growling with hunger as we head towards home, the dog glued to Conor's legs. A string of linking girls pass and they all whisper and giggle at Smart. He laughs and winks at them and I'm so proud to be with him. It's like Smart is shiny and when you're with a shiny person then you shine too. A little bit of the glow rubs off on you.

'See you tomorrow?' I say as we reach the Dock Road.

Smart grins at me, the pop-star grin complete with great teeth and floppy hair. 'Naw, man, I'm going away tomorrow for a while – you know, on holiday.'

I'm disgusted with myself I'm so disappointed. 'No problem. Where are you going?' I ask. Conor's walking ahead of me, the dog skipping beside him. I know already he's going to cause trouble over the dog. There's no way Dad'll have a dog in the flat, especially a scabby one.

'Lahinch. The surf's good for the next week so ...'

'Hey, that's weird! I'm going too – on Friday actually.' It's out before I can help myself. Why the fuck did I fight with Mikey?

'Cool. Man, I'm dying for a surf – you think skating's good? Wait until you surf. See you there,' he says and jumps on his board and rolls off down the road. Conor's standing at the entrance to our apartment block, one hand on his hip, the other on the dog's neck. He has this look in his eye, a look I saw before once when he decided he wasn't going to school any more because Sean Tierney said he had a mouth like a horse crossed with Alan Carr. There was no way he was going to school no matter what Dad and I did. Conor just refused and clung to the chair with both hands welded to it. That's the look he has now.

'No. Fuck off, Conor,' I say.

'We can hide him, Matt. Dad'll never know, I promise. I'll feed him and clean up after him and –'

'No. Impossible, Conor. Out of the question.'

His eyes fill up with tears, huge fat ones that spill down his face. An actor would kill for tears like that.

'Go away, go home,' I shout at the dog. He cowers behind Conor's legs, peeping out at me as if I'm some kind of dog murderer.

'Please, Matt, please?'

The dog knows he's onto a good thing with Conor; he's sitting next to him now offering him his paw.

'Please, Matt – he's the dog in the ad that we love. He was waiting for us to find him.'

Our favourite ad – the dog in the dog pound who understands the art of advertising and has his promo running on ticker tape for prospective owners. And his suitcase packed beside him. Scabby's clever, I'll give him that.

'Look, we'll sneak him in and then I'll – I don't know – I'll think of something,' I say, annoyed with myself. This won't end well and I'm only setting Conor up for heartbreak but I can't say no. I just can't.

So we sneak him up and straight into our bedroom before Dad even knows we're home.

'Rocky,' says Conor, 'his name is Rocky. You're the best, Matt,' he says then and hugs my waist. I pat his head and Rocky/Scabby watches and I swear he's grinning at me.

'You got your wish,' Conor,' Dad says when we go into the kitchen. There's an incredible smell – roast chicken and spuds, Dad has the table set, and there's even serviettes and a candle. It reminds me of when Mrs Chung used to cook our dinners and you could smell it at Murphy's shop, coming home from school. You could nearly taste the gravy by the time you got to the front door.

Conor and I look at each other behind Dad's back. We got away with it. He doesn't know there's a scabby dog in the bedroom. It's going to be a long night.

'You're going to see your mother tomorrow. Jamie too, if that's what he wants. You don't have to go if you don't want to Matt ...'

Dad goes back to carving the chicken, putting the different pieces on plates. Breast for him and me, wings for Conor. I pick a bit of roast skin from my plate and I see Dad looking at the two legs still on the chicken's carved-up body. Jamie's legs. He looks at me and for the first time in ages, I feel sorry for Dad. Then I hear a soft, low bark from the bedroom so I switch on the radio. Spin South West. Cardi B. Enough noise to drown out a whole pack of howling dogs.

6 October 2016

Dad had to go to the school over Fartgate. It wasn't even my fault and I'm always good in school and Dad only ever has to go over Jamie because he's his grades are gone so bad. We were in study and Mikey farted for a joke and the supervisor told Fr. Burke and he lost the plot and banned us all from study until somebody owned up to the fart. Dad was mad when he came home but I still didn't tell him who farted. They wouldn't let the whole class go to study for a week and Mrs Chung went up to Fr. Burke and said it couldn't have been my Michael – he had his fart glands removed with his tonsils and Dad said Mikey doesn't pick it up off the street the smart mouth but Burke let us back to study so it must have worked. I read a book and it made me cry. The boy in the striped pyjamas. Jamie smokes and he drinks beer and I'm not squealing on him really cos you aren't even here. I'm over hating you. Your not worth it.

10

The dog is the newest headache in my life. I'm awake all night trying to work out a plan for Scabby. He's supposed to be asleep under Conor's bed but he's actually worked his way up and now he even has a pillow for himself. I work out a half-arsed plan – bribe Black into minding the dog for some of the time – but still I can't sleep. There are night sounds. The dull whoosh of traffic. The drip of the kitchen tap. I count sheep. No luck. Golf balls. Nope. Girls' tits. Nope – makes me more awake. I hear Dad stirring in the next room, followed by grunts and soft plops. He's lifting weights in the middle of the night. Fucking madman. He can't sleep either and he doesn't even have to worry about the dog. But I know deep down what's keeping us both awake. It's her.

In the morning I'm up first. It's barely light outside and Scabby's eyeing me and wagging his tail. I risk bringing him out to the kitchen, figuring if Dad was lifting weights during the night then he might have a lie-in. Scabby's delighted. He's flying around the kitchen sniffing everything, and when I glare at him for making noise, he stops, sits down and gives me the paw. I feed him cornflakes and he licks the bowl and then does the paw thing again. Too fucking smart. His tail thumps the floor when I smile at him. I make a lead for him out of twine and give him a drink of water.

We head out to find Black before Dad gets up. Finding Black this early could be a problem. He's one of the Living Dead so I don't think I've ever seen him or Hal before lunchtime. Except on dole day. Where the fuck would they sleep? I mean I've never seen them in doorways; they're way above that sort of thing. I try to imagine where I'd sleep if I was homeless. Easy. Under Sarsfield Bridge.

I stroll down by the river, Scabby staying tight to my leg. The sun is rising, striping the sky in pinks and purples. The river stinks. The tide is low and swans avoid bicycle corpses and old tyres, like they have inbuilt satnav. The bridge looms up in front of me. Scabby stops dead and growls, staring into the black mouth of the arch. I drag him in, letting my eyes adjust to the darkness. There is a smell of piss and river and diesel. I spot a bundle of rags in a corner. The rags have a face. Young, dirty, sores on his mouth.

'Do you know Black? Do you know where his ... where he sleeps?'

The eyes flash open. 'Try the house. They won't let me in. Near Subway.' He grins and it makes him look like a kid.

'Thanks,' I say, pulling the dog by the lead. Outside, by the river, I gulp in fresh air. The sun is shining and I head towards Subway, trying to blank out the boy in the bundle of rags.

I know which house it is the minute I set eyes on it. It's easy to find – it has to be the derelict one with the boarded-up windows. I stand on the steps looking at the peeling green paint on the front door. There's a metal stairs running down to a filthy basement – the door almost hidden. What should I do? Knock? Ring the bell? I try knocking but nothing happens. A passer-by eyes me up and down like I'm trying to break into the place or something. I try again, banging louder and longer this time. No good.

'Black? Black – are you there?' I shout as a last attempt at finding him.

I notice a shadow in an upstairs window. The sky has clouded over, fat raindrops begin to plop on my head, and then suddenly the plops become a thunderous shower from nowhere. I look down at the dog, sitting there beside me, fucking grinning up at me, waiting for me to fix everything. I'm tempted to tie him to the railings. Just tie him on with the rope and leave him there. Somebody'll stop and take care of him. Some other fool that isn't me. I take the rope and tie it onto the railing of the basement. Scabby belts his tail up and down on the footpath like I'm being nice to him or something.

I run down the steps but then I make a fatal mistake – I look back. Scabby's there watching me, tail still beating, but now he's got his paw out and he looks like he's calling me. I walk another few paces telling myself it's for the best, that we can't have a dog, that Dad'll find out and Scabby'll go to the pound. But I'm just not able to do it. I turn back and when he sees me coming the tail goes faster and faster and he throws his head back and howls with delight. Fuck sake – he'd better cop himself on with the howling. I untie the rope, Scabby licking my hand to death. I hear a gurgling snot-filled cough coming from the basement and see Black standing below there, pulling on a rollie. He beckons me down and melts in through the rubbish-strewn doorway.

The metal stairs is wonky and shakes as we climb down. I pick my way through the piles of garbage, pulling Scabby behind me. The basement door is open so I just walk in. There's a dark musty hallway. I can barely see and feel my way along with my hands, the walls wet and slimy. I come to a door leading into a dark kitchen. Black is standing at the cooker, stirring something in a pot.

'Want some porridge?' He grins at me, showing off his missing teeth.

'No thanks. You're hard to find.'

He grins again and waves to a rickety chair next to a very old painted table. 'Sit down.'

I sit and watch as he finishes making his porridge. Then he sits down opposite me and eats. He hasn't even noticed the dog yet. I look around the dark, poky room. The bottom part of the window is boarded up but there's light trying its best to peep in through the dirty glass on top. There's a bare bulb dangling from the ceiling and in the corner there's a fuse board with loads of different coloured wires hanging out of it. One wire goes all the way out the window. There's a blue vase on the windowsill, full of white daisies.

'So, why were you looking for me at this unearthly hour of the day? You woke me up with all that fucking banging you were doing – thought it was the law.'

'I ... I wanted to ask you a favour.'

A skinny red-haired girl in pink tracksuit bottoms and a purple bra comes into the kitchen. I don't know where to look but my eyes do. They latch onto the bra. She glares at me as she stands at the sink, drinking water from an old Nutella jar.

'You babysitting, Black?' she says, flicking her greasy hair back from her face. Her skin is covered in tiny pimples with yellow heads. Her forehead is destroyed with them and they're spreading in a V attack down her face.

'What are you looking at, you little bastard?' she says, banging the jar down hard on the worktop and strutting out of the room.

Black smiles at me. 'Morning is not a good time for a lot of people. What's up with you, anyway?'

'I ... there's ... we found a stray dog and my brother wants to keep him and –'

'No.'

'I didn't ask you anything yet.'

'Answer is no. Can't look after myself not to mind a fucking dog. Now fuck off cos it's dole day today.'

I'm about to remind him that he owes me money but decide it's not the right time. Scabby whines again under the table and Black bends down to have a look at him and I'm hoping that Scabby's doing his begging, pleading, poor-me act with the paw out and the eyes all sad. Black sits back up and shakes his head at me.

'Not happening,' he says.

'It'd just be for the mornings. I'll take him at night and –'

'Negative. Now fuck off, it's pushing on.'

Hal comes into the kitchen, her hair standing on her head. She sits down at the table, yawning and rubbing her eyes. Black gets up, puts porridge in a cracked bowl for her and pours her tea in a handleless mug. Scabby whines again and Hal sees him and, fair play to Scabby, the charm works because suddenly Hal's down on all fours talking to the dog and rubbing his head.

'I'd better go so,' I say, standing up. Hal keeps talking to the dog. 'I'd better go and check if the pound is open yet. Come on, Scabby ...'

Hal jumps up and grabs me by the arm. 'The pound? What are you talking about?'

I give Black a sly look. 'Well, we want to keep the dog

but we need somewhere for him to stay when my Dad's around and Black here's too busy...'

'Fuck Black – I'll mind him – I'll mind you, won't I?' She bends to rub the dog and now his tail is whipping in happiness. I grin at Black and he gives me the finger.

'What's his name?' Hal asks.

'Scabby.'

'No, his real name – you can't call a dog Scabby.'

'My brother calls him Rocky.'

'Naw ... Rocky's a shit name – there's hundreds of Rockys. Let's see, fella, what'll we call you?' She scratches the dog's head. Then she beams at him. 'Shep?'

Scabby wags his tail.

'Naw. Too common. There are millions of Sheps. Am ... let's see ... Lassie? Nope. You're a bloke. I have it – Skip, like in *My Dog Skip*.' She hugs Scabby and smiles up at us. 'Remember we went to see that movie and I cried like a baby and when we came out of the cinema there was snow everywhere?'

Black nods. 'Jesus, that was years ago. Your hair was blond then.'

Hal glares at him. 'And you had teeth.'

Black grins now, showing Hal his gummy mouth. 'You still love me though, don't ya?'

Hal stands up and takes Scabby's makeshift lead. 'First stop the pet shop, Skip. I'm not having you going out looking like shit.' She walks to the door, the dog following, his whole body swaying.

'I'll pay for a collar for him and a proper lead and –' I say to Hal's back.

She waves at us as she opens the kitchen door. 'No need, I'm knocking them off, no probs.'

'I'll collect him later,' I say but she's already gone.

Conor's watching TV when I get back. I plop down beside him.

'Where's Rocky?' he asks, not taking his eyes from the telly.

'Rocky is now Skip and he's gone shopping with Hal.'

He glares at me. 'He's Rocky. Who's Hal? I want my dog back.' Conor's eyes water with tears and spill down his face at an awful rate.

'Stop it, you fool. He's grand. We'll collect him later.'

'Are we still going to see Mam? Dad said it last night.' He wipes his face with the sleeve of his pyjamas.

'That was last night.'

Conor begins to full-on wail now and I remember what Mrs Chung used to say about him – that his bladder was very near his eyes. 'You promised. Scout's honour.'

'Yeah, but it's up to Dad too.'

Conor flicks the remote and the room fills with tinny sit-com laughter. 'If he doesn't bring me to see her, then I'm not going swimming. Not ever again.' He blinks at me and turns his gaze back to the TV. The ads have kicked in. It's one of his top ten. Audi.

I go into my bedroom and search for my phone. I have to make friends with Mikey if I'm going to Lahinch with him on Friday, the sneaky shit. I lie on my bed trying to compose a text – I don't want to give in totally. I don't want him to think he can walk all over me and go places and not even tell me but, fuck it, I really want to go to Lahinch now. It'll solve so much. Mam for one. And minding Conor and the stupid dog.

Dad calls us into the kitchen and sits us down at the table. He says he's arranging for us to meet our mother in the afternoon, in the Castletroy Park Hotel. Jamie will be coming too. I barely acknowledge what he's saying. I'm too busy looking at the giant dog shit in the corner of the kitchen near the fridge.

10 *June* 2017

I forget what you look like. Dad took all the photos except for two that Jamie keeps under his mattress and Conor found them and he cried. He let the tears drop onto one and your face went blurry so I had to hide it cos Jamie gets mad very easy. Its over missing Granda Mrs Chung says. Dad found your stash of Vanish in the press. Six bottles and he threw them all out over the smell. Sometimes I think you were like sprayed with the stuff. Three ~~hole~~ whole years. I bet if you saw me on the street you wouldnt know it was me – Mattie. I could be anyone and you wouldnt know. Dads so right about you. I hate myself for thinking about you and writing it down in this stupid fucking Gone Book. Thick I am. Pure dumb. I hate myself. Hate hate hate.

11

I'm nervous. My hands are shaking and I want to piss. We're in a room in the Castletroy Park Hotel. Dad, me, Jamie and Conor. I can't believe Jamie came. Even cleaned himself up and put on his good black shirt. Dad's rolling his neck like he does after a run but it's not helping him. He looks weird, all tight and knotted. We're sitting on dark, red couches trying not to stare at the door. Jamie's pretending to play games on his phone but I can see his eyes snaking over every few minutes. Conor's just pure straight about it, plonked in an armchair, eyes fixed on the door like it's his favourite ad. He's blinking so hard I think it must hurt him. I can hear his breathing, fast and raggy as he rubs his hands up and down his legs. Fuck. I feel sick. Washing-machine stomach as Mikey calls it, and a pain in my chest that I'm sure is a heart attack. Fuck me, this is worse than when Mikey and me got hauled in for pissing in the fountain in UL and Mrs Chung had to get us from security. Shower of pricks.

The door whooshes open and there she is, right in front of us, her perfume wafting across the room like invisible string. Conor is up out of his seat and flying at her at breakneck speed and he throws his arms around her waist and buries himself in her soft cream cardigan. I can hear his sobs and then her tiny little ones. I steal a glance at Dad and his eyes are shiny and he catches me looking at him and tries to rearrange his face but it's too late. A tear sneaks down his cheek.

Mam hugs Conor to her and smiles at Jamie and me. We stand up, as if we rehearsed it beforehand, one of us at each side of Dad, nobody smiling. My heart attack is about to pop, and my breath's shallow. I watch her now, examining our faces, avoiding eye contact with Dad. It feels like we're all frozen in time, like somebody pressed the pause button on a shit film. The air seems too thick to breathe, her perfume making it sickly sweet.

She comes towards us, Conor still glued to her. She has tiny tears under each eye, like someone drew them on. 'Jamie,' she whispers, taking a step closer. I can feel him tense up even though Dad is between us, I can feel his anger fizzing inside him, like a deadly silent time-bomb. Her hair is in a ponytail, streaky blonde like the Laurel Hill schoolgirls, and she's skinny like them too.

She reaches out and touches Jamie's face with her hand. He doesn't move. I hold my breath. Her fingers drop, as if she feels the zing of anger in him.

'I'm sorry,' she says, her fingers stretching out again. Jamie takes a step back. 'I missed you so –'

Jamie leans close and spits into her face. She inhales sharply, her eyes round with surprise, the spit dripping from her nose.

'I hate you. I waited five years to tell you that I hate you. I never want to see your stupid fucking face again,' says Jamie, his voice low.

I think he's going to hit her then, but he just looks at her like she's a piece of shit and he walks out, kicking a potted plant on the way. It falls to the ground with a thud but it's mock so no earth spills or anything. Dad runs over, picks it up and puts it back in its corner.

Mam looks like Jamie did hit her now, tears belting down her face. Conor joins in the crying.

'He's just ... it's ... he's just ...' I can't think of anything to say that isn't a lie.

Mam walks to the door as if she's going to follow Jamie, which is a fucking really bad idea and Dad stops her. He pulls her over to a corner by the window and they whisper-fight. I'd forgotten about whisper-fighting. Worse than real fighting, menace in every hissed word. Mam wipes her eyes with a tissue, but carefully, so she doesn't ruin her mascara. Conor sneaks his hand into mine. Dad touches Mam's arm and she pulls back. She hates him. I can smell it from here. There's more whispering. Fast, urgent murmurs, her soft voice, his deeper one answering. Then a short silence, both of them turning together to look at us. Dad smiles and moves across the room, shoulders straight, like an athlete. She follows, scrunching a tissue in her hands.

'Your mother wants to take you to her house for dinner – would ye like that?'

Conor beams. 'I'd love it.'

Dad looks at me and I shrug. I hate this day and wish Friday'd come so that I can go to Lahinch with Mikey. Away from all this shit.

Her house is perfect. It's all matching and shiny and new. She shows us all the rooms – swinging the doors open on each one, proud of them. She keeps her proudest smile for the little girl's room. It's pink and white and the bed is all flounces and frills. Just like a princess's.

'Taylor's room,' she says, like we're supposed to know who the fuck Taylor is. 'Your little sister – she's adorable and I know you'll love her.' She touches a mobile of tiny white angels. The tinkly sound echoes around the room. Conor's still glued to her, holding her hand tight – like he's afraid that if he lets go she'll bolt all over again.

She even shows us the back garden and, fuck me, there's a skateboard propped up against the garden shed. I run over and pick it up. It's a proper board, Element, I think, but the letters are worn off. There's a yapping sound coming from inside the shed. She opens the shed door and a white ball of fluff with a pink bow yips around our ankles. It's a dog but it looks more like a lamb.

'Ruby – say hello to Matt.' She bends down and rubs the dog's woolly head.

'Who owns the board?' I ask, realising it's the first time I've spoken since the hotel.

She rolls her eyes and shakes her head, a lock of hair falling loose from her ponytail.

'That's Rod's – he used to skate when he was younger.'

Rod brings dinner and our sister. Rod. Kind of looks like Smart, blond, tall and young. Dinner is a takeaway from the Chinese near the university – Mikey's dad would kill me if he knew I was eating it. He says they're not Chinese, can't cook and use horsemeat. Or maybe it's cats. Mam has spread the food out on the glass dining-room table like a buffet, with little bowls at the side and chopsticks. The chopsticks are a bad idea when you have a cream carpet but I don't say this out loud. Our sister hasn't left her father's arms and glares at us crossly. Every time I smile at her, she buries her face in Rod's shoulder. She has a head of white-blonde curls and huge blue eyes. It's the cleanest, shiniest house I've ever been in.

Conor and Mam are inseparable, following each other around and chatting and cuddling, and I feel like a bit of a third wheel. Rod grins at me every few minutes but I can't think of one thing to say to him except for skating and I don't want to talk about skating with him. Any other ideas I have are really bad. Like, *I really like your hair* or *How long are you riding my mother* or *You look the same age as my brother.*

So we circle the table of food and each other, smiling stupidly any time our eyes meet. I'm glad when he takes the little girl upstairs to bed. I do another circle of the table just for something to do and help myself to some chicken, hoping it isn't cat, like Mikey's dad says.

'Mattie.'

Her voice. I drop the chicken skewer onto the carpet. The satay sauce looks like dog shit.

'I'm sorry ... I ... I'll clean it up,' I say. It looks like a Scabby special.

'Don't worry about it, I'll get the Vanish,' she says and leaves for the kitchen.

I'm paralysed, just staring at the mess on the spotless, snowy carpet. She arrives back and starts to clean up, spraying Vanish on the stain. It really works.

'Thanks for coming, Mattie.' She's right behind me. I can smell her – so familiar and strange all at the same time. I stare at a plate of cold greasy spring rolls. I feel her hand on my shoulder. I examine the bowl of egg fried rice next to the spring rolls. Then she's turning me around and pulling me towards her and I want so badly to resist, to stop her dead, to not let her in, but she pulls me close and because I'm such a fool I hug her back. She strokes my head and kisses the top of it and it's the nicest feeling – being hugged. I'd forgotten just how nice that is. 'I want to have a chat before I bring you back to the hotel. Is that alright?' Her voice is soft and whispery in my hair.

We sit on a cream leather couch in the living room, and she sits opposite us on a red velvet chair shaped like a hand. Conor can't take his eyes off it. There's a giant flat-screen telly on the wall and the room smells like the bathroom in Brown Thomas.

She folds her hands on her lap, skinny long fingers knitted together on bony knees. I don't remember the skinniness. Conor beams at her.

'I'm so glad that your father saw sense. I really want this to be a new chapter in our lives.' She pauses and closes her eyes and I nearly snigger. 'We're a new family now and it's going to be great. We can put all the bad stuff behind us.' She smiles at us as if she's waiting for applause or something. I examine her face, smiley and girly and happy. 'We're going to have the best time – holidays, birthdays, Christmas. We'll go shopping for clothes and we'll get you really cool haircuts and, Conor, we'll get braces for your teeth – I can't understand why your father hasn't done something about them up to now.'

I clench and unclench my fist, feeling a knot of black screaming anger inside me. A Jamie-knot of hate and hurt. Conor's all smiles, wrapped up in her picture of shiny, happy holidays – the perfect ad. Her voice is a buzz in my head. I can't make out words, just white noise from her pink, perfect mouth. The buzz continues and some words break through the fizz in my head. *Bad place, needed space, never stopped loving ye. Thought about ye every day, loved ye, loved ye, loved ye ...*

'I don't want a haircut,' I say and Conor stiffens beside me. She does the look that I can remember so clearly from when I was younger. The poor-innocent-me face that makes you feel like it's always your fault. That everything's your fault. 'Dad brought Conor to the dentist ages ago and his fucking name is down for braces,' I say and she flinches at the word *fucking*. Good.

'Mattie –'

'Matt. It's Matt. Don't you know anything?'

'Matt, you've every right to be angry. I understand you're hurt but I had to find myself and heal myself before I could be any good to you –'

'So you lost yourself? Fucking great – our mother is the most careless woman in the world and she manages to lose herself. Imagine that. She wakes up one morning and she can't find herself – fuck sake ... and Granda ... you didn't even come to his funeral, your own father like and –'

'I ... Matt ... please ... Conor's –'

'Conor's what? Conor's here? You walked out on him and you never fucking tried to get in touch, to come and see us, see if we were alive or dead or ... fuck you.' I get up and push out of the room, banging the door hard behind me. I run through the white, spotless kitchen and out into the garden, right down to the back wall. I kick the wall hard and scuff my new skate shoes. Fucking bitch. I wish Mikey was here with his dumb jokes and his belly laugh and his distrust of my mother. I wish Jamie was here too so he could join in. Two of us against her.

I spot the skateboard, still propped up against the shed. I walk towards it, flip it up into my hands and test the wheels. They spin easily, very fluid. It's a well-loved board. I go around the side to the front of the house and do a grind on the footpath followed by a few ollies. It feels lovely and the buzzing in my head starts to fade. I gather speed and go into a beaut of a backslide and a few kids on the green opposite look over at me. So I put on a little show for them, all my tricks in one handy pack. Tony Hawk eat your fucking heart out.

I grind to a stop outside my mother's house and Rod's there, leaning on the wall, watching me. I drop the board and it starts to roll down the footpath and he jumps on it and does a beautiful carve and then a nosegrind and another lovely carve right up to my feet. Then he sits on the wall, takes out a pack of gum and offers me some. A group of kids stand a bit away, shyly watching us. The tallest one, a red-haired boy with a spray-paint of freckles on his face, bounces a football on the ground and rolls it over towards Rod.

'Are you coming out for a game, Rod?' he says.

Rod does a few flicks with the ball and rolls it back to Redhead. 'Not tonight guys, maybe tomorrow.'

He grins at me then, this Rod, my mother's husband. Or maybe it's her boyfriend? I don't know what he is. All I do know is that I could bring him to the skate park and he wouldn't be out of place. The skaters would be asking him to come out and play too.

Dad's waiting at the hotel entrance, and I swear by his face that he went for a quick run while we were gone. Took off around Castletroy in his good clothes. Mam and Conor hug and kiss. I climb out of her flashy jeep and slam the door hard. I don't even look back. Fuck her and her haircuts. Fuck her and her new clothes and her skinny hands. And fuck her boyfriend and just fuck her, fuck her, fuck her. My phone beeps a message but I can't be bothered even looking. I see Dad's battered Fiesta nearby and I climb in. Dad follows with Conor.

'You OK?' he says as he starts the engine.

She waves and honks the horn as she pulls away. Conor presses his face to the window, all goofy-eyed. I give her the finger.

'Matt?' Dad looks at me, his foot revving the dodgy engine, trying to warm it up.

'I'm grand.' I stare out the window.

'We had Chinese, Dad, and Mam has a really cool telly, it's huge and we had ice-cream. She let me sit on the hand chair.' Conor stops to take a breath. 'I had spring rolls and chicken-something and rice. She says I can come and stay next time. Matt too. That'd be fun Matt, wouldn't it? Wouldn't it?'

I shrug, wondering why Conor hasn't mentioned his new sister. I'm sure Dad knows she exists.

'Matt, you dork, wouldn't it?'

'We'll see, Conor,' I say.

'Shut up, you. You're just being all moody and mean. Isn't he, Dad?'

My phone beeps again. I ignore it. There's silence at last. Conor's in a sulk and he's tapping the back of my seat with his foot. Little shit. I turn up the radio. Dad turns it down.

'Can I go, Dad? Can I sleep in Mam's house? She's going to get me a Spiderman duvet and a watch.' Conor's voice is a whining drill now.

'We'll see,' Dad says as he pulls onto O' Connell Street.

'That means no,' says Conor. 'I hate you. The two of you. And Jamie. Hate you.'

'Stop, Conor, don't be a retard.'

'Language,' says Dad.

Conor's kicking the back of my seat, his two legs pounding, making me shake like I'm having some kind of fit. 'Stop!' I say, turning back to give him a death-glare.

He's pointing out the window, face furious, gesturing towards Penneys.

And then I spot him. Poor old Scabby, tied up outside the shop. Fucking Hal. She forgot him. Bitch. If he was a can of Bavaria, she'd have been more careful.

'Dad, I need to get out ... I – I've to meet Mikey to give him ... a book ... no – his phone. I took his phone by accident.'

Dad glances at me and pulls in to the kerb. 'Come straight home. I'm going to a meeting at ten – I'm the guest speaker.'

I run back across the road to Penneys, thinking it's a pity Dad can't get a job as an ex-alcoholic – just going around guest-speaking at meetings.

Scabby wags his tail when he sees me but his eyes are saucers of sadness and betrayal.

'Hey, fella,' I say as I unwrap his lead from the railing. It's a bright blue one with matching collar so at least Hal went shoplifting before she deserted him. I kneel down and hug him. He gives me a half-hearted lick. Just one.

'I'm sorry,' I say, patting his head. He gives me those eyes again. The ones that can read my mind. He can see Lahinch on Friday and Hal langers for the weekend. Fuck. Everything is shit. We walk towards home, me and the Scabinator – his tail at half-mast like he's in mourning for the decent, reliable owner he thought he'd found.

4 July 2017 Tuesday evening

We're moving. I don't know why I keep writing into this dumb fucking book. I mean it's not like you're ever going to read it. Conor asked about you today. He said how will Mam know where to find us if we move? How will she know our new address? I held my breath even though it was hard because I'd just put a full Twix into my mouth and I thought Dad'd lose it with Conor but his eyes filled up with tears and that made mine fill up too. I cry a lot and Jamie says its the fat – that the fatter you are the easier it is to cry. I got an A in English again today. I wrote a story about living in an igloo. Jamie laughed at me and called me a lick-up and a retard and he only stopped calling me names when I cried. Dad told Conor you were like Santa. That you'd just know where we moved to exactly like Santa. I think he believed it. We'll miss the Chungs next door and being able to go in and out to their house whenever we wanted and Mrs Chung's stews when we came home from school frozen and the way sometimes she came in and cleaned our rooms and put on clean sheets that smelled like flowers but what do you care about it anyway. I hate your guts and I wish I could tell you to your face. Burn in Hell.

12

It's finally Friday morning and I'm lying in bed thinking the world knows I'm going to Lahinch today so decides to throw everything at me to stop me going. The fucking dog is first on the list. Hal's promised to mind him but me, her and Scabby all know this is only pretend. Make believe. That she'll tie him up somewhere and go off for a Bavaria party and completely forget about him and he'll be just sitting there waiting for the dog pound van to find him. And the next problem is Conor. Mrs Chung has told Dad to bring him down to Lahinch on Monday so I don't even get a fucking break from him. And Mikey's being cool with me like I'm the one that sneaks off to the movies without even a text. And I can't find Jamie. I've called to the new apartment but there's never anyone there and I haven't seen him in three whole days – not since the time in the hotel. And then there's the rain. The never-ending grey sky, clouds so low you could touch them with your hand and constant rain – sometimes a fine mist – other times it's like the sky is hosing you down.

I can hear it outside now, battering the window pane, the wind howling down the Shannon like it's looking in every corner for the enemy. I climb out of bed thinking that it feels more like December than July. My feet are ice on the wooden floor. Conor's snoring in the bed opposite me. There's something else wrong besides the list of problems that woke me up. I look around the room, missing Steven Gerrard from his perch above my bed all over again. I pull on my jeans and slip my bare feet into my runners and then it hits me. Scabby. There's no Scabby in the room. I lie flat on the floor and look under the beds. Nothing but dust and an old pair of jocks belonging to Jamie. Fuck. Where is the dog? I search under Conor's quilt and mine too, knowing already he's not there. There's no tell-tale lump of dog anywhere.

I sneak out of the room and tiptoe towards the kitchen, hoping Scabby had the good sense to hide somewhere else in the apartment. Then I hear Dad's voice, chatting away to someone. I creep up to the kitchen door, which is open slightly, and peep in. Dad's in full flow, chatting away like he does with his AA pals.

'Rashers are always good, way nicer when it's raining than feckin' muesli. What do think my friend? Rashers it is?'

I push the door as gently as I can to try to get a glimpse of Dad's friend. I nearly die when I see him. Scabby, sitting on his haunches giving Dad the big, sad eyes.

Dad bends down and pats the dog on the head and Scabby gives him the paw. Dad shakes it solemnly and then goes to the cooker. I tiptoe back into my bedroom, unable to interrupt for some reason. I lie in bed listening to the rain for a while as it beats against the window like it's knocking to come in. Then I hear Dad pushing Scabby back into our bedroom, and the front door closing as he leaves for his run and Scabby's tail beating against the floor, almost matching the beating of the rain, happy out, his belly full of rashers.

Anna's being cool with me too. We meet at the park but we don't bring our boards. I texted her to meet up because I won't see her for a week and now I'm sorry I bothered. She has the make-up on again. It's on every day now and I think to myself she's turning into one of those girls – the bitchy ones with the funny high-heeled walks and the eyelashes going like mad and giggling every time a guy passes. Not a guy like me, more a guy like Smart.

'You should try to come down for a day,' I say, picking at my non-existent nails.

'Yeah, right. I'll drive down in my Beemer,' she answers, her voice bitter.

'I'm just saying, that's all.' I look at the sky, obsessed now with the weather. The rain has stopped and there's a tiny bit of blue behind the Strand Hotel. 'You could get the bus – loads of people get the bus to Lahinch. We got it once, Jamie and me, or maybe that was Kilkee. Yep – it was Kilkee.'

Anna kicks her feet off the ground, not looking up at all.

'So I'd better go home ... pack ... you know ...' but I stay frozen to the seat. There's just something about Anna that makes me stay, like an invisible string of sadness that pulls me back. She's crying now, silent little shakes of her skinny, sharp shoulders, her head bent into her hands. I reach out to put my arm around her but I'm too mortified to actually touch her. I wish someone would come along or that Anna's phone would ring. No such luck.

'I can give you the bus money – remember Jamie gave me all that money ... here ...' I root in my pocket for some notes and pull out two twenties. She still has her face in her hands. I'm like a fool now with the money in my fist like I'm trying to pay her to stop crying. She lifts her head then, tears still glistening in her dark eyes. She smiles at me, a tiny smile that makes little commas at each side of her mouth.

'I'm sorry.' Her voice is a whisper.

'For what? There's nothing to be sorry about.'

'Just for being such a bitch. And for sneaking off to the movies ... and other stuff ... like Smart ...'

'What do you mean, Anna? I don't get you.'

She smiles again and then she lifts her face up to mine

so her lips meet mine and her hand pulls suddenly on my back and then my head, pulling me into her. I can taste milk on her mouth, sweet milk, the nicest taste in the world, and I want to stay here doing this for ever. She pulls away just as I'm learning how to do it properly.

'You don't get anything, Matt,' she says and gets up and walks away, leaving me there as high as Hammer Hayes and confused as hell. I want to sing and dance and skate all at the same time.

I'm still in a great mood when Mrs Chung collects me in her already full car. Mikey's sitting in the back seat with a big cranky head on him, his two little brothers in their booster seats, one at each side of him, their faces shiny with excitement.

I'm happy to sit in the front with Mrs Chung, even though I know she'll talk the whole way to Lahinch. Conor and Dad wave us off from the footpath, Scabby – or as Dad calls him now, Bolt, after Usain Bolt – standing between the two of them. The dog looks happy that I'm going away – like I'm the one that keeps making his life uncertain. Fucking thanks you get.

'Jesus, Matt – a dog? Didn't think he'd ever allow a dog,' says Mrs Chung as we pull away. I'm waving frantically at Conor and Dad.

'Neither did I. I think he was forced into it.'

'How?'

'Conor found him and we were hiding him in the bedroom and Dad pretended he didn't know but he knew from the first night.'

'What's his name, Matt?' She smiles at me as she pulls onto the New Bridge.

'Oh he has lots of names, there's Scabby and Skip and Rocky and Bolt – take your pick.'

Mrs Chung laughs and fiddles with the radio. We drive along in silence for a while and the further we go the freer I feel. Except for Anna. I wish she was coming and that I could tell her that I do get things and now maybe I think she likes me just a little bit and the thought of it makes me grin to myself all over again.

I glance back but all three brothers are asleep, Mikey's big bulky body squashed in between the two boys, his mouth open, a thin line of spit running down his chin.

Mrs Chung rolls her eyes at me. It's dusk and the sky is pink and as we bypass Ennis, I notice that we're driving right into the blood-red blinding ball of sun. It's so bright that Mrs Chung has to reach for her sunglasses and I flick down the visor.

'It'll be sunny tomorrow, look at that sky,' she says, pushing the glasses up on her nose.

The sky is weird. Almost navy with streaks of purple and pink cloud and the orange-red disc of sun sinking behind dark-green hills. It doesn't feel a bit like Ireland. It feels like California. What I think California'd feel like.

The sun has dropped behind the hills and I can finally see again without being half-blinded.

Mikey farts in his sleep, a long, low deadly one and Mrs, Chung and I burst out laughing.

'Not too long now – another half an hour,' she says.

I settle back in the seat, enjoying the warmth of the car as it speeds along the road towards Lahinch and the sea. A whole week by the sea. 'I never stayed by the sea before.'

'But you went to the beach loads with your dad. I remember him when ye lived beside us and the day was promised fine – he'd be up at dawn packing the car with tents and baskets and quilts.'

I don't answer. I don't tell her that Dad could never be away from his meetings. Not really. He'd think he could and we'd pack the car and it'd all be grand. We'd get to the beach and swim and eat and play and then as the crowds left and the sun got lower in the sky Dad'd get restless and Conor or me would say, *Come on Dad let's put up the tent, there's a spot over there and we can take out the gas ring and make sausages and …* but we'd all know then it was no good. He wouldn't say it straight out, he'd just start collecting all our stuff, piling the baskets with dirty picnic plates and cutlery and shaking out the tartan rug that was only ever taken out for the beach. Freeing it of every grain of sand and folding it carefully like there was a prize for how exact you could be when folding a blanket. We never slept in that tent. We always went home, sometimes while everybody else was still sprawled out on the hot sand and other times we were the last to leave and the moon shone on the water.

My phone rings suddenly. Jamie. At least he's alive.

'What's up – I got all your messages.' His voice sounds slurred.

'I've been trying to find you since Tuesday and –'

'So, what do you want?'

I take a breath. I feel like hanging up on him, selfish fucker, leaving me to do all the worrying and finding and chasing. 'I just wanted to see if you were OK ... you know – after Tuesday ...'

'What happened on Tuesday?'

I can hear other noises in the background now – shouting and music and high-pitched laughing. 'You know ... the hotel and stuff.' I sneak a look at Mrs Chung. I don't want to bring up my mother with her. I'm afraid she'll have a mam-rant.

'I've no idea why you talk to that fucking bitch at all. Anyway, is that it?'

'Yeah ... well ... call in to Conor to make sure he's OK.'

'Why, where are you?'

'I'm going to Lahinch for a week with Mrs –'

'Well for ya. Lahinch. Might take a spin down there myself – bit of sun, a few beers, a couple of girls ... Hey Hammer – wanna hit Lahinch?' He laughs, a hysterical laugh as if he'd just heard the funniest joke ever and then he hangs up, just like that. I look at the screen on the phone like it's going to offer me an explanation. My stomach is funny. I feel sick.

'What's he up to?' says Mrs Chung, examining the road in front of her.

'Nothing ... I just kept missing him before I left so he rang there just to – just to make sure I was OK.'

The lie sits between us in the car so heavy I can almost see it. I know now that the mam-conversation is going to happen.

She looks across at me quickly and smiles. 'And are you OK?'

I nod and grin like an eejit. I consider turning on the radio but know it'd be rude. I'm praying that Mikey'll wake up suddenly and tell us a few jokes and make us laugh.

'She rang me again. Lucy ... your mother rang me.' I stare straight ahead, watching the road, black now as the sky loses its last sliver of light. 'She's losing the run of herself already.' I say nothing, hoping my silence will stop the rant dead in its tracks. 'Talking about custody – custody, for fuck sake. Walks back after five years and decides she'll pick up where she left off ... Talking about her rights – her *rights* if you don't mind ...'

She stops to negotiate a bad turn in the narrow road. I can see the lights of a town ahead. Ennistymon, I think. I hope. Because that means we're nearly there.

'She should be very grateful your dad is allowing her to see ye at all – do you know that? This is his worst night-mare – her strolling back and claiming you like she has a God-given right after all that happened.' She steals a look at me, I can feel her eyes on me but I continue with my vigil of the road, like our lives depend on it. 'Did she explain why yet?'

This is difficult because it's not part of a rant, it's a direct question.

'No.'

'Least she could do. I told her straight out, I said Lucy, they're not little boys any more, Jamie and Matt are smart and they're hurt and –'

'My head hurts.' I say this to change the subject. And because it does hurt. Like hell.

'Are you coming down with something? I've Panadol in my bag. Anyway, that woman needs to fess up for once in her life. She should own what she's done. And another thing – she should shut the fuck up about Conor's teeth.'

Mikey stirs in the back and then he yawns. I look at him and he winks at me and farts loudly once again.

'Lovely,' says Mrs Chung. 'Just what we need.'

Mikey laughs, 'I'm starving, Mam. Can we stop in Enzo's?'

'I wouldn't doubt you, Mikey,' she says, laughing. 'You hungry, Matt?'

'I'm grand,' I say.

But I'm not. Jamie's phone call sliced my head in half, made my eye sockets burn. I could go to California and it wouldn't be far enough away.

A day in the solar system with Matt Lynch
(December 2017)

Things that are wrong with my life.

1. *Mr Kelly's on my case in Maths. He says I have to do honours but its so fucking hard.*

2. *Jamie. Hes out all the time and lying to Dad and I'm lying to Dad to cover for him and then fighting with him over the lying and its just all getting worse and nobody wants to say it.*

3. *Dad's new food fad. Pulses they're called – lentils and weird beans and shit in curry and they make you fart so bad it burns you.*

4. *The fat. Its getting worse – there's two rings of it now around my waist and Jamie says I've moobs – man tits but Mikey says mine are nothing compared to his – that mine are only fried eggs and his are melons but still I hate the fat. I hate looking at my big fat head in the mirror and my greasy hair and fat fingers. Fuck sake how can you have fat FINGERS? And I hate the way I have to eat fucking everything in sight, every last bar and biscuit and slice of bread. And I hate Dad's eyes examining me, looking at the fat and then at his own toned body. Anyone could have a body like that if they ran around Limerick like a fucking maniac like he does. What's he running away from anyway?*

5. *Girls. They hate me and I like them. Big problem.*

6. *Writing in this stupid fucking Gone Book – like pretending I have a mother. Pretending that one day you'll come back*

and there'll be a miracle explanation of why we didn't hear from you in years like some kind of story on True Movies – you were kidnapped or locked up or in jail in Siberia.

7. *Sharing a room with Jamie. He vomits into his shoe and puts it under the bed. (see 2 above)*

8. *Mikey's new obsession. He wants to be a stand up comedian and I have to listen to all the bad jokes. He couldn't be something quiet like an engineer or even an artist. He never shuts up now and he's not good.*

9. *Gary Hannons mother died from cancer and we all had to go to the Mass and stand guard when they brought out her coffin. Breast cancer and Fr. Ryan said she was noble. I wished it was me instead of Gary Hannon that day and that it was your funeral. Why the fuck couldn't you have been noble and just got cancer and died?*

13

The first thing I notice before I even open my eyes is the stifling heat. It's unbearable and my T-shirt is sticking to me and I feel wet – like I've just come out of the shower. I open my eyes. The room is so tiny. Hobbit sized. Mikey's arse is almost touching me and his legs have kicked the door open at the bottom of our beds. There's a small wardrobe behind us and light beams in through the curtains of the little window above me. I sit up and look out the window and am almost blinded by sunlight. I get up, knocking my leg against the edge of the bed. I have to take my clothes out of the room to get dressed. The living room is in darkness and I whip the curtains back and straight away I'm sorry because there's a woman in the mobile home opposite me looking at me standing there in my jocks. I close the curtains quickly and pull on my jeans.

I make cereal and sit out on the deck. The sun is beating down on my head and I keep scanning the sky for big black clouds. I'm used to the sky being grey and low and all this blue is a novelty. The mobile homes in the caravan park are tiered on a hill, and at the back of ours there's a wooden fence and then behind that there are huge detached houses shaped in triangles exactly like pieces of Toblerone. On the hill down from these giant houses are smaller versions – miniature Toblerone houses, like Toblerone children. You'd want to be rich to own one of the m.

Sun makes you feel happy. My headache's gone and for the first time in ages I feel good.

And the happy feeling gets better and better. Mikey and I walk down the cliff towards the beach. The tide is miles out and the sand is a glistening gold shimmer in front of us. We have our togs with us and I'm whistling like Dad and Mikey's looking at me like I've lost my mind.

'It's only fucking Lahinch, you gowl,' he says, grinning at me.

'Yeah but it's sunny and it's lovely here.'

'You're a wuss, Matt. Just admit it. I had my doubts when you grew your hair and now I'm sure. And the fucking pink go-go in your cute little ponytail makes me double sure.'

'Your mam loaned me one – I can't find mine. So what's the plan today? Will we have a go at surfing?'

Mikey looks out towards the sea. 'One slight problem with that – we'd need a few waves.'

I follow his gaze. The sea is like glass, calm and still and soundless. We walk towards the prom, busy already with families making their way to the beach. Surf school vans are parked up, children queuing to put on wetsuits drying on the prom wall.

'How will they give surfing lessons without waves?' I ask Mikey – like he's some sort of surfing expert, which is highly unlikely ever.

'Dunno – they do it on dry land?'

'No, you fool, how could they?'

But Mikey's lost interest. He's spotted a restaurant and the smell of pasta and pizza wafts over to us.

'I'm fucking starving,' he says, looking longingly at the restaurant. It's called Ricky's.

'No. We're going swimming and then we're having a picnic with your mother, remember?' I head down the slipway towards the beach and Mikey follows me, still looking back over his shoulder every now and again.

He's a really good swimmer in spite of the fat. We race each other out to sea and he beats me hands down and I'm the one now panting and sweating and by the time Mrs Chung arrives with the boys and the picnic Mikey has me completely knackered and I'm looking at him like he's got super powers. How can you swim like that when you're so fat? I couldn't swim two strokes before I got thin.

We're just finishing up the picnic of sandwiches and Taytos and biscuits when I spot them walking down the beach. They're hard to miss. Jamie isn't too bad in his jeans and hoodie but Hammer looks ridiculous with his tracksuit pants and the white socks pulled up over the bottoms and a bright brand-new flashy pair of Nikes that Kanye'd be proud of. I want to hide. I want to slink away into a hole and just hope they go back to Limerick. Fucking bastards – I didn't even get one full day. The knot in my stomach starts up and my head begins to throb. Just a little throb, like a warning. Mikey sees them then and he's just about to call over to them like the big fucking eejit that he is when I kick him, spraying sand into his face.

'Ouch – fuck sake. What was that for?' He glares at me and I glare back, trying to get him to shut up. Jamie and Hammer don't see us. They're deep in conversation, laughing and joking. They both have cans in their hands. Hammer's face looks burnt already. Good.

'They're at it early,' says Mrs Chung. She's lying on a towel sunbathing and as far as I can make out she hasn't raised her head so how does she know that they just passed?

I go over to the United Colours and start to make sand-castles with them. Mikey falls asleep in the sun, exhausted after all the swimming. I try to hold onto my earlier mood, smiling and laughing with the boys and giving myself up to the sun and the heat and the bright holiday feel of the place but I'm jumpy now, watching stick figures miles away on the beach as they walk towards me thinking it'll be Jamie or Conor, some member of my stupid family coming to take my feel-good day away from me.

We're sitting on the rocks watching the sun sink into the sea. It throws a golden glow on the beach, like somebody turned on the lights. We're drinking two cans that Mikey stole from his mother's supply. She likes a beer at night when she's on holidays. The beer is making my head buzz a little, a nice buzz, not like the headache buzz.

'Tastes like more,' says Mikey, looking out towards the sea.

People are walking on the beach still and there's a few straggling swimmers in the water, not wanting to give up the day. It's still bright even though it's gone ten. There isn't a sign of Jamie and Hammer and I'm beginning to relax, thinking they must have headed back to Limerick. A new worry pops into my head – Hammer and the drinking and what if they crash? I shake my head and take a long drink of the warm beer. Not my fucking problem.

'We could try to buy some in the offie,' says Mikey. He leans back on the rock and looks at me. 'You can't go in – you look like a weird cross between a teenage girl and an emo ...'

I thump him in the arm but he doesn't even feel it. He grins at me.

The beach is almost deserted now, just a few people with their dogs. I noticed a sign earlier that said no dogs up to eight o'clock and I had a picture in my head of all the dogs in Lahinch sitting at home watching the clock until they could have their turn on the beach.

'What do you get when you cross Chuck Norris and Vincent Van Gogh? Paintball!' Mikey does his belly laugh now, the flab on his cheeks quivering.

'No more jokes – please!' I say, standing up because one of my legs has pins and needles.

'We need beer,' says Mikey.

'Hang on a minute and I'll shit some.'

He grins. 'If you're going to all that trouble could you make sure it's Heineken?'

Mikey stands up too and then throws his empty can into the rocks behind him. 'Let's pray.'

I look at him like he's finally lost it. 'Pray?'

Mikey kneels down on the dry, dusty sand. He closes his eyes and joins his hands together. 'Dearly beloved God, we are gathered here today to pray for more beer and world peace and a feel of a tit – anyone's tit – please look down on us with mercy and love and lots of beer –'

'What the fuck are ye up to?'

A tall figure is standing over Mikey, casting a long shadow across the sand. My heart starts its stupid little drumbeat and then I recognise the voice. It's Smart. Jesus, the fucking relief.

'Praying for beer. You can do the responsorial psalm – like this: God we have no beer and the world is fucked – response – Lord have mercy on our beerlessness and fuckedupness ...'

Smart laughs out loud and I'm proud of Mikey for the good jokes. 'Your prayers worked – I can get beer no problem. The guy in the offie surfs with me.'

Mikey stands up and bows twice in front of Smart. 'Halleluiah, praise God and his lamb and his ghost and mother. It's a miracle – all our prayers are answered.'

We head to the off-licence and pool our money and Smart comes out with a huge slab. Mikey goes to grab one and Smart pulls the slab away from him. 'The guards'll pull you for drinking on the street. They'll take the can and pour it away. We'll go to the Cliff Bar.'

Smart starts to walk up the main street and we follow like two eager puppies, delighted with the way the night is turning out.

'We should pray more often,' says Mikey.

The Cliff Bar isn't a pub at all. It's just a grassy verge on the edge of a cliff almost opposite the mobile home park. Somebody has already lit a fire and a girl is strumming a guitar and singing an *Adele* song very softly to a guy with longer hair than me. They nod at us and we sit a bit away, forming our own little group. We crack open the cans and drink in silence for a while, enjoying the warm night air and the feel-good factor that has decided to come back in bucket-loads.

'Anyone want to go surfing tomorrow?' Smart says eventually.

'No waves,' says Mikey the surf expert and then lets off a noisy fart. 'Jesus, the beer is full of gas.'

Smart watches the girl over the flames of the fire. She seems to be singing to Smart now and not her boyfriend. This time it's REM's worst song ever – 'Everybody Hurts'.

'The surf's up tomorrow – big waves, shoulder to head high, not messy, nice and clean.' He keeps looking at the girl as he speaks.

Mikey nudges me and throws an eye at Smart. 'Clean, not messy. Got to get all this terminology right.'

'So, you on, Matt?' Smart says, eyes glued to the girl.

I can feel Mikey's disappointment. I catch his eye in the dancing light of the fire and he smiles at me like he doesn't care. I know he does.

'No problem, what time?' I deliberately keep my eyes straight ahead.

'Have you got a board?'

I shake my head.

'Wet suit?'

Another head shake.

'I'll sort you out – we'll go for food afterwards to Ricky's.'

'Ricky's, I'm dying to go there. The pasta looks amazing,' says Mikey.

Smart smiles at the girl and gestures to our slab of beer. She does the giggly thing, then comes over and takes one for herself and one for Long-Haired Guy.

'I'll sort you out with a board and shit, Matt. It's gonna be unreal – you'll never skate again once you surf.'

Mikey takes a beer and slugs it back in two gulps and then he reaches for yet another.

'Jesus, man, slow down. Your mother will fucking kill you if you walk in langers.'

'So lads ...' Mikey says, and I know straight away we're in for a bad routine. I close my eyes, wishing he'd shut the fuck up.

'The local Mr Whippy man was found dead in his ice-cream van covered in hundreds and thousands – the police say he topped himself.'

The girl laughs but I think it's just out of politeness. Smart is too busy flirting to even hear Mikey. But Mikey's on a mission now.

'What do you get when you cross an elephant and a bottle of whiskey? Trunk and disorderly! What do you get if you cross a deer with a hairdresser? A styling moose.'

He stops to drink his beer and I try to distract him. 'You should come surfing too, Mikey. We can like hire a board and a wetsuit and stuff.'

Mikey laughs. 'I'd need four wetsuits stitched together. So, what do you get if you cross a pig with a hedgehog? A porcupine! What do you call a prisoner's pet budgie? A jail-bird. What do you get –'

'Mikey?'

'– if you cross a chicken with a skunk? A fowl smell! Do ye get it – fowl? Foul?'

'Hey, Mikey – maybe we should go? Your mother said we had to be back by eleven.'

'What do you call a hippy's wife? Mississippi. What do get if you cross Dracula with Sir Lancelot? A bite in shining armour.'

I punch Mikey in the arm. 'Enough.'

'What do you call a lifeguard with no legs? Bob. What do –?'

I jump on Mikey's back, making him drop his beer, and suddenly we're rolling along the grass verge and Mikey's trying to choke the living daylights out of me and I'm pushing him off me and I can't breathe. So I pinch his back as hard as I can, taking a whole fistful of flesh and twisting it around until he's yelping with pain. I roll out from under him and then I keep rolling gathering speed as I'm heading towards the cliff and uselessly pulling at tufts of grass. I close my eyes as I feel myself going over the edge, like this is going to help me, like it's going to break my fall or something. I feel myself dropping and then a hard thud as I land. I open my eyes. I can see stars, and I can hear the sea, angry and boiling below me. Then Mikey's voice shouting my name, followed by his head peering over the cliff above me. I smile up at him and he sees that I'm OK, that I've landed on a narrow ledge of rock about ten feet down.

'Don't look down, Matt, I'm coming for you,' says Mikey, and I want to tell him not to because if Mikey comes anywhere near my dangerous perch then we'll both be goners.

Smart appears next to Mikey. 'Jesus, you were lucky,' he says. 'Don't know how we'll get you up.'

But Mikey's leaning down towards me, his big hand almost touching my shoulder and he's yelling at Smart to hold his legs and then I'm being yanked up by one arm and my bunched-up T-shirt, and Mikey's like Superman plucking someone from a cliff edge and everybody claps when he rolls and drags me back up onto the grass. He looks into my face, all worried still. I grin at him and he shakes his head.

'Are my jokes that bad that you had to try to top yourself?' he says, laughing.

'Pretty much,' I say, standing up gingerly, testing my wobbly legs. Smart cracks open a beer and hands it to me. Long-Haired Guy has given up trying to compete with Smart, who's now holding the girl singer's hand. I take a long slug of beer and it's actually delicious.

'Anyway, Matt, what do you get when you cross a cliff with a –'

'NO!' I scream and we all crack up then. We finish our beer and hide the rest of the cans in a little ditch that Smart shows us. He walks off with his arm around the girl and Mikey and me walk across the field towards the caravan park.

'I got a fright when you went over,' he says, staggering a little.

'Not half as big as the fright I got.'

'Yeah but ... you know ... if anything happened you ...'
He stops and looks at me and his eyes are shiny like he's about to cry.

1 January 2018

You can see the river from our new apartment. It feels like we're living in New York or Boston. Somewhere thats on the telly and not Limerick. I like it here. I like being up high and looking down on everything and feeling like God in the world. Jamie got me a skateboard for Christmas and I don't know if he's just having a laugh or what. It's standing propped up against the bedroom wall for two weeks and I'm going to use it today. I've made up my mind and I know if I write it in here then that means I have to. I'm going to take it and bring it to the skate park and I don't give a fuck who laughs at me. And I'm going to do it every day until I'm good. I just want to be good at something. Just one thing so that people won't see me as a fat loser. Dad got me Stephen King The Dark Tower. It's brilliant.

(Notice the way I don't even talk to you any more? Fuck you.)

14

'You go. I'm grand,' says Mikey. We're sitting on the deck of the mobile home and Smart just texted me about surfing. He was right about the waves. We saw them earlier when we walked to town for Mrs Chung's fresh bread rolls.

'You can come too,' I say, playing with my phone.

Mikey looks at me. 'Gee, thanks, I'm fucking honoured.'

'Just saying.'

'I thought we could go to the Cliffs of Moher. Mam says she'll bring us and we can lie flat and hang over the edge and we might get a chase off the rangers.'

I flick the phone on and off. 'I really want to go.'

Mikey shrugs. 'I'm not stopping you.'

'Yeah, but ...' I shrug this time. 'It'll be fun, Mikey, come on.'

'He only asked you to go last night. He didn't say anything about me coming. I'm probably not cool enough to hang out with – big fat-ass fucker like me.' He grins at me but his eyes are deadly serious.

'Come on, we'll have a laugh.'

He shakes his head. I have my backpack ready at my feet. My phone beeps a message. Smart.

Hurry on. Waves cool. Good times.

I pick up my bag and try one last time. 'Come on. You're a brilliant swimmer, you'll love it.'

He glares at me now. 'Just fucking go.'

Then he pulls the worst face I've ever seen and lopes up to the kid at the fence, arms outstretched like a zombie, guttural groans and all and she runs away screaming her head off.

I'm nearly at the beach when he catches up with me, the sweat popping on his forehead.

'Expect a tidal wave,' he says.

I laugh. 'There's Smart, over by that mad-coloured van. Look they've boards to rent – and suits too I bet.'

Smart gives me a knuckle salute and doesn't even say hello to Mikey which pisses me off. He hands me a wetsuit and I talk to the bleach-blond guy in charge of renting the equipment and he's eyeing Mikey dubiously as he roots through the pile of wetsuits on the prom wall. I struggle into mine and retie my ponytail. Mikey, poor Mikey, is nearly doubled in two trying to fit into his. Smart is itching to get in the water but I stay there until Mikey's stuffed into the wetsuit and I force the zip up for him, catching his flesh in it a few times before managing to close it.

'Perfect,' I say, grabbing the board that Smart left for me.

Mikey looks down at his body, whale-like in the skin-tight suit, showing every ripple and contour of fat – on show for the whole world. I feel lousy now for all this surfing shit.

'Get your board there,' I say, picking mine up and heading down the concrete steps to the beach. I can see Smart way down at the shoreline doing stretches. The sea is dotted with surfers, like little ants climbing hills of water. I look behind me and Mikey's struggling with the board, his breathing so loud I can hear it over the roar of the waves.

'Wait up, man,' he says. Mikey arrives, drops his board on the sand, and tries to wipe sweat from his face with his rubber-clad arm. 'Jesus, the fucking heat in these things – pure murder,' he says.

'OK, short lesson,' says Smart, all authority. He lies flat on his board, arms to the side of his waist, and then rises to his knees and then his feet in an incredibly fluid movement, hands out, balancing his body. 'See? It's all about balance. Now try it.'

Mikey snorts with laughter. I lie down on the board and try to remember the sequence of movements. Smart shakes his head. 'OK. Watch again. I'll talk you through it this time.' He lies flat on the board, hands tight by his side. 'It has to be one smooth motion – it's called popping up.

You have to keep your centre of gravity low. Good flexed balance in the middle of the board – just like skating, Matt.' He begins to rise off the board like a dancer. 'Arch up, slide feet under you and pop up, feet planted – but stay low, hands out, balanced and relaxed. Exactly like skating.'

I get up on the second attempt. I don't exactly catch a wave – it's more a glide into the shore on the choppy sea – but already I can feel the attraction. Like skating but better, more physical, more dangerous.

I grin at Smart and search for Mikey. He's waist deep in water, trying really hard to get on his board. He's not even watching the waves coming in behind him. It's like the goal is to just get up on the board any old way at all. A group of kids are standing a bit away from him laughing and nudging each other. Smart is calling me to paddle out to the bigger waves.

'Mikey,' I call out but the noise of the waves drowns out my voice. He tries to grip the board and push his knees on and the board sinks straight away. The kids get into hysterics, falling around laughing. Poor Mikey's so intent on getting on the board that he doesn't even notice. He finally gets both knees on the board and of course it goes down like concrete and Mikey with it. The kids are screaming with laughter by now and I can feel my temper rising and my fists clenching.

'Fucking *Titanic*,' one kid yells.

'Sumo-surfing,' says another, cracking up laughing.

Mikey rises out of the water like a huge black whale and starts all over again. And now I want to hit Mikey. I don't know why. I want to hit him for making a fucking ape out of himself and not caring.

I catch my first real wave an hour later. Smart has taken me over towards the rocks, way out on the left-hand side of the beach. Beautiful clean curling waves. I see a big one coming in and Smart yells at me and suddenly I'm doing it, I'm popping up and holding my balance and cutting through the water like I'm on my skateboard, and all I can see zipping by me is bits of blue sky and sea and white foam. The wave carries me right in and Smart glides in behind me. He's beaming from ear to ear.

'I knew it, I knew you'd get it,' he says, shaking his head at me.

'It's the most fucking incredible feeling in the world. Fucking unbelievable buzz.'

Smart laughs. 'Good isn't it?'

'Understatement. Best thing ever.'

Smart smiles at me and flicks his hair out of his eyes. 'Dude, you have it bad. Let's get lunch, I'm starving.'

'No – I want to do it again. I want to keep going.'

He laughs. 'No. The beach is good for surf for another few hours – it's a spring tide. We need carbs for energy. Let's go.'

We walk to Ricky's cafe with our wetsuits pulled down to our waists, the hot sun drying us as we go. A group of girls pass in tight shorts and stringy little tops, giggling and whispering. Smart winks at them and one of them pretends to faint. He grins at me. I watch the girls once they pass and a small dark-haired one with plaited hair and a great arse turns around and waves at me. I think my heart is going to burst with feel-good.

We're sitting outside with huge platefuls of the best pasta I've ever had in my whole life when I think of Mikey. Fuck it, I'd completely forgotten about him with all the surfing. I look over towards the prom and it's like the fact that he popped into my head makes him appear in front of me like magic. He's walking towards us, kind of loping across the road, the belly wobbling in a too-tight pink T-shirt. He smiles hello and sits down at the table, making it shake and spill our Cokes.

'That looks good – what is it?' says Mikey, eyeing my plate with absolute lust.

'Carbonara – best in town,' says Smart.

'Gonna get me some of that. I'll be right back,' he says.

We eat away in silence, lifting our heads to watch every time a decent-looking girl passes.

And the girls look at us which is a real novelty for me.

Mikey arrives back, his tray piled so high I can barely see his face. He lowers the tray precariously onto the table and I can nearly hear the table inhale with the weight of it all. There's the pasta and garlic bread, some other side dish, a pack of Taytos, two chocolate desserts and some yoghurt.

'Surfing makes you hungry,' he says as myself and Smart look on, speechless at his spread.

'OK, time to go – let's catch some waves, man,' Smart says, getting up and walking away without waiting for an answer.

Mikey glances at me, while stuffing pasta into his mouth. I'm itching to get back into the water. He takes a gulp of Coke and belches loudly. 'This is the life,' he says, looking across towards the now packed prom. The traffic moves like a snake past the cafe, in search of an elusive parking space as close as possible to the beachfront. I will Mikey to eat faster and he seems to know this because for once in his life he's not shovelling the food in like it's some kind of race. He has his hands behind his head now, body stretched out, legs crossed, eyes closed, enjoying the sun. Fucking bastard.

'So – what'll we do now?' he says, eyes still closed.

'Am ... well ... I'm going back in.'

He sits up straight and starts eating again. He eats now like a Dyson, hoovering up everything in front of him. 'So, what the fuck are you waiting for?' He glances up at me, and then back down to the plate.

'You.'

He laughs. 'Like fuck. I know you can't wait to go off with Smart – oh, here come the surfer dudes – well off you go.'

'Mikey, stop being a bitch.'

'Fuck off.'

'Do you want to come?'

'You're joking, aren't you? I should never have come in the first place. You're just too cool for me now – too cool by a fucking mile.'

'Cop on, Mikey. I like surfing, that's all. I fucking love it, actually.'

'Then fuck off back into the sea, Mr Fucking Cool.'

I stand up and push the table. 'Exactly what I plan to do. Beats hanging out with a bitch.'

We're in the water, even further out now, me and Smart and a few of the regulars. The waves are getting bigger as the tide comes in hard and fast. I can feel the power in the waves building and building and then Smart signals me to go out a bit more and I know instinctively that there's a big one on the way. The other surfers head out too and I imagine I can hear our collective heartbeats as we paddle furiously against the incoming tide.

'She's a-coming,' Smart screams as a huge wave approaches. I try to stay relaxed, imagining I'm on my skateboard, watching for the exact right moment to start the ride. And then I'm up and on it and riding it just at the right point before it barrels and I chase and chase and chase and then I let it barrel over me but I'm in control, it's my choice. I'm inside the wave and I can't stop laughing and I think I'm screaming too and then I crash into the sea, right under the wave, trying not to let my board strike me. I pop up and Smart is right beside me and he high-fives me and the other surfers come over and do the same thing and I think I'm the happiest fucker in the whole world.

'Man, you're a natural,' shouts Smart over the thundering noise of the sea.

I'm beaming. I can't stop beaming. 'That was it, wasn't it?' I scream at him. 'That was the green room.'

He grins back. 'Poor fucker you – hooked already. I knew you'd be good.'

We call it a day then and paddle back towards the beach and still I'm smiling like a lunatic and I feel drunk and happy and bursting with excitement. We're walking with the boards up towards the rocks when I spot Mikey, sitting with a couple of lads. They all have cans and Mikey's laughing – I can hear his belly laugh from here. I'm just about to go over when I realise he's with Jamie and Hammer. Having cans in the sun like it's the most normal thing in the world.

I keep walking, hoping they haven't seen me, and I'm motor-mouthing to Smart. Just talking shite to fill the silence. And all the time while I'm dressing I'm scanning the place for Jamie and Hammer. Smart spots them then and waves. Hammer climbs up the rocks to the pier wall and I can see him handing a baggie to Smart. They high five and Hammer skitters back down to the others. I want to say something to Smart as he stuffs the bag of pills into his backpack but instead I make plans to meet him later and I walk like a fugitive along the prom. I look down towards the rocks where the lads had been sitting. Mikey's on his own now, a big hulking lump of loneliness, watching toddlers splashing in a rock pool nearby. Their parents are glaring at him like he's some kind of pervert and of course Mikey doesn't even realise it. He smiles as one of the kids stamps on a beautifully constructed sandcastle freshly made by Daddy.

I call him and he beams when he sees me, and jumps up and tries to run up the steps towards the prom, his belly and arms quivering with the effort.

'You were fucking awesome – I saw you do the big wave,' he says, punching me in the arm.

'Ouch! You don't realise your own strength,' I say.

'I met Jamie and Hammer – they're actually dead sound when they're not in Limerick.'

We're walking up the hill towards the caravan park. The old familiar knot in my stomach is back, and a throbbing pain over my left ear is needling me. Just reminding me that no matter how big a wave I caught today they are still around and watching.

'So, I told them about the Cliff Bar. I told them we'd see them there later.'

'You fucking gowl, Mikey – why did you do that?'

He looks at me, all offended. 'Jesus, who's the bitch now? It's just a few cans and a laugh. They want me to do a bit of a routine for them.'

'Yeah. Right.'

'Why the fuck did you come to Lahinch with me? Why didn't you go with Smart altogether?'

'Shut up, Mikey. This isn't about Smart. It's about Hammer Hayes – he's a scumbag.'

Mikey stops dead and pokes me hard in the chest with a sausage finger. 'This is about you thinking you're fucking special. So special you won't even say hello to your own brother. You're a fucking gowl sometimes, Matt. An absolute gowl.' He marches off up the hill, the back of his T-shirt soaked with sweat.

The tide is in now, crashing against the sea wall over and over. I wish I was in the sea where nobody can follow me. Where I can be safe from the whole lot of them.

April Fool's Day 2018

Skating. It's my life. End of. Heaven is a fucking half pipe.

15

We have our dinner on the deck in the warm sun. Mikey's cranky and I can't be bothered trying to humour him. So I tell Mrs Chung all about the surfing and she's delighted for me, I know she is and then she asks Mikey how he got on and that's the end of the surfing conversation.

'Are you right?' Mikey says after we clear the dishes.

'For what?' I ask, wiping down the table with a cloth. There's ketchup everywhere. It looks like blood. My headache's back, tapping little sharp stabs of pain into my eyeball.

'The Cliff Bar, gowl – it's time to party.' He grins at me and I know this is a peace offering.

'Don't feel like it.' I keep wiping the table even when the ketchup is well scrubbed off.

'What's up with you?'

'I've a headache and –'

'Fuck sake. You're either gay or a girl. Big fucking girly head on you.'

'Girl, girl, girl,' says Leon, the older brother. 'Matt's a girl.'

I shrug. 'Is that supposed to be an insult? Being gay or a girl? It's the opposite actually.'

Mikey stands up, but I can feel his eyes boring into me while I'm still bent over the now spotless table. 'Good luck, I'm outta here,' he says, stamping down the wooden steps of the deck. It shakes.

'What does gay mean?' says Leon.

'It just means happy.'

'No, it doesn't, you fool. It means sexy – Tyrone Mac told me in school.' Leon gives me a withering look and goes off in search of his pals, football under his arm.

Mrs Chung comes out with a bottle of beer and a glass full of ice. 'Matt, how do you think Mikey is?'

I look away, fixing my eyes on the tiny clothesline beyond the deck, on the row of beach towels, pinned and still. She's in rant mode – I can feel her building up.

'Mikey's Mikey.'

She looks at me over the rim of her glass. 'Mikey's sad. Quiet. Didn't you notice?'

This is too heavy for me and I'm sorry now that I didn't go with him. Mrs Chung likes to talk. Especially when she's having a beer.

'He's stopped talking to me – you know, sitting down with a cup of tea and having a laugh and stuff. And he sits in his room and God only knows what he does up there and more so now because you go skating. It's just a bit worrying, that's all.'

The sun is sinking fast, although the air still feels warm.

'It's just you never know these days – you hear all sorts of stories. A boy from Galbally hung himself last week – he was Anne Gubbins's husband's nephew.'

My phone beeps a text. It's Smart. He's in town.

'You're off, I suppose? You're dead right too – you're only young once, Matt. Ye can have an extra hour.'

Smart texts again as I head across the road but I know where I'm going. I can't let Mikey on his own with Hammer and Jamie.

Mikey's sitting on the cliff edge – a can of Dutch Gold in his hand. He's looking out to sea and doesn't hear me until the last second. 'Fuck, Matt, you frightened the life out of me,' he says, but I know he's delighted I came. 'Do you want one?' Mikey reaches for the slab of beer.

'In a while,' I say, gazing up at the sky. The sea laps at the cliff below. It's peaceful. 'I'm sorry,' I say to the pink sky.

'For what?' says Mikey.

'For fucking off on you today. It's just the surfing – I can't resist it ...'

'I didn't get it until I saw you on that big wave – you looked like you'd been surfing for years.'

I laugh. 'The skating helps – same principle.'

'Jamie was so fucking proud of you.'

I blink. Just like Conor. The sky is an even deeper pink. Almost red.

'He didn't know it was you at first, wouldn't believe me, and then he took out his iPhone to video you but I think he was too late. He just got you crashing under the wave. What was it like?'

'Wet.'

'Gowl. I mean what was it like being able to do it? Actually surf a whopper like that?'

I close my eyes. I can feel the water curling around me, the board underneath me, the screech of seagulls. I can smell sea, wax, fear, and feel-good, all wrapped around me in the wave capsule. The green room. What a great name for that feeling.

'Perfect.'

'What?'

'They call it the green room.'

'I thought they called it surfing.'

'Hilarious, Mikey. No, that's what they call the feeling you get when you catch a whopper and ride it in.'

'Green room? Dumb name. Green room, my hole.'

I sit up and reach for a can from the slab. I pop the tab and slug back the warm beer. It tastes good.

Mikey grins at me and fixes his eyes on a yellow fishing boat way out on the horizon. 'This is the life, Matt. Fuck Limerick.'

'You said it. I wish I could live here.'

A knot of people walks towards the cliff, talking loudly. Mikey waves at them and I know there is no Limerick to

183

fuck because it's coming right over to us. Jamie. Hammer. Smart with two girls hanging off him. They all sit down and Mikey throws cans at them as if they're his long-lost buddies.

Jamie sits next to me. 'Man,' he says and takes a long drink of beer. 'You were awesome today out there.'

I nod. I'm too fucking shocked to speak. Jamie said something that wasn't angry or insulting. It's true for Mikey. Lahinch changes people.

'I'll bring you out if you want.' I blurt this out before I can stop myself.

Jamie looks at me. His pupils are huge. Glassy. 'Want to see something?' he says.

'What?'

'Come on.' He gets up and I follow. We climb over a low stone wall. There's a group of three tents set up in a deep hollow in the middle of the field.

I beam at him. 'Dad's tent? It finally saw the light of day!'

Jamie laughs. 'Cool, isn't it? I called in today and I thought of the tent. First time it's actually been put up.'

'It's bigger than I thought.' I pull down the zipper and a belt of heat rises towards me.

'Remember the day he bought it? A Lidl special. Conor nearly pissed himself with excitement.'

I grin. 'Weird we never used it. Not once.'

Jamie bends down and crawls inside. I follow. We sit cross-legged in the space, facing each other, and there's something cosy and surreal about it. The light is beige in here and it's warm from the sun. We smile at each other in the weird cocoon.

'It's like he loved the idea of camping, getting away from it all, but he just couldn't be away from home.'

Jamie laughs. 'He'd miss his meeting. Those fucking meetings were worse than drinking!'

'Look – the price tag is still on it.' I pull off the tag, which is trapped under a steel pole.

'I called in to him today.'

'Why?'

'He was gone for a run with the dog.' Jamie looks at his hands as he speaks. 'He loves that dog.'

'I know.'

'I wanted to wait until he got home and ... you know the way he's always in a good mood after running.'

I look at the zipped-up door of the tent, not wanting to interrupt Jamie.

'It's just ... all this shit is going down and Dad ... I want him to – oh fuck ...' He starts to cry, little dry sobs with no tears. The heat is suffocating.

'What's going on?' I ask. I don't want to hear the answer. If I could close my ears, I would. And it's like Jamie senses this. He shakes his head.

'I couldn't wait for him. I couldn't tell him ...'

'Tell him what?'

'Just ... stuff is happening ... and I thought he'd know what to do.' He pulls at the string of his hoodie, yanks on it so hard he rips it out completely. Then he twists it around his wrist. Tight. 'Remember when Mark Tierney was bullying you?'

'That was years ago.'

'Yeah. He called you Fatballs and made jokes about you.'

'And you beat the living shit out of him behind the bike sheds.'

'And Mr Tierney called in his guard's uniform and Dad said I was right and told him that he was very proud of me. That I sorted out a bully.'

'I remember. Just after Mam ... I remember.' I want to take the Mam word back but it's too late. I can feel her in the tent with us.

'Dad was cool that day.'

'He's alright.'

'He stood up to Tierney's dad. Called him a bully too. Said, *Like father, like son.*'

'You should have waited for him. Talked to him. He'd –'

'Forget it. It's nothing – it's the weed. Always does that to me. Same with Hammer – turns us weird.' He laughs and stretches his legs out in front of him.

We listen in silence. The sea pushes and pulls against the cliff outside and the birds haven't realised that the day is over. There's a low rumble of voices in the distance, followed by screams and guffaws.

'I'd love to stay here for ever.' Jamie tucks his knees up to his chest and rocks back and forth.

'I said the same thing earlier. Lahinch is cool.'

'Not Lahinch. Here, in this place. Right here.' His eyes are fixed on the roof of the tent and he's rubbing his fingers like Mrs Chung when she makes cakes.

'Are you OK, Jamie?'

He doesn't hear me.

'Jamie, are you –?'

'More beers are in order, come on, bro,' he says and zips down the door. He crawls out and I follow him, beaming like a fucking ape. He called me bro. He jumps the wall and puts a hand back to pull me up. I grab it and we stumble towards the cliff and the glow of a fire.

Hammer and Mikey are huddled together, laughing at nothing. Smart has an arm around each girl. Greedy fucker. The girls look like twins – weird made-up eyebrows, long fair hair, matching screechy voices.

'Give Matt some,' says Mikey.

'Some what?' I say, sitting down opposite them. The fading light is a thin line low on the navy-blue horizon. I can just make out the black shadow of the fishing boat.

'Yokes,' says Mikey, breaking into another fit of laughing.

Hammer takes a bag out of his pocket and passes it to me as if it's a pack of Haribo. Uppers. I know what they are. Hal and Black warned us off them ages ago. Happy pills that bring you down to hell.

I pretend to take one and hand the bag to Jamie. He scoops a few and passes it on to Smart and the girls. Mikey holds a finger up to the sky and Hammer guffaws and spits like it's some hilarious joke. I take another beer. One of the girls smiles shyly at me. I smile back. Jamie's eyes dart from face to face. He sucks at a fag, and then realises he hasn't lit it. Mikey's on laughing duty now, cracking up at nothing, Hammer egging him on.

I pop the beer and feel light-headed as I take a huge slug. I lie back down on the grass. The whole sky is pinpricked with stars. Conversation buzzes around me and I try to make out whose voice belongs to who and my eyes close and all the voices are one now, a continuous, comforting drone. I doze for a little while and when I wake the murmuring soundtrack in the background has stopped.

Hammer has Mikey in a headlock and they're rolling around the ground. As I run over, Hammer punches and punches Mikey, tears running down Hammer's face. I pull him off and he collapses in a heap, sobbing like a small child.

Mikey sits up, rubbing his eyes. 'Fuck,' he says, 'they should call those pills downers instead of uppers. Fuck sake – he was crying and I put my arm around him and he tried to kiss me? A proper shift, like? Then he beats the crap out of me? Fucking mad.' Mikey wipes his nose with his sleeve. Jamie's still snoring, oblivious to all the commotion.

Hammer has stopped crying and I think he's asleep now too. What a great fucking night this is turning out to be. I knew we shouldn't have bothered coming. I knew once Jamie was here it'd all go to shit.

I throw another piece of wood on the dying embers of the fire. It sparks to life, spitting and crackling.

Mikey reaches for the bag of pills. 'These things are useless – they didn't knock a stir out of me.' He pours a few into his palm. 'I'd need ten times more than you skinny fuckers.' He grins at me and throws the handful of pills down his throat.

I stare at him, shocked. 'What did you do that for you fucking gowl?'

He shrugs. 'They're like Love Hearts or Skittles – there's nothing in them at all. Relax. Chill.'

'No, I won't relax. Look what they've fucking well done already – everyone conking out and bawling and freaking. You're a gowl sometimes, Mikey, do you know that?'

He grins in the firelight. He looks like a monster, eyes huge and glassy, just like Jamie's earlier.

'That's me – king of the gowls,' says Mikey, his voice all sorrowful.

'Here comes the downer now, Mikey. Have a good cry about it like Hammer did – that'd be really clever.'

Then he does exactly that. He starts bawling his head off too – not fucking Love Hearts after all. I know I should comfort him but I can't because it's all so fucking mock anyway. All brought on by popping the stupid pills. Why would you take something that was going to make you unhappy? So dumb. So unbelievably dumb.

'How many did you take when I was gone?'

He wipes snot from his nose and looks at me, eyes glassy and unseeing.

'How many? Fuck sake.'

Mikey gets up unsteadily, wiping his face with the back of his hand. 'I'll show you, you fucker. Watch me. I'll show you what I can do when I want to. Think you're great with your surfing.'

I laugh. 'Look at the state of you. Go home to bed, you fool.'

'I'm going to swim the bay. Right this minute. I'll swim the whole way over to Liscannor.'

'Off you go. Enjoy it, you gowl.' I lie back on the grass. I can hear Mikey walking away, I close my eyes. Swim the bay, my hole. He's heading straight for home, the big eejit. He'll probably get a three-in-one in the Pagoda first. I try to get up but I feel too tired. So tired I can't open my eyes.

6 May 2018

I still dream about you. I hate myself for doing that. Giving you space in my head. Seeing you dream-smiling at me. It makes me think you fucking care. Even though it's only a dream.

16

There's a ringing noise and first I think it's a smoke alarm. I open my eyes and I haven't a clue where I am. I'm staring up at a pink-blue sky. I'm shivering with the cold. I sit up and look around, trying to get my bearings. The fire has gone out a long time ago and the place is deserted. Bits of the night come back to me as I stagger over to the stone wall to piss. The ringing starts again once I'm doing up my fly and then I realise what it is. My phone. I search my pockets but I know already it's not there and then I see it jumping as it rings over by the bag that had been full of cans last night.

'Hello?' I mumble.

'Matt? Oh, thank God. I've been ringing Mikey for ages – where are ye?'

Oh, fuck.

'We're ... I'm ... we – we went to a party and ...'

'And never texted or rang me or answered your phones?'

'It was only a few of the lads and they had a tent and –'

'Come straight up now – both of you.'

I take a deep breath. I have to tell her. 'I don't know where Mikey is.'

'What? What do you mean?'

'He stormed off last night – said he was swimming the bay ...'

'And you left him?' Her voice is quiet and steady and terrifying.

'I ... he ... I thought he was joking – I thought he'd go straight home. I'm sorry, Mrs Chung, I'm sorry.'

'Oh God, no. Please no.'

She hangs up and I'm left there looking at the phone like it has answers. And then panic sets in and I'm off across the field and down the hill as fast as my legs will carry me. She's on the beach already. She's running down the long stretch of sand calling Mikey's name over and over. There's nobody about at all. I try to catch up with her but she's like a mad woman, flying along the beach screaming *Mikey! Mikey! Mikey!*

My lungs feel like they're about to burst and I finally catch up with her just where the beach meets the river.

'We should ... we need to call the coastguard,' I say, gulping in air.

She looks at me, not understanding, and then she shakes her head. 'No. No, Mikey's not ... he's fine, he's – we'll find him, we'll ...' She scans the sea in front of us, then screams his name at the top of her lungs.

Mikey. Mikey. Mikey. The words echo across the empty beach.

'We have to call the coastguard, we have to –'

'Mikey! Michael Francis Chung! Mikey!' Mrs Chung yells up to the sky. Then she whimpers, low soft cries.

I can't feel my feet under me, can't feel a thing. I know I need to do something but my brain won't work.

'Mikey,' says Mrs Chung, her voice a whisper now.

I see him first. He's across the river, barely a trickle now at low tide, lying on the sand, very still. I can hear Mrs Chung's sobs and I realise that she's holding my hand so tight it hurts. My legs won't move. He's dead. I know he is. And it's my fault.

Then, like in a dream, Mikey moves. He stands up slowly, stretches his body, dusts sand from his jeans. He turns to face us but it's as if he can't see us. He walks into the water, not realising that it's water. He walks slowly over to us, his hands outstretched like Jesus. The crossing seems to take ages, like it's in slow motion and dreamlike. 'I told you I could, dickhead,' he says as he reaches us.

Mrs Chung throws herself at him and I join in and we do a little circular dance on the beach as the sun rises over the town. I'm crying but I'm so delighted, I don't care.

'You swam the bay in the middle of the night?' I say.

'Weirdest thing. I swam out and then I got caught in a

current and I prayed to St Anthony, Mam – do you know the way you do when you can't find the car keys? And then I woke up over on that beach.'

'You were stupid to swim in the dark, Mikey. I could kill you,' says Mrs Chung. 'And you left him do it, Matt Lynch.'

'Ah, cop on, Mam, it's not Matt's fault. I'm a big fella – in every sense of the word. And I'm fucking starving.'

We're sitting on the deck having a big fry-up when a jeep pulls into one of the big Toblerone houses behind our mobile home. I'm too busy tucking in to the sausages and rashers to cop the jeep but I'd recognise the fucking lamb-dog anywhere. My mother and Rod spill out and I push my patio chair back in against the caravan wall so they can't see me. Mikey is too busy stuffing his face to even notice. My head starts to throb, a small little tap of a headache, just behind my eyeball. Of all the fucking houses she could have picked she decides to rent the one right next to us. Mrs Chung comes on to the deck with more rashers and sausages and loads them on to our plates. I'm wishing her back into the caravan but she pulls up a chair and pours herself a mug of tea.

'Don't ye ever again pull the stunts ye pulled last night – is that clear?' she says as she butters toast for herself. The small boys have gone off already with their bellies full of cornflakes and their footballs under their arms.

'We know, Mam – give it a rest,' says Mikey, grinning at me. He's in great form, considering the pills and alcohol he consumed last night. Maybe the swim in the dark cleared his head. My mother and Rod seem to have gone inside but I can't relax. And the lamb-dog is still yelping from inside the kitchen window.

Mrs Chung hears her and looks across. 'Will you look at the dog? He's like a toy,' she says.

I see my mother inside in the kitchen, her face excited, her girly ponytail swishing as she laughs at something Rod says. Then he pulls her towards him and nuzzles her neck and his hand moves under her T-shirt and up to her tits. I want to vomit.

I try to melt further into the side of the caravan. Mrs Chung gives me a funny look. She doesn't miss a trick. Well, except maybe for last night.

'I want to do the Edinburgh Fringe next year,' says Mikey, completely out of the blue.

'Is that like Movember except you grow a fringe instead of a moustache?' I say, laughing.

Mikey eyes me. 'Matt, stick to the skating and let me tell the jokes. OK – how about a quick-fire selection of Edinburgh's best?'

I drop my head into my hands and groan. 'It's almost time to go surfing.'

Mikey dead-eyes me, then stands up ceremoniously and clears his throat. 'OK – best joke at Edinburgh last year? It's by a guy called Nick Helm – very funny guy – I needed a password eight characters long so I picked Snow White and the Seven Dwarfs.'

Mrs Chung laughs. I don't.

Mikey starts off again. 'Crime in multi-story car parks. That is wrong on so many different levels.'

Mrs Chung laughs again. I'm thinking they're not very funny at Edinburgh so Mikey might do grand there.

'People say, "I'm taking it a day at a time." You know what? So is everybody. That's how time works.' He grins at me. I grin back. Just because he isn't drowned.

'Drive-Thru McDonald's was more expensive than I thought. Once you've hired the car ...'

Mrs Chung laughs. And so does somebody else. It's Rod – my mother's boyfriend. He's standing in the garden of the holiday home, arms folded, chuckling away to himself. Mikey sees him and that fucks it. Mikey has an audience that isn't his mother or me – we could be here all day.

'I was playing chess with my friend and he said, "Let's make this interesting." So we stopped playing chess.'

Rod and Mrs Chung laugh harder.

'I admire these phone hackers. I think they have a lot of patience. I can't even be bothered to check my *own* voicemails.'

Mikey's running out of steam. I can see the panic thing in his eyes. That thing that first appeared at the St Colm's Talent Show. Motormouth is about to happen.

'My friend died doing what he loved ... heroin. We have our own local version of *Big Brother* round my way – it's called jail ... Am ... am ... oh – a good one from Karl Spain, he's from Limerick too. I joined a dating agency and went out on a load of dates that didn't work out. I went back to the woman who ran the agency and said, "Have you not got somebody on your books who doesn't care about how I look or what job I have and has a nice big pair of boobs?" And she checked on her computer and said: "Actually, we have one, but unfortunately, it's you."'

I snigger at this one – even though Mikey flies through it way too fast. Just then my mother comes out of the Toblerone house, the little girl – Taylor – on her hip. She's smiling as she walks towards us. She's wearing denim shorts and a pink T-shirt and flip-flops.

'Terry, I don't believe it!'

'I do,' says Mrs Chung. There's a sharpness in her voice, like earlier on the beach.

'We got a cancellation, and the weather is so nice and Rod has a few days off so ...'

Mrs Chung says nothing. She just picks up her mug and sips her tea and eyes my mother.

'This is Rod – my partner. And this is Taylor.'

Mrs Chung smiles at the boyfriend and the child. I want to die.

'Mattie – Matt. You look so tanned.' She smiles at me and I have a *déjà vu* moment, like I dreamed this exact scene – her face, the sun, the pink T-shirt, all of it. 'Conor's coming today too. It's just so lovely here. So pretty.' Again the smile. I smile back – I just can't help myself.

'You should be here when it's pissing out of the heavens,' says Mrs Chung.

Mam nods, not knowing if she's being nice or not. Taylor cries and puts out her chubby arms towards her father and Rod takes her and nuzzles my mother's neck as he does so. Pervert.

'I have a great idea!' says my mother and she does a little girly dance with her feet. Mrs Chung rolls her eyes. 'A great idea!' Mam says again, looking at me. And there's something in the way she does that that makes me want to hug her. It's the way she makes me feel like I'm the only person in the world that she cares about.

'Can't wait to hear this,' says Mrs Chung.

'How about we do a big barbecue here tonight? Rod's a great cook and there's a huge deck up here. I'd love to have the kids around.' She looks directly at Mrs Chung, like this is a challenge. 'You'd like that, wouldn't you, Matt?'

I nod because it's true. I would like it. And I know Conor would love it. Mrs Chung nods too.

'Settled! I can't wait – it'll be the best ever.' She does the little dance thing again and it's funny. Rod hugs her and nibbles her ear. Puke.

'Jamie's around too. You should ask him,' says Mrs Chung.

My mother's face changes. Mikey farts and grins at everyone. 'Oops,' he says.

'Of course,' says my mother. 'Jamie's welcome too. I'd love to see him.'

'Good. See you later so,' says Mrs Chung.

Mam nods and gives me a little wave. I feel sorry for her. Mrs Chung is being such a fucking bitch to her and it's really annoying. Mam and Rod walk arm in arm back into their house.

'Are you OK, Matt? You don't have to go to the barbecue if you don't want to. I've a good mind to go over there and tell her she has no right –'

'I want to go and Conor will want to go.'

'I don't believe her for a minute – she knew exactly what house she was picking. Right beside my caravan. She knew exactly what she was doing. Ingratiating herself back in with ye and trying to ...'

She looks at me. I'm rubbing the side of my head with my fist. I want to scream at Mrs Chung. I want to scream at her that I want my mother to care. To want to be with us. To fight for us. That's what I want. She's my mother, for fuck sake. My mother.

'Let's go surfing, dude – I need to brush up on my surf-speak,' says Mikey. He punches me lightly in the arm. 'I'm getting the dried-out bleached hair and the babe-magnet pecs very soon – if I can find them on eBay!'

We go get our stuff and head down the hill. Mikey talks and talks and I'm thinking all the time what a fucking great friend he really is. He hates surfing, he hates Smart and he's still willing to come with me.

30 June 2019

Today I met my cousin that I never knew existed. She told me where you live. I know you'll hate me. I just know you will. But I can't help it. I'm going to find you.

17

We're walking home from surfing and I drag Mikey into the surf shop to show him a board that Smart just told me about. It's a gorgeous one, a Sam Egan Resin 8 – Smart says it's perfect for me. Mikey whistles when he sees the price – almost six hundred euro. It's a beauty. I want it so much it hurts.

'We could try to rob it,' says Mikey, pretending to lift it up.

'I'd do anything for it,' I say, running my hand down the side of the board.

'Anything?' he says.

My phone beeps. A text from Anna.

See you Thursday! Cant wait.

The kiss pops into my head. The lovely, unexpected kiss that tasted like milk and coco pops. I go bright red and of course Mikey notices.

'What's up with you? Are you sexting somebody?' He tries to grab the phone but I punch his hand away.

Dad's old Fiesta passes us as we climb up the hill. He's looking straight ahead, his body upright and stiff. He doesn't see me. Mikey waves but he keeps going. Scabby is looking out the back window and he spots me, no problem. He gives me one look and then ducks his head, afraid he'll be landed back with me. Dad's done a drop-and-run with Conor.

'He could have fucking waited for me.' I don't realise I say this out loud until Mikey looks at me.

'He probably has an AA meeting – or ten. Or maybe a couple of marathons to run,' he says.

I shrug.

Conor's found my mother already. I can see him inside in the kitchen, Mam fussing over him. He spots me on the deck of the caravan and waves. The lamb-dog is going ape in the garden, jumping up and down like she's on a spring, barking at the comings and goings in the caravan park. My phone rings. Jamie.

'What's up?'

'Nothing. Just back from surfing.'

'Heard the bitch was around. Heard she's having a little party.'

The little drumming pain wakes up in my head. 'Don't come, Jamie.'

He laughs. A cold hard laugh that drills through my head. 'See you later,' he says and hangs up.

I go inside the mobile home and head straight to the tiny bedroom. I flop onto the narrow bed, cover my face with a pillow and close my eyes. Fucking hell. How could a few days by the sea get so complicated? When I leave Limerick why does everyone have to follow me? A holiday is supposed to be about getting away from it all. Lahinch is a joke. Limerick just shifts itself down here for the summer. This morning when Smart and me were surfing I met our postman, Ray, and my English teacher from St Colm's. I wouldn't be surprised if I met Hal and Black sunbathing on the rocks. I mean, for fuck sake, this isn't a holiday any more – it's a fucking endurance test.

Her voice wakes me up. I think first that I'm dreaming but then I hear my mother talking to Mikey in a low voice.

'Can you come and show me which one?' she says.

'Course I can, Mrs – am ... Mrs ...' Mikey says and I laugh to myself. He doesn't know what to call her, the fucking eejit.

'Lucy. Call me Lucy,' says my mother, her voice like a soft cuddle.

'Lucy,' says Mikey.

'Let's go,' says my mother.

I sit up in the hot tiny cell of a room and wonder if I dreamed the conversation. The caravan is dead quiet. Mrs Chung is probably gone to the beach. I get up and sit on the deck, enjoying the peace. The caravan park is deserted.

Gulls call out to each other over my head and I imagine as I watch their snow-white bodies against the blue sky that they're doing an aerial recce for food while everybody's out. The headache has disappeared and I decide to have a shower before the crowd come back.

The shower is another endurance test. I can barely climb in, it's that small, and I wonder how Mikey manages to fit in here. Although there are a few dents in the plastic shower casing that look like they got a belt of Mikey. The water is hot, though, and a ton of sand comes out of my hair and now I know why all the surfers that I met with Smart have such crap hair. I think about Smart while I dry myself and how he wants to surf for ever. And how when I didn't know surfing – a few days ago, even – I thought it so dumb to think you could have a job surfing. Like trying to have a job skating. But all these surf guys with the dried-out hair have jobs surfing. Teaching it, selling surf gear, doing competitions. They travel all over the place and one guy with very bad dreadlocks will fly anywhere in the world if there's a big wave coming. That's so cool.

As I get dressed I think how much I miss being by myself. I pull out my gear bag from under the bed and root around in it for my favourite blue T-shirt. Instead, I take out the book. The Gone Book. I can't even remember putting it in there.

I flick the pages to the last entry. The day I discovered she came home.

Today I met my cousin that I never knew existed. She told me where you live. I know you'll hate me. I just know you will. But I can't help it. I'm going to find you.

Words I wrote only a few weeks ago but so much has changed already. I hate the way things are always changing. Things you believe are the absolute law and a week later the opposite is true, depending on who's around at the time. It's like there's tons of versions of the same thing – like the poem we learnt in primary school about the blind man and the elephant. I scrunch my wet hair up in a ponytail. I can do it now without even looking. I put the book away, pull on my T-shirt, and look at myself in the long mirror stuck to the back of the door. And even though I say so myself I'm looking damn fucking handsome. I wink at myself and think again how nice it is to be on my own. Then I can hear shouts and screams and laughing and they're all tumbling back into the caravan as if they'd heard me thinking about how good it felt to be alone.

Mam is nervous. I can hear it in her voice, a tiny little shake, especially when she's talking to Mrs Chung. We're sitting out on the deck of the holiday home. There's a fabulous sea view and the sun is an orange ball in the sky. The barbecue – a state of the art one that Rod brought with him – is all fired up and Rod's cooking steaks and burgers. The small kids are flying around the garden, chasing a bright pink Peppa Pig ball and screaming in tinny voices. Even Conor's playing and I'm glad about that. Every few minutes he goes and finds Mam and stands next to her, almost touching her and then he runs off again.

'Hey, Matt, can you help me for a minute?' Mam calls from inside the house. I get up and stretch. Mrs Chung sips her wine and I can see Mikey eyeing beer but I've warned him already about drinking. I couldn't face another morning like this morning.

'Yeah?' I say as I go into the dim kitchen. She's standing by the sink and she does the smile thing, and I feel very shy.

'I'm so glad you're ... I'm so glad this happened,' she says.

I look at her from under my eyebrows. I know what she means and it's not the party she's talking about. I feel myself going red from the neck up.

'Come with me,' she says then and grabs me by the arm. I follow. I don't have a choice. She pulls me outside, down towards the little garden shed. I can see Mikey looking at us, and Rod too. Even the kids seem to stop and stare.

'Open the door,' she says. She's wearing a long dress with no sleeves. It's the colour of sand.

'Why?' I ask.

'Just open the door, Matt. Open it.'

I do it and first I can't see anything and then my eyes adjust and I can't believe it. I just can't believe it. It's the board. The very one I looked at today except now it has ribbons and a red balloon on it.

'It's ... I can't ...'

'You can, Matt. You deserve it.'

'But how did you ... how ...?'

'Mikey told me. The minute he said it I just knew I had to get it for you. Do you like it?'

I look at the surfboard and then at my mother and then back at the board again and I can't decide which I love the most.

'I love it,' I say and I hug her.

'I loved you the most,' she whispers into my still damp hair. I pull away but she's smiling at me and I think maybe I imagined it. Those exact words. Like the versions of things I was thinking about earlier.

'You were always the sweetest. I'm sorry, Matt. I'm sorry I missed out on so much. Sometimes I'd try to imagine you – your life now – how you were coping and ...'

She starts to cry.

'Look at me – I'm a mess,' she says, dabbing her eyes with her fingers. But the tears keep coming. Her shoulders shake a little and I can hear sobs caught in her throat. Fuck.

'I missed ... you ... so much ...' The tears form make-up tracks down her face and she doesn't try to fix it. She just cries and I want her to stop.

'Did you miss me? Your father said you didn't ... that you'd all moved on ...' A tiny sob catches in her throat. 'That hurt so much, Matt. That broke me.'

'I'll be back in a sec.' I run down towards our caravan and leap the wall. I go in, pull out my gear bag from under the bed and grope inside. I feel the book, feel the weight of it in my hands. I pull it out quickly. No. I can't give it to her. I drop it on the bed like it's a bomb. I back away from it, sitting in raggy glory on a worn Superman duvet. She should know though. She should. She should know what it was like without her. My version. She should know my version. What missing is really like. I grab it and run before I change my mind again.

She's in the kitchen when I get back, stirring something in a huge pot.

'Mam ...'

Fuck. that slipped out.

She turns, looks at me and then down at the book in my hands. She reaches out for it, feels the thickness of it.

'What's this?' she says, reading the front of it in my baby ten-year-old writing. *The Gone Book.* She flicks through the first few pages, then lets out a little groan and closes her eyes. She hugs the book to her chest. Her eyes are full of tears. I have a big choky lump in my throat too.

'You wrote all of this?' she says, pulling back from me to examine my face. 'All those years?'

I nod, regretting now that I gave it to her at all. She'll read all the horrible stuff I said about her over the years. All the names I called her. She'll read my private thoughts.

'I'll treasure this,' she says. 'I'll read every word.'

The kids burst in to the kitchen, followed by the dog. The room is filled with barks and shrieks as they circle the table, chasing each other. Mam lifts the book to her lips, kisses it and puts it into a stripy beach bag on the floor. 'Thank you, Matt,' she says, smiling now. She fixed her face while I was gone. 'Will you help me with plates?'

I nod and we gather plates and cutlery and bring the stuff outside. Then we all sit down and Rod begins dishing out the barbecued meat. Mam has strung up fairy lights above the patio table. Candles glow in the dusky light. Mrs Chung laughs and jokes with Mam at the far end of the table. Conor's stuffing Pringles into his mouth and showing the contents to Leon and Troy. I can't see Mikey – there's a wine bottle in the way – but I can hear him horsing into the burgers and chicken. This night feels special and normal, all at the same time.

The desserts are amazing. There's cheesecake and pavlova and a coffee cake that Mrs Chung bought in Centra earlier. I have two slices of pavlova, dripping with cream and strawberries, and a giant dollop of ice-cream. I'm considering a third slice when I see them. Jamie and Hammer are sauntering up the driveway. Hammer's smoking a rollie. Jamie has his hands in his pockets. He's wearing a white T-shirt that says *I'm a right fucker* across the front.

'Look at this – happy fucking families,' Jamie says. He laughs then, but the laugh has a hard edge. 'Hi, Mommy,' he says, smiling at our mother. He gestures at Rod. 'Is this your new fuck buddy?'

The little kids stop their chatter, sensing the menace in Jamie's voice. I drop my eyes and stare at the burger on my plate. Lamb-dog has even stopped her endless barking.

Mrs Chung is on her feet and she goes and gives Jamie a hug and pulls him over by the wall. Rod continues to play host but there's a weird atmosphere now. I just want the night to be over. And the holiday. It's just too hard.

18

Jamie sits next to Mrs Chung. She finds a plate for him and fills it with food. He folds his arms across his chest and just stares at everyone so that we're all afraid to open our mouths. Conor's speed-blinking and he's giving me this look like I can fix it all. Mam is hiding behind Rod, running in and out of the kitchen, getting imaginary things for the table. Hammer is sitting on the wall, drinking a can of Bud and smoking a cigarette. The neighbours in the house across the way glare at him from their garden. He grins and waves. 'How's it goin'? Fucking great weather, isn't it? Come on over and have a can,' he shouts.

The neighbours run back inside. Mikey laughs and I kick him under the table. Leon and Troy have a fight over a slice of cheesecake and we're all glad of something to watch. Mrs Chung separates them and takes them inside to talk to them. Jamie cracks open a can of Heineken and comes and sits next to me. Somebody has put on music, Ed fucking Sheeran.

Jamie takes a slug of beer. Mam watches us from the other side of the table. She's pushing her cake around her plate but really she's watching Jamie like he's some kind of bomb ticking away at the dinner table.

'So, did you surf today?' Jamie asks. His voice is light, fun, interested.

'Yeah, it was awesome. Smart's taking me to Crab Island tomorrow – over by Doolin. He says I'm ready.'

'Must be all the skating – it's all about balance, isn't it?'

I nod at my brother and notice that his eyes look red. There's a vibe off him and I can't put my finger on it. A new vibe or feeling. I scramble in my head for things to talk about. Ordinary brother things. Mam is still watching us, but I don't think she can hear what we're saying. Ed Sheeran has some uses. The vein above my eye is acting up like it has something live inside it that desperately wants to get out. 'Yeah. I just took to it straight away. It's the best thing I ever did in my whole life. I'm, like, addicted already.' I smile at Jamie but he's looking at the small kids who are once again running around the garden. I follow his eyes. He's looking at Taylor, who's trying to wrestle the Peppa Pig ball from Troy. She wins, pushes him onto the ground and runs off. Jamie laughs.

'She's lovely, isn't she?' I say.

He shrugs. 'What's her name?'

'Taylor. I always wanted a sister.'

'That's because you're a girl, Matt, you always were.' He grins at me.

I dig him in the arm.

'She doesn't feel like my sister.' He takes a slug of beer.

'She will once you get to know her.'

He shrugs and I get that awful vibe off him again. 'You don't get her, do you, Matt?'

'She's only a kid, a baby, she –'

'Our mother. You don't get our mother.'

I pick up the last piece of pavlova and take a bite. It's dry and powdery in my mouth. Mrs Chung and Mikey are chatting to Mam and Rod. Mam smiles and nods but she's watching us. I feel sorry for her. I know I shouldn't really but I do. The music has shuffled to Westlife. Mam's favourite.

'She'll go again. In fact, she's planning it already. I can see it in her eyes.' Jamie's staring at Mam now, just staring down the table, over the bottles and the jugs and the bowls of salad. It's like they're having a wrestling match but just using their eyes. 'Mam is like the weird kid in *Interview with a Vampire* – that's our mother.'

I haven't a clue what Jamie's talking about. And I don't want to know.

'She bought me a surfboard.'

'Oh, how fucking generous! So she walks out on her kids and then strolls back and buys you a toy and all is forgiven?' Jamie's voice is getting louder and I'm afraid everybody'll hear. 'Just don't fall for it again, Matt. Don't give her a fucking inch.'

I bite my lip and the beetle that lives in the vein over my eye is having a dance party at this stage.

'So where's this surfboard?' he says after a while.

'Come on, I'll show you.' I get up and Jamie follows me to the shed. I open the door.

'Nice,' he says. 'I'd say that cost a few bob.'

'Nearly six hundred.'

He whistles and strokes the board. 'You'll catch some fucking waves with that.'

'Yeah. I can't wait to try it out.'

'Don't leave it outside the caravan – it'll be robbed. Lock it in here at night.'

'I'll mind it with my life.'

He strokes the board again. 'It's beautiful.'

'You should come for a surf with us. Smart'll sort you out with gear and stuff.'

'I think we're sorting him out with gear.' Jamie grins. 'He's on his way up here. Told him to call in.'

I look at Jamie. He shrugs and then walks away, his hands in his pockets, shoulders slumped.

I steal a bottle of beer even though nobody except Dad would object to me having one. And maybe Mrs Chung. But she's in great form now, herself and Mam are having the chats, slugging back the wine and giggling. Hammer's playing drunk football with the kids and the vein over my eye has gone to sleep. Mikey gets up and tries to play football, the big ape. He's waddling around the garden, his little brothers ducking and darting around him, and then he's in a huddle with Hammer. They're walking towards the shed and then they're actually in the shed. What the fuck is he doing? If he's popping more of the psycho pills, I'll beat the living crap out of him. They're laughing when they come back out. Mikey plonks into the chair beside me, shaking the table full of food and drinks.

'What were you doing with Hammer?' I say it quietly, so Jamie doesn't hear.

Mikey grins. 'Nothing. Just shooting the shit – showing him the surfboard and stuff. That's all.'

'Weird.'

'Why? I wanted him to feel OK about all that shit last night. No big deal.'

'He's a scumbag, Mikey. He'd stab you in the back in a second.'

'So would a lot of people,' Mikey says and picks up a whole bowl of Pringles and starts to munch his way through them.

Smart arrives then, strolls into the garden like a boss, his hair damp from a recent shower. No fear of him getting surfer hair. Hammer spots him straight away and they both go off to the bottom of the garden in deep conversation. Hammer's shaking his head over and over. I don't think they're discussing the surfing conditions for tomorrow. Then Hammer kicks the ground, glares at Smart and walks away. He looks pissed off. I walk down to Smart.

'Well, how goes it?' he says.

His voice is funny. Slurred.

'What was that about?'

'What?'

'Hammer.'

He shrugs. 'Nothing. Crab Island, tomorrow, man?'

And of course now all I want to do is show off my board.

'Look!' I throw open the shed door and Smart goes in.

'Fuck me, I'd ride this baby every way I could.' He's leaning into the board, pretending he's jumping it, caressing and groaning and kissing it.

'Perv,' I say, laughing.

'Man, she's a beaut.'

'Yeah. I can't wait to surf with it. Come on, do you want a beer?'

I close the shed door and Smart whistles. 'Hey, fucker – is that your Mam? The blondie one? You never told me your mother was a hot mama. She looks about sixteen.'

'You're some perv – she's my mother and she's ancient.'

He grins and we stroll out of the shed and up towards what's left of the party. The small kids are in bed. Mikey's sipping a beer but seems to be falling asleep in his chair. All the fucking uppers must be catching up with him. And the bay swim.

I sit drinking beer with Jamie and Smart. Mam and Mrs Chung are still chatting and laughing – louder now since the small kids went to bed. Rod's disappeared too.

'And who's this young man?' says my mother as she pours more wine.

'I'm Smart – I mean that's my name, Aaron Smart – but I am actually smart too.' He grins at my mother and she smiles and giggles.

I can feel Jamie stiffen beside me. Mikey's fallen asleep and is snoring loudly in the chair across from me. I try to think of something to say but I have brain freeze. I look at Mrs Chung but she's a little bit pissed. Hammer's laid out on the grass looking at the dark night sky and laughing to himself.

'Have another beer, boys,' says my mother.

'No way, they've had enough. It's twelve o'clock,' says Mrs Chung.

'Twelve? *So* late,' says my mother, giggling.

Only Smart giggles back. I can feel Jamie's body fizzing with nerves. Or anger. I don't know what it is but it's horrible.

'So, mother dear, where's my surfboard?' says Jamie.

Mam giggles again. 'Jamie, I ... if you want one I'll –'

Jamie shakes the patio table so that all the bottles crash and fall. 'Don't fucking bother. Just give me the money instead.'

There's a dripping noise from where a bottle of beer has fallen on its side.

'Calm down, Jamie,' Mrs Chung says but it has the opposite effect on him. His body is wound up like a tight spring.

'I'll have my money now. My little pay-off,' he says.

Mam looks like he's slapped her.

'Now, Jamie –' says Mrs Chung.

'Stay out of it,' he says.

'I ... I'll get my purse,' says Mam, just like that.

Jamie smiles at me. 'See how easy it is, Matt? I'm gonna screw her for every fucking penny she's got. She's going to be paying for all those missed birthdays for a very fucking long time.'

'Jamie, please. This isn't right ...' Mrs Chung says, but for the first time I notice that she's a tiny bit scared of him.

Smart reaches for another bottle of beer.

Mam comes back with her purse and hands Jamie some notes. 'It's all I have in cash. I'll give you some more tomorrow.'

Jamie takes the cash, counts it and puts it into his pocket. Then he kicks Hammer to rouse him. Hammer gets up groggily and Jamie lights a fag and then turns and grins at us. Mam is crying. Mrs Chung is sitting there with a face like thunder.

'Thanks for the food, the beer, the mother love,' says Jamie. He winks at me. Then he walks away, with Hammer following like a drunk dog, and I get that vibe thing again and now I know what it is – the feeling I'm getting all night from Jamie. Hopeless. Jamie is hopeless – no matter what happens, shit's going down. Mean, hopeless, certain shit. And there's no stopping it. I shiver.

'You shouldn't have done that,' says Mrs Chung.

My mother starts to cry.

'Time to go,' says Smart, standing up and almost knocking the table again.

I get up too and walk towards the caravan. I know what's coming. Mrs. Chung and her showdown.

'He – he makes me feel guilty ...'

I stop and sink down on the springy grass near the wall. I want to hear it but don't want to. Wanting to wins.

'He has a right to be angry.' Mrs Chung takes a slug of her wine. 'He has a right to be mad but buying him off is not the way to solve it.'

'You have all the answers, Terry, don't you?' Mam's voice is quiet.

'You left them. You got up one morning and decided you were running off with ... a boy.'

'You know my reasons. Men walk out all the time for far less, but that's OK in your world.'

'You deserted them and none of it was their fault.' Mrs Chung's using her quiet and deadly voice now.

'I deserted him, not the kids.' Mam flicks her head so that her ponytail swings from side to side. Mikey farts but it's a quiet one, almost silent.

'Five years, Lucy. Conor was five years old for fuck sake – that's half his life you've missed.'

Mam looks at her nails. 'I tried. He stopped it. The letters, the calls, he wouldn't let me see my children and my solicitor says it was all wrong, that I have a case –'

'It was all John's fault, was it? He stopped you contacting them?'

'You don't know everything, Terry. You think you do but all you know is John's version. You don't know mine.'

'I know the most important version, Lucy Meehan. I know your children's version and it broke my heart to watch them every day, day in, day out, their faces – the fucking pain in their faces – and now you've the cheek to want them back?'

Mam looks up from her nails. 'They're my children.'

'You didn't think of that when you left them.'

'I should have stayed out in Woodbine Avenue and rotted in that house with him and ...?' She looks down at her nails again.

'And them, Lucy, the kids – is that what you were going to say?'

'No, it wasn't – you know that's not true. You were my friend, Terry, you knew I loved them.'

'The only thing I know now is that talk is cheap. So you're going to fight for them?'

Mam nods.

'Jamie too?'

Mam says nothing.

'Thought as much. He's too much trouble, isn't he, Lucy – and we don't do trouble very well. We do happy and shiny and sexy and girly but we don't do trouble.'

'You're drunk.'

'So are you. *In vino veritas* – isn't that what they say?'

I almost laugh at this – at Mrs Chung spouting Latin.

'I'm going to bed. Fuck you.' Mrs Chung stands up and Mikey wakes with a start. Then she leans onto the table, making it wobble something terrible. 'One last thing, Lucy.

The difference between you and me? I don't need a man to fix my life. You should try it sometime. Try being an adult. Mikey? Come on.'

I duck over the wall and towards the caravan before she realises I was there all the time. I pretend to be asleep on a deckchair. She bends down and shakes me gently. 'Bed, you,' she says.

I get up, rubbing my eyes. I'll make a class actor someday.

'Night,' I say and go into the tiny bedroom after Mikey. He's already crashed out in his clothes. I lie down in mine. As I drift off to sleep I hear Mrs Chung in the next room. She's crying softly. It sounds a tiny bit like rain.

19

Smart's being a dick. He doesn't show up to go surfing off Crab Island and I'm there like a fool with my brand-new board. I'm like a total fucking novice. One of his friends – the bad-dreadlock guy – feels sorry for me so he comes over. Mikey's sitting on the wall of the prom. I can see his bulky silhouette from the shoreline. It's early morning. My favourite time of day.

'He's not coming, man. He's, like, fucked.'

'He'll be here. He's probably in some strange girl's house – you know the way he is,' I say, laughing.

The guy shakes his bad dreadlocks. 'He was out of it last night – took something, I don't know – wasted, totally.' He bends down to wax his board. Then he hands me the tin of wax. It's called Sex Wax for some strange reason. I wax my board too.

'Coming in? Waves are good on the left-hand side,' he says.

As I paddle out beside Dreadlock I think back to last night and Hammer and Smart and I've a good idea of what's going on. And weirdly I feel it's my fault – if Smart hadn't met Hammer then he'd be OK just having a few beers.

The surfing's good and soon I'm on a roll. I'm catching every wave and Dreadlock's amazed – I can see it in his face. It's almost too easy. In some ways it's easier than skating – water's more pliable, easier to master. We finally call it a day and when I reach Mikey I'm shocked to see Anna standing beside him. Glaring at me.

'Anna. Jesus – what are you doing here?'

'It's Thursday, Matt,' she says, her voice flat. She looks lovely in a pale-blue summer dress with tiny white flowers and blue flip-flops. Her hair looks longer and her skin is a golden colour. My little pal in the vein above my eye wakes up. How could I have forgotten she was coming?

'I'm sorry, it's just you lose all sense of time here – don't you, Mikey?'

He's glaring at me too and I know exactly what he's glaring about. I never told him she was coming. I didn't tell him because I'd decided to deal with it when it actually happened instead of causing friction for ages beforehand. So it's actually happening now.

'Let's go swimming,' I say.

Both of them look me up and down. I have a wetsuit pulled down to my waist, I'm carrying the surfboard and I've been in the water for four hours. They walk away up the hill towards the caravan park and I trail after them like a lurk.

Mrs Chung makes a huge fuss of Anna and I love that about her. The way she makes you feel so welcome, like one of the family, and Anna's beaming and I think the visit might be OK after all. We have lunch on the deck and the sun is still shining and Conor's all chat, hopping over the wall to Mam's like a yo-yo. Mam appears at one stage and calls me over to the wall. Mrs Chung gives her a filthy look and then marches off into the caravan.

We go back to the beach for the afternoon. The tide is almost in so we go to the far end, near the sand dunes, and while Mikey dozes on a pink stripy towel, I lie down right next to Anna. She's in a red bikini and her skin is the colour of weak tea. She's sunbathing; her eyes are closed. I lean over her, admiring her face. Anna opens her eyes suddenly and smiles at me. There are tiny flecks of gold in her eyes. I want to kiss her but I haven't the nerve.

'I'm glad you came.'

Anna rolls her eyes. 'You forgot I was coming.'

'No, I didn't. I lost track of the days, that's all.'

'Another way of saying you forgot.'

'How's your mother?'

She closes her eyes. 'OK. She's having more chemo next week so she'll be really sick again.'

'It'll be over soon. The chemo'll work –'

Anna sits up and dusts sand from her legs. 'Stop, Matt. Please.'

'I'm sorry.'

She examines her nails – she's wearing nail polish and I think that's a first for Anna. She looks at me from under her eyebrows and then she grins. My heart does a backflip. I love her smile. It makes me happy. I reach up and touch her face and lean towards her. And then we're kissing, our lips barely touching. When we pull away, we both laugh. She lies down on the sand and I lean over her and kiss the tip of her nose and then her lips once again. And then Mikey lets off a huge fart and the two of us crack up – we're rolling around the sand. Mikey sits up then and watches us for a minute.

'Fuck sake,' he says.

We stop messing. 'What's up?' says Anna.

'I'm fucking starving,' he says.

We crack up all over again. Mikey stands up and dusts himself down. 'Are you two coming?'

Giggles from us. Mikey gives us the finger and marches off down the beach. We collect the towels and walk after him in our bare feet. The sand is hot and dry and the tide is right up now, leaving only a tiny strip of beach to walk on before we're forced to climb onto the path that skirts the golf course. Mikey's still walking ahead like a bold child who's had a fight with his parents. Anna slips her arm in mine.

'I hate going back. It's really nice here. It's so perfect.'

'What time is the last bus?'

'Around nine, I think.'

'Couldn't you pretend you missed it and go tomorrow? You could stay with us.'

She says nothing, like she's having a think about it.

'We could go to the Cliff Bar tonight. It's not really a bar – it's the edge of the cliff – I rolled off it the other night. Come on, Anna – it'd be a great laugh.'

'I can't.'

'Why not? They wouldn't miss you for one night – your dad said you needed a break. Come on,' I stop on the path and look at her. She looks out towards the sea.

'I can't. Mam needs me at night – she wouldn't settle. I can't.'

'Maybe it's you that wouldn't settle.'

She pulls her arm away from mine. 'What do you mean, Matt?'

'Just that maybe you can't be away from her and not the other way around.'

'That's so fucking unfair. Your mother hasn't got cancer, what the fuck would you know about it?' She glares at me, her chin sticking out, her eyes flashing with anger. Then she storms ahead. I swallow, sweat popping from my forehead. There's something about the way she throws this dagger of a look over her shoulder at me, like it's my fault her mother is sick. A black lump of anger burns in my chest.

'I know a lot about it, Anna. I know a lot about mothers fucking off,' I say to her back. Then I push past her and then past Mikey and run the rest of the pathway back to town.

I sit on the prom wall to try to calm myself down. The prom is packed out – there are throngs of people walking up and down in the hot afternoon sun. The surf-school vans are parked at the kerb, their business finished for the day. I spot Smart at the mad-coloured van, in bright orange swimming trunks. He's leaning against a board, talking to Hammer and Jamie. What the fuck is he talking to them about? Jamie waves at me and I walk over. Hammer's eyes are all weird and he looks at me like he only half-recognises me.

'Where were you this morning?' I ask Smart.

Jamie and Hammer guffaw.

'Did I say something funny?'

Smart grins at me. 'We had a bit of a mad night.'

'Mad isn't the fucking word,' says Jamie. 'Smart's some cunt when he gets going – he'd fucking take anything.'

'Gowl,' I say to Smart.

'Chill,' says Jamie. 'Smart's all right.'

'We were supposed to surf Crab Island.'

Smart shrugs. 'There's always tomorrow. Look who it is – the lovely, sexy Anna – bet I could,' he says then as Anna and Mikey come towards us. I want to stamp on his stupid fucking head.

'Shut up,' I say.

'Ooh – Matt has a little crush,' says Jamie.

'No, I haven't,' I say.

'So you don't mind if I help myself?' says Smart, going towards Anna and kissing her on each cheek. I can see she's kind of flattered by the attention. I think she's grown a full foot in the few days since I saw her last.

'Fancy an ice-cream?' says Smart to Anna.

'Love one,' says Anna, glaring at me.

'Two secs,' says Smart.

He goes into the back of the van. Anna sits on the wall swinging her legs. Mikey sits beside her. Mikey's glaring at me too. Fuck sake.

'What does Rod do?' Jamie says, out of the blue.

'Bank or something – why?' I answer but I'm watching Smart jump out of the van like a fucking ad for California.

'Because our mother is rolling in it – I just tapped her half an hour ago for a ton. Nice one, Mammy.'

'Another hundred after what she gave you last night? That's not on.'

Jamie laughs. 'Listen to yourself with your kick-ass board. Least she fucking owes me.'

Anna jumps down off the wall and walks away with Smart. I watch them disappear up the prom.

'Are we going to Ricky's?' asks Mikey.

'No,' I say but it comes out as a shout. Jamie watches me curiously. Hammer spits a big gob of snot onto the prom, almost hitting a baby in a buggy. The mother glares at him. He winks at her.

'Come on, Mikey, we'll get some grub – you look like you're fading away,' says Jamie.

I walk off up the road almost at a jog. I walk and walk, past the caravan park and out the road until I come to a small deserted beach. I climb down and sit on the rocks and flick stones into a large rock pool. The stones make patterns in the water. I don't know how long I sit there. It feels like hours and my arse is numb but it's great to be on my own again, not pulled all over the place by people and their shit. My phone beeps eventually. Anna. A text.

Leaving soon. Friends?

I get up straight away and climb over the rocks and run like a lunatic down the hill and back towards town. She's sitting by herself on the wall, waiting for the bus to Limerick. She's wearing a blue fleece hoodie over her dress and she looks gorgeous with her pixie face and her too-big sweatshirt.

'Where's Smart?' I blurt out.

She smiles at me. 'We had ice-cream and I told him I had to leave. He's weird, a bit pervy.'

I grin at her and nod. 'I'm sorry.' I sit up on the wall beside her.

'Me too. You were right.'

'So were you.'

We laugh and then we kiss and don't stop, even when the bus pulls up.

We don't say goodbye. She climbs on the bus and gives me a little wave and then she's gone from my view but I'm happy all over again and I wonder will it always be like this once there's a girl in the picture. The bus revs its engine, and the driver checks in his rear-view mirror, his indicator flashing loudly. I walk away, trying to catch a glimpse of her on the crowded bus.

At the corner I take one last look. The bus has pulled away and there she is standing by the wall, arms folded tightly across her chest, her flowery backpack at her feet. She grins. I am so feel-good I'm in the green room again.

20

The main street is busy, cars snailing past, as if the heat of the day has made them lazy too. I can smell tar and sea and chips. And my heart still wants to explode. We spent hours in Ricky's, eating chips and talking. Just the two of us.

'Dad believed me – about missing the bus,' she says, swinging our joined hands gently.

'Told you – it's grand,' I say. I'm grinning like an eejit.

'So, where's this Cliff Bar?' she says.

We're heading up the hill. The sea is glass this evening and the sun is setting over it. Everything glows orange.

'Just over there,' I say.

'Let's go,' she says.

I don't want to break the spell of her but we walk towards the cliff. Already I can hear loud voices and music from a speaker. As we round the bend we see them all clustered around a small crackling fire. Mikey's beaming but he has that glazed look again. Hammer's together for once, smoking a cigarette and eyeing up Anna. Jamie and Smart are huddled in deep conversation. Smart looks up as we approach.

'Hey, do ye want a beer?' says Smart. He's staring at Anna. Looking her up and down like she's his dinner. Fucking bastard. 'Or some sweets? Pick and mix, Anna – you like pick and mix don't ya?' Smart's grinning now and holding out a bag full of pills. 'Go on, live a little, these'll make you –'

I launch myself at Smart before he has the sentence finished, scattering the fire embers everywhere. I sit on Smart, my hands around his throat, squeezing as tightly as I can. My mind is blank and my hands are my brain, with an iron grip on his narrow neck.

Suddenly Jamie's on top of me, prising my hands from Smart, screaming into my face. 'Man, stop, man, fuck sake, you'll kill him, stop it ...' He punches me hard into the side of the head and I topple off Smart, who's choking and coughing and spluttering.

'Jesus, man,' Jamie says, pulling me away by the arm. 'Fuck sake, Matt, what's with you? He was only having a laugh ... fucking hell.'

I kick the ground in front of me. I want to go back and do it all over again. Do it properly and scare the living shit out of him. I can still hear him coughing.

'Listen to the cunt, doing a fucking Neymar on it – he should be an actor, fucking pervy bastard.'

'Hey, calm down, Matt. Have a beer, relax, OK?'

I glare at Jamie.

He grins at me. 'Makes a change – me telling you to calm down.'

My breathing is normal now. I look over at the group, huddled around the now scattered fire. The air smells of burnt hair and Hammer is rubbing his head and then looking at his hand as if he's trying to wipe away the damage. Smart glares at me while popping a beer. Miraculous Neymar-like recovery, though. Mikey's sitting next to Hammer, arse-licking the shit out of him. Fucking eejit. And Anna's gone. I search for her and spot her running over the hill towards the road.

'Mikey, we've to go,' I say, remembering Mrs Chung's warnings.

'I'm busy, Mam,' says Mikey.

Hammer guffaws. Mikey grins like a gowl. I give him the finger and walk away. He can do what he likes from now on. I leap over the wall and catch up with Anna. She's on the phone to her dad. I sit on the wall next to her as she talks rapidly in Polish into the phone. She hangs up and examines her nails.

'That was weird.' She keeps examining her nails. Girls always do that when things are awkward.

'Why – what did your dad say?'

'Oh, not that – I mean what happened with Smart.'

'I'm sorry, I just lost it ... I ...'

She looks me straight in the eye. 'You scared me.'

'He was being a prick, Anna, insulting you and –'

'You scared me, Matt. The look on your face, the ... what's the word? Fury? Madness?'

'Look, I lost my temper, I ...'

She shakes her head and drops her eyes back to her nails. Her dark lashes are thick and long. 'I thought you were going to kill him. I really did.'

I examine my nails. Those girl genes are strong. 'I'm sorry. What can I say?'

She shrugs. 'I knew I should have gone home.'

'How do you mean?'

'The sun, the great day. You.'

'I'm still here, I'm still me. Let's forget we ever went there – let's do something else, fuck them.'

A tiny shake of her head again. 'I want to go home.'

'Anna, please ...'

She jumps down from the wall and faces me. 'I can't do this, Matt. You scare me and I can't have more scare in my life right now. I just can't.'

This time I shrug and I can feel my old friend, anger, begin to bubble and crackle inside me again. I get off the wall and walk up the hill. I can hear her behind me but I ignore her. I even whistle a little as I turn in to the caravan park.

Mrs Chung is out on the deck, reading a magazine. 'Did you miss the bus, Anna? You can stay here, no problem.'

'Thank you, Mrs Chung. My dad wants you to ring him.'

'No problem. Are ye hungry? There's ham in the fridge. The boys are all conked. Conor's staying over there,' she says, throwing a dagger look at the holiday home.

I nod. Anna sits down next to Mrs Chung. I feel like a total spare now.

'Where's Mikey? I told him ten o'clock,' says Mrs Chung, checking her phone on the table beside her.

'I'll go get him – he's down at the chipper,' I say. I walk away, leaving Anna on the deck. I can feel her confusion. And her disappointment. I can really feel that, like it has long skinny fingers that rub it in to me over and over again. The fingers follow me like shadows.

I try to walk back down to the Cliff Bar but my legs insist on walking up to my mother's place. They insist like they have a mind of their own. It's all quiet – even the yippy dog is silent. I go around the back and look in through the open patio doors. She's alone in the kitchen. The lighting is soft, and she's smiling to herself as she wipes the table. She looks up and sees me and her smile is like a hug. Before I can stop myself, I'm in her arms and I'm bawling and she's rubbing my head and holding me so tight that the disappointment-fingers have no room to poke me. We stay like that for a long time. Eventually she pulls away and hands me a tissue. We both blow our noses at the same time. And then we laugh, tears coming again, but this time the good ones.

'Are you hungry?' she says. 'There's pizza in the freezer. Conor's asleep since eight. He's exhausted. He went swimming with Rod and then Rod had to go to work – delivery time.' She winks at me like I know what she's talking about.

'What's being delivered?' I ask, taking a banana from the fruit bowl on the table.

'Money,' she whispers, 'he's in charge of the bank deliveries. It's a very responsible job.'

I nod but all I can think of is Rod and his boyish head and his skateboard. He doesn't look responsible but what do I know?

She makes two cups of tea and she's forgotten about the offer of pizza and the banana has made me realise I'm starving. I take another one.

'Jamie called?'

She smiles and nods. 'I made him coffee and he smiled at Taylor.'

That was fucking big of him considering he tapped you for a ton, I think, but I don't say it out loud. I'm remembering things about my mother that I used to know. Like how she creates her own version of stuff for herself. Maybe we all do. Maybe I do too.

She's chattering on now about the holiday and seeing us and she's smiling and giggling but my mind is wandering like a fucking snake. Anna and Mikey and Rocky the dog. Will Dad have to bring him on the half-marathon with him? Where's Mikey anyway at nearly eleven o'clock? Now she's moved on to Taylor and how Taylor was a gift from God. I see the striped beach bag that she put my book into yesterday. It's still dumped in the same corner of the kitchen. I can even see a bit of the book peeping out.

'Who was he? I remember that day. I was sick and –'

'Matt, please. Not now. It'll spoil the –'

'Who was he? I should at least know that. I should know what was so fucking bad that you had to leave us. Or maybe what was so fucking good?'

She pulls back from the table and I realise that I shouted the last bit. I can feel the anger inside me again, black and smouldering and deadly.

'It was just a guy. It meant nothing – it was just a way out.'

The clock on the wall ticks loudly. The lamb-dog has woken up and I can see her outside peeing on a plant and then sniffing it.

'That's worse,' I say. I ignore the tea she made for me. 'It wasn't even for love?'

She looks at her nails. Big surprise there. 'It's complicated, Matt.'

'Who the fuck was he? Why all the secrecy? Was he famous or something?'

'He was a student in St Colm's. A repeat student. He helped me find Jamie one day when Jamie had forgotten his rugby gear, and he was fun and kind and a laugh and he ... he got me. Your dad never got me ...' Her voice trails off or else I switch her out of my head and all I can see is a Colm's school uniform on the floor of my mother's bedroom in that house right beside Chung's. And Dad's face like somebody stabbed him in the gut over and over again.

'Pervert,' I say, and again it comes out as a shout. 'Weirdo pervert.'

She closes her eyes and two of the perfect little tears she keeps for these moments pop out and roll slowly down her cheeks. I want to hit her. Choke her hard like I did to Smart. Thump her until she can't talk any more. Can't talk about St Colm's and schoolboys and rugby gear.

'Poor Dad.'

'You don't know everything, Matt. Don't judge until you know the truth.'

'How can I ever know the truth when you fucked off and didn't even contact us?'

'He had a temper, your father. Did he ever tell you that?' She picks up her tea and takes a long sip. 'I bet he didn't. When he was drinking, he'd ... well, he'd hit me, and the worst part was that he wouldn't even remember the next day –'

I put my hands over my ears and block out her voice completely and all I can hear is a drone and a noise like the sea. I look at her and only take my hands away when her lips stop moving.

'Versions,' I say.

'What?'

'Nothing. You wouldn't get it ... get me.'

'You wanted the truth, Matt.'

I stand up, shake my head at her and run out through the open doors, almost falling over the lamb-dog on my way over the back wall.

The caravan is quiet. Anna's asleep on a bed couch in the living area. She sits up when she hears me and rubs her eyes, spreading mascara all over them.

'Mrs Chung's gone searching for Mikey – he's not answering his phone. Hey, what's up?'

'I ... nothing,' I say and escape to the tiny bedroom. I get into bed fully dressed and the tears come straight away and I cover my head with a pillow so that she won't hear me but it feels like the whole caravan shakes because of the crying. I can't stop it.

21

Anna's gone again. She's like the disappearing girl. I'm up first and climb over a snoring Mikey's body to get to the loo. The bed in the living area is a couch again and the quilts are gone. It's like I dreamt she was there last night. She could have waited. She could have said goodbye. I take my phone out of my pocket and check it. No messages.

I notice something odd in the garden next door. The shed door is wide open. It's flapping in the breeze, tapping against the wall. I jump the wall and run to the shed. The padlock lies smashed on the dry brown grass. I go into the murky gloom and almost trip over a spade. The board's gone. Of course the board's gone. Even that couldn't fucking last. I punch the shed wall so hard with my fist that it splinters.

'Fuck. Fuck. Fuck. Fuck.' I punch the wall a second time and hear the satisfying crack of timber. My hand is bleeding. I watch the blood drip onto the concrete, dark and shiny in the dim light.

'Matt, what's up? What happened?' says my mother from the doorway. She's wearing pyjama shorts and a string top. Pink, showing way too much tit.

'The surfboard. It's stolen. Gone. Fuck sake.'

'Ruby's gone too.'

Who'd have stolen a surfboard? Hammer. It had to be Hammer. I remember then himself and Mikey down by the shed the night before last. I leap over the wall and tear into the caravan. I push open the bedroom door and jump on Mikey. I get his neck in a vice grip and he struggles under my weight. But he's no Smart and with one heave he manages to push me off.

'Good fucking morning to you too, psycho,' he says, sitting up.

'Where's my board? What the fuck did ye do last night?' I whisper. I don't want Mrs Chung to hear.

'What the fuck are you talking about? You've had too much sun, Matt. You've, like, lost the plot – trying to choke people and murdering them and stuff.'

'They broke into the shed and stole my fucking new surfboard and they took the dog too – probably for a laugh. And you were with them, you gowl.'

'Fuck.'

I sit down on the bed, my head in my hands.

'Hey, look, I'll sort it, Matt. It's probably a joke or something. I'll sort it out.'

'Who was it? I know it was one of them.'

'Jamie was conked out and then I conked and Hammer was gone and –'

'Hammer. Fucking cunt. It's your fault. You fucking invited him to steal it, showing it to him the other night. Why? Why'd you do that, you gowl?'

Mikey shrugs and heaves his body out of the bed. 'I'll fix it. I promise I will.'

'I want it back, Mikey. My board. It's your fault.'

I get up and go back next door. Mam is sitting at the table crying, phone glued to her ear. Conor's sitting at the kitchen table, crying too. There's no sign yet of the little girl. My sister.

'OK, OK, I will. I love you too,' she says and hangs up.

'Rod's coming back. He says not to call the police yet – that it could be just a prank – or maybe ...' She looks away but I know what she was going to say. Jamie. Jamie stole my board and her dog.

'It wasn't Jamie,' I say.

Conor sniffles. Mam wipes a tear away. 'How do you know?'

'He's my brother. He wouldn't.' I glare at her, willing it to be true. It is true. I know it is.

'Poor Ruby,' says Conor. 'She'll be so lonely.'

His voice trembles. Mam doesn't even look at him.

'I'll find her, Conor, don't worry. I'll find her and she'll be grand.'

'Promise me, Matt?'

'Scout's honour.'

He gives me a watery grin. 'You were never ...'

'A scout!' We say it in unison.

Mam's furiously texting on her phone.

'Can I go over to Mrs Chung's?' Conor says.

'Course you can. Get dressed and hop over the wall.'

She's talking to someone on the phone, hysterical over the missing dog – Neymar-style also. She doesn't see me leave.

I check the cliff but I know before I even go there that they'll be gone. That there will be a brown circle of earth where the tent had been, a splash of oil where the car had been parked, beer cans and bottles thrown around the ground, the dead black ashes of last night's fire. And of course I'm right and I head into town, my anger on red alert. I know that if I even smell Hammer, I'll actually kill him. I march down the hill, not seeing anything, just blurs of sea and sky and people and cars. And blurs of noise, girls and seagulls screeching, tinny music from an arcade, a car pumping a heavy beat through open windows.

I scan the beach and prom for the familiar hunch of my brother's shoulders or the lanky, dopey lope of Hammer. Not a sign. And no sign of the car. I ring Mikey. No answer. I try Jamie. Straight to voicemail. I do one more round of the beach and prom, my T-shirt sticky with sweat, my boxers glued to me in the stifling heat. There's a shimmer before my eyes and I don't know if it's the sun or my temper or both. I want to puke. I buy a bottle of water in the supermarket and sit on the prom wall and sip it slowly, hoping the urge to vomit will stop. Somebody thumps me in the back and I almost fall onto the rocks below. 'Fuck, watch it,' I say, turning around.

Mikey's grinning at me, his big stupid grin, sweat bubbling on his forehead like glass acne. 'So Paddy dies and goes to Heaven and St Peter is there at the door and Heaven's a bar – a big huge bar – and there's Elvis having a drink with John Lennon and there's Phil Lynott hanging with Kurt Cobain. And then Paddy spots Bono. He grabs St Peter's arm and says that can't be right – Bono was alive and kicking when Paddy had his heart attack. St Peter smiles and says that's God – he just thinks he's Bono ...' Mikey guffaws, then grins at me. 'Get it?'

'Mikey? Where's my board?'

Mikey puts his finger to his lips. 'I'm sorting it.' He gives me a huge wink.

'What did you do, Mikey? What the fuck did you do?'

Mikey beams this time and does the finger to the lip thing again. I jump off the wall, spilling my water onto the ground. I think I hear it sizzling.

'It's sorted. Like you told me. I didn't find the board yet, or the dog, but I got Hammer. I got him good.'

'What did you do?'

Mikey's face loses the grin. 'I don't get you.'

'Just tell me what you did?' My voice is low and threatening.

'I ... got him – that's all. I got the snakey little fucker where it hurt.'

'What did you do?'

'Shopped him.'

'What?'

'To the shades. I shopped him.' He smiles like he's done a great thing. I kick the sea wall so hard that I yelp in pain. 'Are you mad, Mikey? Seriously? Are you mad?'

Mikey goes all sulky. 'I told the cops and they – and they hauled him in and they're searching the car and all and, and, they'll find the board and the stupid dog, and –'

'No. No no no. What about Jamie? Is Jamie with him?'

'I, am ... I ... I didn't think ...'

'Of course you didn't think, because that would require something that you don't have, you fat useless fuck – that would require a brain and instead of a brain all you have up there in your thick stupid head is fat cells.'

'Shut up, Matt, just shut the fuck –'

'Do you know what you've done?'

'I'm getting your surfboard back like you told me, like you said, it was my fault for showing it to him in the first place and –'

'God, I give up.'

'And the guards were very nice and they said they'd haul him in casual like, and ask him a few questions and,

and I lied a bit – I said I saw him take the board and the dog, and I signed the statement. Simples.'

'Simples? What about Jamie? What about the fucking drugs you threw into your gob the past few nights? What about that?'

'I ... well ... I only said about the board and the fucking dog, I said nothing about drugs.'

'You are one thick fool.' I stare at him, at his scrunched-up eyes, his fat cheeks, his big dumb face. I shake my head and walk away.

'I did it for you, man. I tried to fix it for you ...'

He's shouting after me, and people on the prom are watching us. I begin to run, almost pushing the crowds out of my way. I run down the slipway and onto the sand, trashing sandcastles and picnic rugs and shell paintings as I run, the sand dry as a bone under my feet. I stop by the estuary, the one where Mikey crossed like Jesus, and I have to sink down on my knees because of the stitch in my side. A horse and rider gallop past. My breath won't come and then I puke. It's mostly water, with a few cornflakes.

22

The lamb-dog is home. I hear her before I see her, the whiney bark, ear-piercing in the quiet late afternoon sun. I can just about see her tail from the deck as she bounces up and down, like she has trampolines for legs. I leap the wall and she runs in a circle at my feet like a ball of white fur in orbit.

I bend down and rub her tight curls. She licks my hand, then leaps into my arms, and sits there looking up at me. I realise I'm delighted to see her. Taylor and Conor are playing in a splash pool, placed under a tree. Conor is sitting in the pool and Taylor is pouring water over his head from a Winnie the Pooh teapot. Conor looks miserable and I can't help thinking why you'd come all the way to a beach in the sunshine only to stick your kids in a plastic pool in the yard.

My mother's doing her nails in the kitchen and Rod's sitting beside her, eyes glued to her face as she chatters away.

'Oh,' she says, when she sees me.

I feel like an intruder. A spy.

'She's back,' I say, nodding at the dog in my arms.

'She was found in Ennis,' she says, blowing on her now purple nails. Rod takes her hand and blows too. She giggles.

'Ennis? How did she get to Ennis?'

'On the surfboard?' says Rod. She giggles hysterically at this. There are roses in a vase on the table and a bottle of wine is chilling in a silver holder.

'The Old Ground Hotel. She was found wandering around the grounds and Rod ...' She pats Rod's arm and smiles at him. 'Well he'd contacted all the animal welfare people and somebody recognised Ruby ... and there you are!' She leans into Rod and they kiss, right there in front of me, tongues and all.

I put Ruby down and she goes off to sniff something outside. Taylor begins to scream at Conor, 'My the mammy, my the mammy, my the mammy.'

Still the kiss goes on. He has a hand up her jumper now and I want to look away like I did years ago when Jamie made me watch *Jeepers Creepers*. But my eyes stay fixed on this girl-woman that is my mother and her boyfriend. Conor arrives in, hair wet from the pool, Taylor trailing water after him.

'Want to go for a swim in the sea?' I say. Conor blinks and looks at our mother. She isn't even listening to the conversation.

He nods. 'Just us?'

'Yep. Just you and me. We'll go to the beach up the road.'
Just as I'm about to hop the wall she calls me.

'Matt?'

'Yeah?'

She smiles and flutters her eyelashes like the young wans in Limerick.

'We were like, Rod and I were wondering if you might babysit tonight? Rod wants to take me to dinner ... well it's been so stressful ... and it's our anniversary ...'

Taylor gives me the evil eye from her mother's arms. I want to say no. I want to say fuck off and die. But the thought of Mikey and the fuck-up he created make up my mind for me.

'Yeah – what time?'

'Around nine?'

'Grand. Have that little tyrant in bed though.' I look at my mother's hurt face, give her a thumbs-up and leap the wall.

The beach is deserted and Conor's doubtful about swimming there but I finally coax him in. I swim right out to the horizon, past the skeleton of rocks, past a huge seaweed bed. The further out I go, the calmer I get. I think that maybe I've exaggerated it all. I haven't heard from Jamie or from Hammer. I haven't seen them or the car. Maybe they got off home before the guards caught up with them? And if

Hammer did rob the board and the dog, then maybe that explains how the dog ended up in Ennis. They got sick of her on the way back to Limerick and dumped her at the Old Ground Hotel.

I swim back in, tasting salt on my lips. I still can't believe it – that Jamie would allow Hammer to steal my board. He knew what it meant to me. I get out of the water, letting the still-warm evening sun dry me off like a giant hand drier. There are two guys sitting on the sand near our gear. Standard Lahinch surfer dudes, tanned skin, bleached hair, surfer tees and shorts.

'Yo,' says the nearest one. *Yo*, like he's on a stoop in New York.

I nod and sit down on my towel. I watch Conor as he leaps over the waves, which are coming in faster now. 'We'll have swell here soon,' the guy says. He sounds like he's talking to himself or an imaginary person right in front of him. I nod anyway just to be on the safe side.

I sit and watch Conor playing in the water and already in my head I'm seeing the wave, watching it build and then roll and crash against the cliffs. I walk down to the shore and call Conor. Then we pack up our stuff and as we walk up the rocky hill we pass the two lads carrying their surfboards. They're wetsuited now, and the one I was talking to grins at me as we pass.

Conor chatters away as we walk down the road. I barely hear him. I'm too worried again about Jamie and the cops. Everything is getting fucked up. I can't seem to stop it and sometimes I think that I actually cause it. I kick a stone along the soft tarry road. I'll fuck up Conor too. I should just stay away from everyone and everything. If I hadn't come here then none of this would have happened. Jamie and Hammer wouldn't have had the bright idea to follow us down. Then Mikey wouldn't have taken those stupid pills and neither would Smart and I wouldn't feel like shit now. And Anna would like me and not be scared. All my fault. The whole thing. You can't have a holiday from shit. It just follows you and gets you anyway. Long fingers.

We have takeaway for dinner. Mikey eats in his room and I'm glad. Troy and Leon have gobbled their chips and are already running off to join their new pals. We can hear them laughing and shouting as we eat on the deck.

'So, nice day?' says Mrs Chung, looking straight at me. Eyes like lasers.

'Great. We went swimming – didn't we, Conor?'

She's eyeballing me so hard I have to look down at my burger. 'What happened between you and Mikey?'

I know she's still staring, though I don't look up. I give a tiny shrug. I can hear Conor chewing.

'Tell me.' Her voice is low.

Another little shrug from me. I pick up the burger and take a bite from it, never raising my eyes to hers.

'I know there's something up, Matt. I know it in my waters, so you might as well tell me now before the shit hits the fan.'

This time I look up and meet her eyes – eyes like tweezers pulling stuff out of you. 'We had a fight, that's all.'

'About what?'

'About me surfing all the time – that's all, I swear.'

'Make him do scout's honour, that always works,' says Conor through a mouthful of chips.

'I don't believe you.'

I shrug again. 'It's true.'

'We'll see, Matt. I'll get it out of Mikey. The truth.'

I take a drink of water. 'There's no truth. Nothing happened.'

'Do you think Rocky's OK?' Conor asks, as he dips a giant chip into ketchup. 'He's collecting me tomorrow. My dad is. I want to see Rocky.'

I watch as he dips another chip and blinks twice at it before he eats it. I hope Dad hasn't forgotten. I hope he hasn't forgotten the dog. And one other thing niggles at me. Conor actually wants to go home. He wants to go home with Dad.

Our mother is so glammed up I don't recognise her at first. She's wearing a short black dress with heels and a shimmery necklace. Her hair is up but with bits falling down on purpose. She smells lovely, like Brown Thomas, and she hugs us both but not too close in case we mess her up. Taylor is in bed and Ruby's banished to the garden.

'There are treats in the fridge and Taylor's fast asleep since seven. It's like she knew we were going out and we needed time to get dressed – such a doll.' She beams at us and Rod comes in to the kitchen. His hair is all gelled the way Jamie used to do his before he became a shit. He's wearing really nice jeans and a Hollister T-shirt. A peach one that doesn't look a bit girly on him.

'Hey dudes, thanks for babysitting,' he says, and then he puts his arms around our mother and she pulls him real close, not a bit worried that he'll mess her up. I push Conor into the sitting room. He flicks on the telly. They're giggling in the kitchen like two teenagers. I turn up the volume on the telly. It's an ad – one for bottled water with rapids and volcanos. Conor is glued to it.

Our mother walks in and puts a baby monitor on the coffee table in front of me. 'See you later – and you could turn down the sound on the TV.'

Conor and I stay glued to the ad. He turns up the volume. We grin at each other.

'Popcorn?'

Conor nods, never taking his eyes from the telly. I go to the kitchen and put the popcorn in the microwave. It takes me a few seconds to recognise the face at the patio doors. A face so freaked out I just know the shit has finally found a target.

Jamie.

23

I want him to go away. To just disappear out of my life. I blink, a Conor blink, and I wonder if that's why Conor does it. If he blinks hard enough the shit will be gone? But Jamie's still there, his face ghost white, his eyes huge in his head. He points at the lock.

I walk over to the door, Ruby scampering behind my legs, like she knows crap is coming too.

'Hey, what's up?' I say as he slides in the door. He's all hunched up, hands in pockets, face like somebody terrified the living shit out of him. *Jeepers Creepers* face.

'Man, what's up?' I ask again. The air smells buttery from the popcorn. Jamie sinks into a chair and puts his head in his hands. 'Are you OK? There's pizza in the freezer and rolls and ham and ... there's popcorn ...'

He starts to cry but it's not like crying or sobbing. It's more like a wail, like something a ghost would do. Fuck.

I don't know what to say or do. And the worst thing is I don't want to know.

'What happened?'

Jamie looks at me now, straight into my eyes, and I want to cry too. He shakes his head. 'I am so fucked.'

'How do you mean? Fucked as in drugs?'

Another desperate shake of his head. 'I'm a dead man walking. I am so fucked that I might as well die now. Save myself the fucking pain. Oh God, I am so dead ...' He starts crying again, laying his head on the table and just wailing softly. It's almost like a chant, like the Muslims on telly after a bomb blows up their neighbourhood.

'How? What happened exactly?'

Jamie looks up at me and wipes snot and tears from his face with the sleeve of his hoodie. 'You should fucking know, Matt. Mikey shopped us.'

'Not you, just Hammer and he stole –'

'You haven't a clue, have you?' he shouts, banging his fist on the table and making the vase of roses shake. 'They took all the gear. They found it in the car.'

'But he'll get out on bail and ...'

Jamie shakes his head. 'None of that matters. What matters is we're playing with the big guys and we lost their gear and we don't have three grand to give them. We're dead men walking – simple as that.'

The vein above my left eye gives a little tremor. I feel sick and the buttery smell is not helping. Now I see it all. I see all the shit that I spent the day not looking at.

'They hauled Hammer in, got him in the car when he came out of Centra – I'd gone for a piss in SeaWorld – and they hauled him in and stripped the car and he's gone to Limerick in a fucking squad car and I'm dead. They'll have heard already and they'll kill me, man.'

'They might give you time to sort it out?'

Jamie laughs. A horrible bitter laugh. 'Do you know what these people are? Time? They'll kill me and they'll go after you and Conor if they have to.'

'I want my dad.' Conor is standing in the doorway, blinking at us. His voice is calm.

'Conor, look, just go back into the living room. Here, I'll get the popcorn and you can watch a movie and ...' I jump up and run to the microwave and pop the door. I dump the popcorn into a bowl and push it into Conor's hands. He's staring and blinking at Jamie, who's leaning into his hands again. Conor lets the bowl slip. There's an almighty crash as it hits the floor and popcorn flies everywhere in a white cloud. Ruby yelps.

'I want my dad. He stops all of this. He stops the crazy stuff. He does.' Conor looks at me, his eyes spilling huge fat tears. 'He stops all the stuff, Matt. He doesn't let it come into the flat. He does, Matt, he does.'

'Conor, Dad'll be here tomorrow. Go into the living room, put on a movie. I'll –'

'Shut up. I hate you.' Conor marches out and bangs the door hard. My head hurts, the fucking dog barks.

Jamie groans. 'Fuck, fuck, fuck,' he says, then belts the

table again. This time the vase gives up and falls, spilling water and red roses all over the floor. The vase rolls along the table and stops at the edge.

'This is so fucked up, Jamie. Why did you let Hammer steal the board in the first place? If that hadn't happened, then –'

Jamie pounds the table again and the vase plops onto the tiles and smashes into a million pieces. 'Are you thick? Hammer never stole the board or the stupid dog. He was comatose last night. He never took the board. And if he had, Matt, I'd have killed him, made him bring it back to you. Don't you believe that?'

I shrug. 'He was looking at it with Mikey the other night, he ... he ...'

'It wasn't him.'

'Then who did it?'

Jamie sniffed and wiped his snotty nose again. 'No idea. But it wasn't Hammer. And now he's done for a shit load of gear and I'm dead because the gear is fucking gone.'

'Jesus Christ. Look, maybe we can get the money.'

Jamie laughs. A tight, mean laugh. 'From where? From Dad. Not fucking likely. Mam?'

'I'll ask her.'

Jamie looks at me. 'Really? Do you think she might give it to me? I'd pay her back eventually – I'm done with this shit anyway. It's killing me.'

'I'll ask when she comes home.'

'They're, like, loaded, aren't they?' Jamie seems brighter, happier, hopeful even.

'Well, Rod's got a huge job in the bank – she told me about it the other day – real big noise, so they've got money. I mean, she doesn't seem short, does she?'

Jamie gave me a tiny smile. 'Do you think she'd help me?'

'Actually, I think she will. Let's get this place cleaned up and I'll ask her as soon as she comes home.'

We're almost finished the cleaning when the screaming starts. We both look at each other in confusion and then I remember Taylor. I go up to her bedroom, dreading going in. I stand outside, hoping that the screams will stop and she'll go back to sleep. No such luck. I open the door and stumble into the room. There's a nightlight casting a haunting shadow of patterns across the ceiling. No wonder she was screaming.

'Taylor?' I whisper.

The screams quieten.

'Taylor?' I say again. This time they stop altogether. I lean over the cot and lift her out. She snuggles into my chest.

'Daddy, I scared,' she says.

I carry her downstairs, dreading the second she realises that I'm not Rod. I bring her into the living room. Jamie and Conor are sitting watching a movie. Taylor looks at the two faces and starts to cry, burying her head in my shoulder. Then she pulls back and looks at me and the screams start all over again. Piercing screams that make Ruby hide behind the couch and Conor cover his ears.

'Fuck,' I say.

'Do something to shut her up,' shouts Conor.

Taylor raises the volume another notch. Then Jamie comes over and takes her in his arms and starts to walk up and down with her, patting her back and just walking and walking and walking. And the screams stop and now they're just tiny sobs and Jamie tries to sit down but we won't let him, Conor and me.

'I'm wrecked,' says Jamie after about twenty minutes.

'Keep going,' says Conor, 'but don't walk in front of the telly – I love this film.'

'Is she asleep yet?' I ask, stretching my legs.

'Nope. Every time I think she is and I stop then the eyes open again.'

'So keep it up,' I say.

'Man, she's heavy.'

I shrug.

The movie is nearly over by the time Taylor falls asleep properly. And Conor and Ruby are asleep too. I throw a rug over them and then go to the kitchen with Jamie in search of food. We find coco pops and a half a carton of milk. We stuff the cereal into our mouths and it reminds me of years ago in the old house next to Chung's when Jamie and I'd race each other eating cereal. He always won.

We hear voices before the key turns in the front door. Mam's voice like an excited girl's and Rod's voice, deeper, quieter. They stumble into the kitchen, eyes bright, voices giggly.

'I asked him if he knew, Rod, and he just smiled and ...' My mother's voice trails off as soon as she sees Jamie.

'Oh,' says Rod.

You'd swear Jamie was a disease that had popped in for a bowl of cereal.

'Jamie called – lucky he did. He was the only one that Taylor'd go to when she woke up – for nearly three hours,' I say.

My mother doesn't look at me. She busies herself making tea. Jamie's just sitting there like a stray dog. My anger volcano rumbles and the vein over my eye twitches. A silence falls in the kitchen, except for the tea making. Rod throws Ruby into the garden and she whines now at the door, standing up on her hind legs like a human trying to get back in.

'I'd like you to leave, Jamie.' My mother's voice is low and calm.

Jamie sits there, frozen to the seat. My vein is dancing now.

'We talked. Rod and I talked and we feel you're not in the right place to have a relationship with me.' She keeps her back to him while she says this. Rod leans against the doorway, looking at his nails. I know that trick. The nail trick.

'Please give me some space, Jamie. Maybe down the road ...'

'You're a fucking bitch, do you know that? A fucking bitch is all you are and you shouldn't be allowed to have children – space? You had four years of space you f–'

'Stop it,' shouts Rod. 'This is what I told Lucy tonight. This shit has to stop. This is my family and I will not have any more of these bust-ups and upsets and robbery.'

'Robbery?' says Jamie. 'I didn't rob anything.'

Rod glares at him. 'You did. You guilt-tripped your mother until she handed you money and it's over. No more. Leave her alone.'

Mam's pretending to wash the dishes but I know she's crying. Her shoulders are shaking. Jamie stands up slowly, looks at me as if to say I told you so. I told you the hope wouldn't last. I told you that the long fingers were flexing themselves, waiting to pounce. I told you I'm a dead man walking.

'Have the guts to say it. Don't let your boyfriend do your dirty work. Have the guts to say it. To his face,' I say, walking towards her. She flinches as if I'm going to hit her or something. Rod puts up a warning hand to me.

The patio door slides open and Ruby bounds in as Jamie leaves.

The vein over my eye is about to burst.

'I hate you for that. I hate you and I wish you were dead.'
I whisper this into her ear.

'Enough,' says Rod.

'I agree,' I say. 'I'm getting my brother before I leave.'

I march into the living room and shake Conor awake.

'What's wrong? Where are we?' he mumbles, rubbing his eyes. 'Are we at home?'

'No, that's the last place we are. Come on, get up, let's go,' I say, dragging him to his feet. I pull him after me into the kitchen. Mam and Rod are hugging and he's kissing her tears. I almost fall over the stripy beach bag with my Gone Book still inside. Never opened. I pick up the bag and take out the book. She looks over in time to see me drop the empty bag on the floor.

'Fuck you,' I say.

'Stop it right now,' says Rod.

'Fuck you too, Rod.' I drag Conor out the door.

Things are supposed to be better in the morning but it's not true. The rain arrives for a start. Heavy, non-stop rain pouring from a grey-black sky. Lahinch looks different now. Desolate and miserable. The streets are empty and I keep thinking that tumbleweed should roll down the hill like in *Red Dead Redemption*.

Conor and I are in the caravan waiting for Dad. His phone is off and I'm praying that he'll remember to collect

Conor. I've packed my bag too. Mikey and I are barely talking and I just want to get away now. The shit seems way more concentrated here than in Limerick.

It's five now and I'm losing hope. We've been playing cards, Conor and me. Mrs Chung took the others to the cinema in Ennis. She couldn't bear the noise of the children and the rain in the caravan. I try Dad's number again and Conor watches, eyes blinking. No luck. I try Jamie's number and that's off too. I should have handled Mam better. I could have coaxed her. Guilted her.

'Let's play Snap again,' says Conor.

I roll my eyes but deal the cards anyway. As we play, he glances out the window whenever a car passes by.

'You hungry?' I ask eventually.

He shakes his head and studies his cards.

'We could get a Chinese? I've money.'

'Where's Jamie?' He's still studying his cards.

'He's gone home.'

'Why's he a dead man walking? What does it mean?'

Jesus. Fuck.

'Am, it doesn't mean anything really. It's like ... he's fallen out with someone and –'

'Are you a dead man walking?'

'No.'

'You've fallen out with Mikey, so why aren't you a dead man walking?'

Christ. I pull off the go-go on my ponytail and put it back on again. Just for something to do.

'Well ... I'm not –'

Conor jumps up and cards fly into the air. He's smiling, as he runs to the door. For a second, I think that I've sorted him out and then I hear a car horn beep and there's Dad and Rocky, standing on the deck. Conor hurls down the steps and throws himself full force at Dad. He hugs Conor to him, a real hug, and beams at me in the flogging rain. Rocky joins the love-in, licking any body parts he can. I drag our bags down the steps. Rain empties itself on me as I load up the boot.

'You coming home too?' Dad says.

I nod and rub Rocky's wet snout. His scabby back has cleared up. He looks handsome now. And happy. He tries to give me the paw.

'I came third.' Dad high-fives Conor. 'That's good, isn't it?' I watch him as he pushes Rocky by the wet arse into the back seat. 'I'm happy with that. Big race like. So, was Lahinch fun?'

'Yeah. Grand.' I sit into the car. It smells of wet dog and sweaty runners and Deep Heat. It smells like home. We pass rows of mobile homes; they look miserable and lonely without the sun. Children's faces press against the windows, waiting for a break in the clouds. Grey sea and sky roll into each other, broken only by a few white-horse waves in the distance. It feels like summer is over. I want to go home.

24

It's like a week since Lahinch and the last time I saw Jamie. It's Saturday and I stand on the balcony playing God, watching the tiny people and the traffic below me. Dad and Conor are gone to UL swimming and then they're taking Rocky for a walk along the bank. I'm tempted to call at Anna's, ask her to come with me searching for Jamie. She has a boyfriend now, some posh lad from Adare.

Mikey – fucking cheek of him. He sends me a text out of the blue this morning.

Wanna go cinema later?

After all the shit he's caused, he wants me to go on a fucking man-date to the cinema with him? I spit over the edge of the balcony and watch as it plummets to the pavement below. I go inside and close the door. I love this flat now. It's like a nest, a cocoon away from everything. No neighbours unless you want them. No passers-by. No small talk or bullshit. I go in and lie on my bed. The room is spotless – Dad was on a cleaning spree this morning. I notice something sticking out of my wardrobe. I go over and pull it out. It's my Gone Book. I was sure I'd left that under the bed. Right under the bed – so far in you had to crawl under to reach it. I take it out and touch it and pray Dad didn't see it. Read it. I open it up at the last page and search for a pen. I stare then at the blank page. I write one word – *Lahinch* – and then cross it out. I've nothing to say. Nothing at all. I fling the book under the bed and try Jamie's number again. It rings out. I lie back down on the bed and start dozing. I'm turning into such a lazy fucker lately. I don't go skating in case I meet Anna and her lovely not angry or scary boyfriend from Adare. My eyes close and I nearly scream when my phone rings.

I fumble for it on the bed and nearly drop it when I see Jamie's name on the screen.

'Man, I ... sorry, man ... I just, like ... I ...'

'Jamie? Jamie? Where are you?'

'They fucked me over ... man ... help me ...'

'Where are you?'

'At the flat ... just got back now ... God, I'm dizzy ... fuck ...'

I hang up and run out the door, forgetting to close it and having to double back.

I'm ages standing at the door ringing the bell. I think now that Jamie was lying to me, maybe he was out of his head somewhere, talking through his arse. I'm just about to leave when the door opens slowly. His face is a mess – one eye closed shut and swollen, fat and purple, scrapes and bruises on his arms. He's walking slowly, like an old man, hissing groans as he moves.

'Fuck sake – what happened?'

He eases himself onto a leather couch. There's a space on the wall where the huge flat screen used to be. The room looks bare.

He shrugs. 'They were OK about it.'

'OK about beating the shit out of you?'

'It could have been a lot worse.'

'I've been ringing and texting. Where the fuck were you?'

'Hammer and me hid out in Ennis but you have to face it sometime. You can't run away from them.' He groans again and tries to cough.

'You need to go to the hospital. I'll ring Dad, he'll –'

'No, you fucking won't. He'll be all AA and holy and shit. I'm grand. They've given me a bit of time. Took pity on me.'

'Nice of them.'

Jamie smiles. 'It is, really. Look, I was going to try Mam again – you know, on my own.'

'Jesus – not looking like that you can't.'

'I was going to write a letter. Look – I even bought paper and envelopes and stuff.'

I glance to the floor beside him. Envelopes. A copybook. A packet of biros.

'I'm going to write to her. Explain it all. And ask if I can see her. Just to talk.' He drops his head into his hands. His shoulders shake. 'I'm so fucked Matt, so fucked ... I want to die. I should just kill myself ...'

'Shut up, Jamie.'

'No, seriously. I fucking hate myself. This is all so shit.'

He looks up at me, his eyes fill with tears, his face elastic with the effort of not crying. He swallows hard and sniffs.

I stand there, like a gowl, not knowing what to say or do. I've never seen Jamie like this. Before he turned into a shit, he was funny, clever and quiet. After he turned into a shit, he became arrogant, cocky and stupid. When he turned into a giant shit, in recent weeks, the stupidity grew and kind of swamped everything else.

But I believe him now. I think that the old Jamie, the real Jamie, wants to come back and that this horrible version's time is up. I know by the hurt in his face. Fuck Mikey anyway. And fuck me too. Fuck me being a selfish bastard. Running off to Lahinch, thinking I was entitled to stuff – like a holiday, a surfboard. A fucking mother. I shouldn't have said anything to Mikey. It wasn't his fault – it was mine.

'I want to help. I'll talk to Mam. I'll sort it out. I swear I will, Jamie, I promise you. Scout's honour ...'

'Do you think there's a chance?'

'It'll work. I'll talk to her, arse-lick Rod. Then she'll get the letter – a fucking letter? Nobody gets letters these days – she'll be delighted and she can tell everyone about it and then she'll help. She can't say no to both of us. I'll bring the letter.'

'No. It should be posted,' Jamie says. 'Much better if it's posted.'

'Good idea. Do it today. I think it'll work. And if it doesn't then we have to tell Dad.'

Jamie cracks his knuckles. 'That's never happening.'

'Where's Hammer?'

'Out on bail and hiding. They're gunning for him in case he snitched. I'm starving, Matt.'

'Do you want a takeaway?'

He nods and closes his eyes. I search my pockets, hoping I have cash, and find a tenner rolled in a tight ball.

'Garlic chips,' says Jamie, his eyes still closed. 'And a battered sausage.' Then he laughs but it sounds like a groan.

I run down the street to the brilliantly named Chip Shop and order our food. It's empty except for me. The greasy smell is thick in the air. The only sound is the fat fryer bubbling. While I'm waiting for the food, I try to think of ways to get money. I've three hundred euro in the Credit Union and I wonder now if I could get a loan? And the letter to our mother might work. All I need is three grand.

I let myself back into the apartment, wondering how long more Hammer and Jamie can stay here without paying rent. The hallways smell new and unlived in. He sits up as I come into the room. He looks better. Or maybe I'm just getting used to the bruised eye and battered face. We eat in silence, except for the munching. Jamie's starving, wolfing down the hot food as fast as he can shove it into his mouth.

'Sgood,' he says, mouth full of sausage. 'Fucking shtarving.'

I give him my chips too and he hoovers them up. Then belches loudly.

'Feel better now,' he says.

'Nothing like a feed when you're hungry.'

'No, I don't mean that. I mean about the plan. Mam and stuff. The letter.'

'Yeah.'

He curls up on the couch. I'm sitting on the floor by his feet. He drops off to sleep and I tidy up a bit and stick his phone into the wall to charge. I'm just heading towards the door when he calls me.

'Hey, man, you forgot something.'

'No, I didn't,' I say, patting myself down.

'Her address. Mam's address. I don't have it. Here, write it down.'

He throws me the pack of envelopes and I catch them. Then the pack of biros follows. He goes back to sleep. I open the pack and take out a snow-white envelope. Then a biro. A red one. I stop for a second, just a split second, and wonder should I give him the address at all. But my doubt only lasts an instant. This is his last chance. I scribble her address on the white rectangle. Just as I'm walking out the door, Hammer comes in.

'Fucking bastard,' he says, launching himself at me. I try to push him off but I stumble and then he's on my back trying to stick his fingers in my eyes. Then he finds the ponytail, the stupid fucking ponytail, and he swings out of it like Tarzan and I actually think he's going to pull it off along with my whole face. Then Jamie's pulling him away and Hammer loses the plot completely and he's roaring like a mad man and I pick up the nearest thing I can find, a stainless-steel lamp, and belt Hammer full force across the head, just missing Jamie's good eye. They both fall to the ground. Jamie rolls off Hammer. The air is full of the fight, sweat and anger and hate.

Hammer isn't moving. His face is white. So white he looks like he has vampire make-up on. Jamie staggers to his feet. 'Jesus, my ribs,' he says.

'Look, Jamie.'

'What?'

'The blood. There's blood coming out of his nose.'

'Where?' He bends down again, groaning with the effort. 'Fuck.'

'Is he ...? Did I ...?'

Jamie lays his head on Hammer's heart, and then shakes him hard.

'Is he dead? Oh fuck, what'll we do? Oh man, I killed someone – I'm a fucking murderer.' I punch the wall beside me. Punch it so hard I think my fingers crack.

'Stop, you ape, calm the fuck down,' says Jamie, grabbing my hand before I can land another punch at the wall. The punch lands on him instead. 'Jesus, how many more beatings in one day?' he says, grabbing my two hands this time.

Then the tears come. Stupid tears. I lay my head on Jamie's shoulder and cry. Jamie pats me awkwardly on the back. 'It's OK, Matt, fuck it, it's OK,' he says.

'How? How is it OK? I killed Hammer,' I say into his shoulder, the words mumbly because of the snot and tears.

'I'll say it was an accident. That you weren't here. I'll take the blame,' he says but that only makes me cry harder. There's a loud groan.

'You all right?' I ask, lifting my face and looking at him.

He nods. Another groan and we both look down at Hammer. He's sitting up, blood pouring from his nose like somebody turned on a tap in his nostril.

'Fuck sake,' says Hammer. 'My nose is fucked from coke.'

I grin at Jamie.

'Any gear?' says Hammer.

That makes us crack up.

25

I see Anna out of the corner of my eye. She's in the skate park. She's never in the park on a Sunday, she has to do Mass and shit with her parents. But there she is now showing off for Adare Boy, grinding and ollying and being a bitch and Adare Boy's loving it, sitting there watching her little display and loving every minute of it.

So I jump on my board and give a little wave like I'm just passing by and I keep going, not stopping until I hit the lights at Henry Street. Fuck. I can't even skate now in my own skate park. I glide up O'Connell Street, Sunday-afternoon quiet, and head towards Tait's Clock. I skate slowly, finding a rhythm. All I can hear is the soft thunk of the board on concrete, the whir of the wheels, the low hum of traffic. I don't know how much time passes, it could be minutes or hours but all the stuff in my head settles down, relaxes. I know what I have to do. I have to talk to Mam. Tonight.

I sit on the steps of the clock and text Mam.

Calling over tonight. 8 OK?

I break out my water and my badly squashed Nutella sandwich. I'm starving and wolf down the bread in two bites. I throw the water bottle into my backpack and check my phone. Nothing. I plan what I'm going to say to her in my head. I'll bring the Gone Book and read it to her if things don't go my way. Although she'll just block out anything she doesn't want to hear. My phone beeps a text.

Please call wd love to see you.

First contact with her since Lahinch.

I jump on my board and head down Cecil Street. Early drinkers knot outside Collins's, pulling on fags. A black cat skirts by me, expertly dodging the board. I wobble and almost crash into a pair of legs sticking out of a doorway. Fuck sake. Junkies. I'm almost past when something bothers me. The shoes. Dark red Etnies that cost a lot of money. And you can't get them in Ireland – you have to get them online. Smart's favourites. I double back. He seems to be asleep, head drooping onto his chest, hair matted and dirty.

'Hey.' I kneel down and shake him gently.

Smart opens his eyes. They're unfocused, glazed, like he's a million miles away. He's grinning though, and his eyes are closing.

'You OK?' I shake him again.

His eyes open and he squints in concentration at my face. 'Man ...'

'Smart – what are you doing? Fuck sake.'

'Man, I took your board, man. I'm sorry. I took it man ... needed money ...'

I drop my hand from his shoulder.

He smiles at me – a spaced-out goofy grin. 'I'll pay you back, swear ... scout's honour bro ...' His eyes close. I stand up and jump on my skateboard, afraid that if I stay I'll thump him like I did Hammer and this time I won't be able to stop. Smart. Smart took the fucking board. Anger boils inside me, black and murderous. No amount of skating will calm it.

Dad's made fajitas. He has the table set and Conor's already eating and Rocky's in his favourite place under the table, his head on Conor's lap.

'Hungry?' Dad says.

I nod.

'Mikey called.' Conor says this through a huge mouthful of bread.

'So?' I pile my fajita with salad and salsa. This is my favourite dinner. Dad's whistling a song, 'Golden Brown', by an ancient band called The Stranglers. He sits down opposite me, his plate piled high with food.

'Just saying,' says Conor.

'What did he want?' I take more garlic bread. Rocky nudges me under the table.

'You,' says Dad, putting salsa on his salad but dead-eyeing me.

I shrug.

'Talk to him, Matt. He's your oldest friend – they're hard to come by,' says Dad.

I ignore him, just feed Rocky instead.

I'm just around the corner from my building when he comes at me from out of thin air.

'Fuck off,' I say, walking faster.

'Hello to you too,' Mikey says, trying to keep up with me.

'Fuck off, you bastard.'

'I miss you.'

'Shut up, weirdo.' I speed up and he's panting now trying to stay with me. We're down by Arthur's Quay and I'm walking like those walker fellas in the Olympics, arms flying, legs almost breaking into a run. Why the fuck didn't I bring my board?

'I'm going to follow you until you talk to me,' he pants.

'Best of luck with that,' I say.

'You miss me too. Go on, admit it – you miss my jokes.'

'Never.'

'Bet you do. How many amoebas does it take to change a light bulb? One, no two, no four, no eight, no –'

'Shut up.'

'How many women with PMS does it take to change a light bulb? None – you can do it yourself, dammit. How many heterosexual males does it take to change a light bulb in San Francisco? Both of them. How many –'

'Shut the fuck up, you retard,' I shout, turning to face him.

He grins. 'A break, at last – knew it'd work.'

'Gowl.'

'Douche. My Little Ponytail.'

I smile in spite of myself at this. Mikey takes this as encouragement and grins back. 'Fuckwit.' His grin scrunches up his face.

'Dipstick.' I don't smile.

'Prick.' He's still grinning.

'Fuckbag. Tell-tale-fucker-upper. Retard thick-bastard fuckhead.'

'You're cheating,' he says.

'How?'

'Repeating. You can't repeat them or just put fuck before words. That's cheating – shows an awful lack of imagination, like something Hammer would do ...'

The minute he has the name out, he knows he's made a mistake. The word hangs in the air like pollution.

'I'm sorry.' He drops his eyes to the ground.

I shrug. 'What's done is done.'

Mikey seems to brighten at this. Like it's forgiveness.

'Where are you going?'

'My mother's.'

'I'll walk with you – could do with the exercise.'

I shrug again.

It's only nine o'clock but already the nights are getting shorter. Summer is nearly over. Thank fuck for that. We walk in silence for a while but I up the pace every now and again, just to make him sweat.

'Story with Anna?' he says, his breath raspy.

I shrug again. It's a night for shrugs.

'Saw her with that skinny fella – face like a hamster?'

I can hear the grin in Mikey's voice. Along with the panting.

'Bet he doesn't kiss her, bet he nibbles her,' he says.

I smile at this. At the idea of it.

'Bet he keeps his nuts in his cheeks,' he says.

I want to laugh but swallow it. I'm still mad at Mikey – at his sheer dumbness.

'Bet he sleeps in a hutch and skates on a wheel and pisses himself – hamsters piss themselves all the time. We had a hamster once – Nuthead – and I swear he pissed himself to death.' Mikey guffaws, a high-pitched screechy sound, and I know he's trying way too hard now. I want him to go. Too much too soon.

'I know who took my board.'

Mikey stops dead in the street. 'Hammer took it. I know he did.'

I shake my head.

'He defo took it – nobody else would, Matt. I know he did. I know he fucking did.'

I shake my head again. Mikey looks like he's about to cry.

'Hammer took it and sold it and ...' Mikey pleads.

'Smart.'

Mikey inhales sharply. 'Smart?' His voice is a whisper. He knows it's true.

I nod. 'I met him – out of his tree – and he said it straight out.'

'Fuck me – fuck me pink and sideways too. Fuck me.' Mikey pats his pockets and takes out a packet of fags and a lighter. 'Fuck me pink,' he says as he lights up a fag.

I start walking again.

'This is so fucked up, Matt. I want to fix it – I want ...'

I keep walking. There's nothing to say, no fixing, no words to help with the fixing.

'Look, I'll go to the guards and tell them Hammer is innocent and I lied to get him in trouble and –'

'What about the gear they found in Hammer's car?' I stop dead and face him. 'What about the fucking gear?'

'I'll tell them it was mine. I'll tell them I stashed it and ... and ... and why would I shop him if I knew it was stashed in his car?'

'You're finally getting the picture.'

'I'll think of something.'

'Think of this. The shades are the least of our worries. Who really owned the gear?'

'Hammer and Jamie?' he says, but I can hear the doubt in his voice.

I laugh, a mean laugh that makes Mikey look away from me. 'Three grand's worth gone, belonging to the big guys – the guys who'd chop off your dick and stir their tea with it.'

'Stop, Matt, shut up ...' Mikey's crying now, his voice shrill and choked up.

'So that's what you did, Mikey, with your great idea. That's how you fixed it.'

'I'll fix it, Matt, I'll ask my dad for the money, I'll ask my mother, she could go to the credit union, she –' He stops and looks at me, tears and snot running down his face. He shakes his head. He knows it's useless. 'Man, I'm sorry. I'm a lousy friend, aren't I?'

I shrug.

'Say it out loud, Matt. Go on, say it. I'm a lousy fucking friend – a fuck-up.'

It's not true. Mikey is an ace friend. I try to say this but the words won't come out. Pictures of Jamie's broken face flick in my head like a comic book. 'I have to go.'

'What are you going to do?' Mikey starts to trot beside me again. He wipes snot and tears with the sleeve of his hoodie.

'Beg.'

'From who?'

'Anyone that'll listen. My mother, my father, the big guys if I have to ...'

'Fuck.'

'Fuck is right.' We've reached the turn-off to my mother's estate. I look at Mikey. 'Go home.'

He wipes his face again but misses a string of snot on his cheek. 'I'm sorry, Matt.' His voice is a whisper, a desperate whisper. He wants me to say it's OK. That things are OK between us.

'It's ... what's done is done, man.' I can almost feel his pain but something inside me won't let me make it OK for him. He has to suffer too. I walk up the path towards Mam's. Mikey's standing outside under a streetlight, still trying to wipe snot from his face. I try to say it again. No words come, just a little half-wave. Maybe I'll be able to say it next week. Or the week after.

26

I ring the doorbell. Mikey's still standing like a fucking eejit on the footpath. Just standing there looking at me. I turn my back on him and watch the hanging baskets sway slightly in the night breeze. The flowers are dying and I think that Mrs Chung would never allow that in her flower baskets – dying flowers mixed in with the good ones.

There's no answer and I wonder now if Mam forgot I was calling. Just completely forgot even though I'd texted and all. Maybe something really important came up – like a fucking manicure or a night out with Rod. I put my ear to the door and hear a faint yipping. Lamb-dog is there. Then the door opens and I almost fall into the hallway.

'I rang the bell but –' The sight of my mother's face stops me talking. She's been crying and did a hasty job of trying to clean up streaked mascara.

'Matt.' Her voice quivers.

'Are you all right?' I ask as I push past her into the hall. I can smell air freshener. Lots of it. And some kind of polish. There's a lamp turned over on the glass and steel hall table. I pick it up and straighten it and turn around again to face my mother.

'Oh fuck,' I say as a shadow emerges from the stairway. 'What's going on?'

She starts to cry then, tiny jerky little-girl sobs. The shadow, a tall man in a rubber rabbit mask, pushes her towards me.

'Kitchen,' he says in a very bad American accent.

I obey, my knees buckling with the effort of walking. I want to piss so badly I think my insides are going to burst. The kitchen is dark, just one lamp on, but I can see Rod in a chair, his hands bound tight in front of him with a plastic tie. He has a cut over his forehead. He looks terrified. Another man, wearing a Donald Trump mask, stands by the sink, arms folded across his chest. There's a knife gleaming on the worktop next to him. A long, thin, deadly looking one.

'There's no need for no-one to get hurt,' says Trump. 'This bastard just needs to get the money from the bank.' He's trying too for the American accent with less success than Rabbit.

'I don't *have* keys for the bank. I'm just security – that's all. We have no money –'

Trump shuts Rod up with a closed-fist punch into the head. 'Shut up. This is a fucking tiger kidnapping and we're not leaving here without the money. I don't care if you have to shit it. We don't give a fuck, sure we don't J–'

He stops himself saying the name but he doesn't have to. I know who he is. Who they are.

I turn around to face Rabbit. He won't look at me.

'Bastard.' I stare at him but he keeps his eyes on the floor.

'I swear, we have no money – we live on credit cards. Tell them, Lucy, tell them,' says Rod.

My mother is crying hard, her make-up sliding down her face like a mask melting. 'Don't hurt us, don't hurt our baby, please don't. Rod's just a security guard, that's all ...' She starts wailing then and Trump looks from one to the other and then punches Rod again, a full-force blow to the jaw. Rod's nose spouts a spray of blood over the shiny white tiles in a perfect arc.

'Stop it. Stop it now,' I say to Rabbit, stepping closer to him. 'Leave now, and we'll say nothing about any of this. I promise. Scout's honour.'

A tiny cry escapes from Rabbit's throat.

'Don't listen to him, he's lying, they're all lying,' says Trump. 'This fucker has a fancy job in the bank and he can get us the money – can't you, fuckface?'

Rod gets another slap across the head. Then Trump picks up a can of Coke and tries to drink some, forgetting he has the mask on.

'Fucking hell,' he splutters as Coke joins the blood on the floor. It's almost funny, the whole thing, if I was watching it and not in it. These two must be the worst tiger kidnappers in history. More cubs than tigers.

'You tricked me,' I say to Rabbit. He shakes his head.

'Do you know them?' Rod asks. He gets another belt into the ear.

'You tricked me. Your own brother.' I'm so close to him now I can smell the rubber from the mask.

'Jamie?' says Mam, her badger-eyes round. 'Jamie?'

'Fuck up,' says Trump.

'The address,' I say. 'You were never going to write a letter. You had this fucked-up plan in your head all the time, you were never –'

'You know fuck all. Nothing. Do you hear me? You know fuck all about fuck all. We are dead men walking and you think I've the time to write letters and rely on that bitch's help?' Jamie's voice is low and menacing.

'It's not her fault, Jamie. Ye drove around Lahinch with a car load of gear. It's ...'

Jamie picks up an ornament, a silver teddy with a picture of Taylor inserted in his belly. He looks at it and then at Mam.

'Don't, Jamie, or I'll –' Before I can finish he's hurled it at me, missing my head by a fraction but managing to shatter the glass door of a kitchen press instead.

'Oh God,' says Mam.

'Leave us alone. Please just go and we'll –' Rod is stopped again in mid-sentence by a clatter to his cheek.

'Her fault,' Jamie says, inclining his rabbit head towards

our mother. 'She fucked a sixth year in my school. Do you know that? A schoolboy, for fuck sake.'

This time I drop my eyes.

'She fucked him in Dad's bed and I came home early and she told me not to tell and gave me a tenner. That's our mother for you.'

'Shut it, Jamie. This isn't the time.' I still can't look at him.

Jamie whips off his mask. I sneak a look and his hair is stuck to his head with sweat. It makes him look like a kid.

'Man, why did you take off your mask? Now they saw your face, you retard,' says Trump.

'But I didn't keep quiet, sure I didn't, Mammy dear? I told Dad straight away and he caught them the next time. See Matt, she had times all worked out – she even had the calendar marked. Her fuck-dates with her little boy.'

'Jamie, please.' Mam's voice is a whisper. Rod's head is sunken into his chest and I think he might actually be unconscious. Trump aka Hammer is all ears.

Jamie's crying, tears streaming down his face. 'And do you know what she did, Matt? Her revenge?'

I shake my head and close my eyes. *No, I don't*, my brain whispers. *No, I don't.*

'She told Dad I wasn't his son. She told him that. Didn't you, bitch? Didn't you?'

'Man, I need a hit,' says Trump. His body is shaking.

I look at our mother and her eyes are vacant. She has tuned out. Closed her ears.

'Answer me, Mam. Tell the truth.' Jamie's crying again and the menace has gone from his voice. 'Please tell me, Mam. Dad won't do the DNA shit. Tell me if it's true. Tell me tell me tell me ...' He sinks to the floor, sobbing.

'It's OK, Jamie.' I slide down beside him and his crying gets harder. 'Hey man, it's OK. Dad's your dad – you're the head off him.' I put my arm around him and he cries into my shoulder. The rabbit mask grins up at me from the floor.

'It's her fault,' he mumbles into my shoulder. 'You were upstairs with a green blanket wrapped around you so tight and I told you and you just moaned and moaned and didn't hear me ...'

I close my eyes and see green. Everything is green and I can hear Jamie's voice, a child's voice, and our mother and Dad downstairs screaming at each other and Jamie crying and me not letting the words in, holding the blanket so tight around me that I can't breathe.

'And then she fucks off, Matt. Just like that. And she took my good gear bag with her. My Ireland gear bag.'

A new cry begins from the baby monitor on the table. A sniffly cry that develops very quickly into a wail. Our mother tunes back in and stares at the monitor. 'Taylor,' she whispers.

The dog takes the new crying as a signal to carry on. She bangs her fluffy white body against the back door.

'Fuck,' screams Trump, lunging towards the door. He fumbles with the lock. Mam makes a run for the hall. There's a face outside the back door. Mikey. I jump up from the floor and follow Trump as he lunges at the door. I tackle him just as he opens it and we crash out onto the patio.

We're in a circle. Me, Hammer with his Trump head and Mikey. There's a kind of calm, a silence, broken by Taylor's sobs and Jamie's matching ones. I reach out a hand towards Hammer. 'It's over.'

'Over? I'm in deep shit over that fucker,' says Hammer. He throws himself at Mikey and I jump on his back.

'Get off me, get the fuck away from me,' Hammer says, elbowing me into the ribs. I stumble backwards. Jamie's just crying, the gowl, sitting there bawling. Hammer's flexing his fists and launching himself at Mikey.

'Mikey, run,' I say, and wangle myself in front of Hammer. I put up my hands. 'Come on, Hammer. Chill, come on, man,' I say. Hammer dips his Trump head and I feel relief. Fucking hell.

'I'm going to fuck the two of you up, bastards, dead men walking.' Hammer says in a low mean voice. He leans into my face, fist raised and pulled back. Mikey pushes himself in front of me.

'Hit me. Leave Matt out of it. Go on, fuck me up,' Mikey says.

'Shut up, Mikey,' I say but it's too late. Hammer screams and punches Mikey full force into the head, fist closed. Mikey falls backward and his head hits the patio slabs with a sickening thud.

I'm staring at Mikey, sprawled on the flagstones, blood seeping from his ear. 'No,' I say. 'Please. No.'

Hammer looks at me and then at his still curled fist. 'Fuck. Fuck it – I didn't mean it, I swear,' he says, flexing his fist like it'll turn back the clock. He peels off his mask. 'I didn't mean it. I didn't, I didn't.' He sinks down and curls into a tight ball, holding his legs up to his chest. 'I didn't mean to hurt no-one, I didn't mean it. He hit his head on the ground. I didn't ...'

I crawl over to Mikey, swallowing vomit. Piss drenches my legs. So much piss and it makes me think of Mikey's hamster. 'Man,' I say, when I reach him.

'Hey,' says Mikey, trying to smile.

'Hey. You OK?'

He tries a grin. 'Fuck me pink – I just got decked by Trump.'

I laugh. There's a huge black patch of blood on Mikey's hoodie. His favourite Rip Curl hoodie. White. I'd warned him about white hoodies. You could never keep them clean.

Hammer's crying now, like a little kid. 'I want my dad, Jamie, will you call my dad? Jamie? I want my father. I didn't mean, I swear.'

'Call an ambulance, Jamie, for fuck sake,' I say, over my shoulder. Jamie doesn't move.

'Now,' I scream. 'Call a fucking ambulance.'

'Come closer,' says Mikey. His voice is a whisper.

'I'm here, man,' I say, lying down beside him, my face next to his. Jamie's above me, phone in hand, wet dark eyes staring down.

'I'm sorry, Matt,' says Jamie. 'I'm sorry. It's my fault. Mikey? Mikey? Are you OK?'

'Shut the fuck up, Jamie,' I say and turn my face towards Mikey.

'Buddies?' whispers Mikey. 'Right?'

I nod, gulp back stupid tears. 'Always.'

'I helped, didn't I? I helped you stop it.'

I nod. 'I know, Mikey. You're ... you're the best, like.'

'Got something for you,' he whispers. Then he smiles and lets off a huge fart. A long, low Mikey special.

Then Mikey coughs once and reaches for my hand. I hear the wail of an ambulance in the distance. Mikey closes his eyes. Like he's asleep.

'Don't, Mikey. Wake up. The ambulance is coming – listen, can you hear it? Wake up, Mikey, please wake up.'

Mikey's eyes are closed tight. I lie there, Hammer crying and calling for his dad, Jamie's ghost face above me, the ambulance screaming its arrival. My mother's voice is there too in the mix and a neighbour's TV blares tinny voices into the night. There are no stars in the sky.

24 September 2019

I miss you. Everybody said it'd get easier but it hasn't. I miss you so fucking much it hurts. You'll be happy to know I haven't surfed since Lahinch. Haven't skated either. I just can't because I'm afraid it'll make me feel good and I can't feel good. Not ever again. And guess what? The fat is creeping back. There's a nice new ring of it around my waist. I love that ring of fat like a drowning man loves a lifebuoy. What would you call a lifeguard with no legs? Bob! Fat is good because it makes me feel bad. The fatter the better. Rocky's here beside me on the couch. You'd love him now – he's the king here.

Shit happens. What's done is done. Forgive and forget. Onwards and upwards. These are the things that people keep saying to me. None of them are true. They're just phrases people use because they don't know what to say or do. Dad's the best though. He says none of those stupid fucking things. He says nothing at all. But he's there. All the time. And he's there for Jamie too.

Your Mam was right. She doesn't give a fuck really. It's all about her. Do you know what she did? She fucked off again. Just like that. A week after it all happened she was gone. I went back out there. To the house. Not to see her or anything. Just to stand in the garden for a while. Talk to you a bit maybe and the house was deserted. I looked in the windows and everything was cleared out. Nothing left except a toy elephant on the shiny kitchen floor. I climbed over the wall into the garden.

But I couldn't feel you there at all. It just looked like a brown piece of grass and a stone patio. That's all. So ordinary and harmless looking. I'm not angry though about her any more. Dad is right. She sees the world the way a teenager does. Her growing-up gene is fucked, mutated.

I went to see your mother too – hardest thing I ever did in my whole life. She got a shock when she saw me and then she cried. So did I. Bet you love all this crying shit! She looked different – so quiet and not alive? Does that sound mad? She looked the way I feel. The United Colours were quiet too.

She made me stir-fry. Asked about Jamie – which was big of her. I told her he's like a new man – back at school all focused and shit – I'm the fuck-up in the family now. Him and Dad are best buds – imagine that. She liked that – your mother. We never mentioned other stuff. Hammer. That night. You. I cried the whole way home. See? I'm turning into a pussy for sure.

School is shit without you. You did good in your Junior Cert man. I did better but then you've shit for brains, right? I can't bear anywhere that reminds me of you. So that means every-where – like the whole of Limerick – is out of bounds. Skate Park, town, UL, McDonalds – especially McDonalds. And The Chopstick – man I can't even think of going in there – looking at your dad. And school. You're all over that school and I have to go there every day. Yesterday Ryano called your name during roll call by mistake. He went bright red and they all laughed and looked at me. I don't know what they thought I'd do – cry maybe – but I smiled at them. Grinned even.

You were right about the credit union and I laughed when you said it. Dad got a loan from them and paid off the big guys. Said it was for a new bathroom. Hammer's on remand. Don't kill me (joke ha ha!) for saying this but I feel sorry for him. I think you would too. He took the blame for everything, never shopped Jamie at all. He tried to kill himself two weeks ago but that could be a rumour. Jails are desperate for rumours. Dad says that, though how would he know seeing as he was never in jail? AA maybe. Sure they know everything! I'm getting worse than you with the bad jokes. I never thought I'd say this but I miss the jokes. Even the dumb ones. This is like the longest thing I ever wrote in my life – man – my hand hurts. It feels good – talking to you like this I mean – not the pain in my hand. And yeah I know – I'm a pussy but ... hang on there's someone ringing the stupid doorbell over and over brb ...

27

I get up from the couch and shove the book down the back of it. The doorbell buzzes non-stop; the person just keeps a finger on it all the time. I go out to the hall and open the door. Anna.

'Yeah?' I say, looking her up and down. She's taller, skinny and her hair is longer. She has a ponytail just like mine. Curly eyelashes and no baseball cap. She's turned into a girl. She's still carrying her skateboard, though.

'Aren't you going to ask me to come in?' She smiles. She has the nicest eyes ever. The colour of Galaxy chocolate.

I shrug and go back into the living room. She follows.

Anna opens the patio door and hangs over the balcony.

'What are you doing?'

She grins at me. 'Checking to see who's in the skate park.'

'Why?'

She comes back in but leaves the door open. I can hear the dull whoosh of traffic below. 'Avoiding somebody – but I'm dying for a skate. Want to come?'

I shake my head. 'Nope. Who are you avoiding?'

'Long story.'

'So tell me.'

She cocks her head to one side and examines me with her eyes – exactly like Ryano does in maths class when he knows you've no homework done. 'Naw. You're not interested.'

'Bit harsh.' I stare at her.

'Not harsh enough, Matt.'

'What do you mean?'

She shrugs. 'I'm just sick of you, moping and moaning and sitting on your arse all the time. You're such a waste of space these days. You never go out, never text me back, never –'

'Fuck off.' I stand up and point at the door. Rocky jumps off the couch and heads for the door. He thinks he's in trouble.

She's brazen now: hand on her hip, eyes blazing anger, like lasers directed straight at me. 'No, I won't fuck off. Not this time. You've told me that since ... since he died ... and I'm sick of it. Sick of you.'

'So why do you keep calling?' I take a step towards her.

She drops her head and when she looks up, I see tears. Tiny ones squeezing out of her eyes. 'I lost a friend too, you know,' she says, her voice low. 'In fact, I lost two friends. I lost him and I lost you.'

This stuns me. I don't know what to say. She wipes her tears away with her sleeve but more spring out to take their place. 'I'm sorry,' I say.

She cries harder.

'I'm sorry, Anna. For all of it. I'm a useless friend – a fuck-up of a friend.' Mikey's face is in my head, a collection of images, smiling, laughing, mad, eating. 'He was a great friend.'

She nods.

'He ... that night he wanted me to tell him that we were OK – pals again – and I couldn't. He stood in front of me ... Hammer was going for me first and Mikey ...' My voice chokes.

'Where's your board?' she says.

'Hall, but –'

She's gone. I follow her and Rocky follows me, and before I know what's happening we're out on the street carrying our boards, walking towards the park. The sun is low on the river, making the whole place golden.

'Jasper,' she says, as she hops on her board and does an ollie almost on top of me.

'Jasper?' I jump on my board too. I'm a little shaky, though. It's been a while.

'Avoiding him. Jasper from Adare?' She stops and I crash right into her. 'You're a newbie, Matt – you're like a learner all over again.'

'So you ditched him? You ditched the Hamster?'

She grins. 'The Hamster? Oh my God the Hamster? That's brilliant – oh my God, that's hilarious.' She's holding her stomach, doubled over laughing.

'Thank Mikey for that one,' I say, jumping on my board. I'm steady this time and I try a kickflip. It's perfect. I glide away towards the park, Rocky at my heels.

'Wait up,' she calls from behind.

I go faster.

Hal and Black are sitting on one of the benches, a slab of beer between them. Black is stroking the slab as if it's his child. He grins when he sees me. He's lost more teeth, just two left on top now. 'It's the man,' he says, standing up. He sways on his feet. Hal pulls him back down and calls Rocky over to her. He sits at her feet, forgetting that she ever abandoned him outside Penneys.

Black eyes Anna and me. 'Want one?' he asks.

We shake our heads in unison.

'We're celebrating,' says Black.

'What's new?' I say, laughing. 'Ye're always celebrating.'

'Everything changes and nothing changes. Isn't that right, Hal?' Black says but keeps his eyes on me.

Hal cackles and lights up a rollie. 'Too right, Black, too right.'

'Cast a cold eye, my friend, cast a cold eye ...'

'Shut up, Black, spouting shit when you're drunk. You and your fancy words,' says Hal.

'On life, on death. Horseman, pass by!' says Black, making a sweeping gesture towards the river with his hand. We all follow his pointing finger and for a second I have a mad notion that a horseman will rise out of the water. The sun is very low and the Shannon is still and shimmery and glassy. A small boat glides down the river, a dark silhouette inside rowing and making ripples on the golden water. Anna slips her hand into mine, then leans in and kisses me lightly on the lips. I can taste lip gloss and banana. It's delicious. Then she punches me quickly in the stomach, jumps on her board and takes off skating. She does a beaut of a kickflip followed by a nollie, and then she comes back and circles me, teasing me.

'Race ya,' she says.

And I do.

ACKNOWLEDGEMENTS

I'd like to thank the Shannon Fields where I did the hard work, the thinking, plotting, untangling, all while shouting at the dogs to stay out of the river. I'd also like to thank the Chicken Hut – best gravy chips in Ireland. My Spanish Point bolthole deserves a mention as do my Bose noise-cancelling headphones. And Emmet and Sonia B's gaff for the edits. My publisher, Siobhán Parkinson of Little Island and my brilliant editor, Matthew Parkinson-Bennett: thank you for your brave, cutting-edge attitude. Huge thanks to Arts Council of Ireland for financial support while writing *The Gone Book*.

ABOUT HELENA CLOSE

Helena Close is a native of Limerick City in Ireland. She has been writing full-time for twenty years. She has written or co-written seven novels, published by Hodder Headline, Hachette Ireland and Blackstaff Press. She is Munster Rugby obsessed, and she loves cats and dogs and sometimes people. *The Gone Book* is her first young adult novel.

PRAISE FOR HELENA CLOSE

'Extraordinary, a remarkable book that expands the frontiers of Irish popular fiction.'

THE IRISH TIMES (for *The Cut of Love*)

'An impressive, relevant, and entertaining read. An absolute page turner.'

THE IRISH INDEPENDENT (for *The Clever One*)

ABOUT LITTLE ISLAND

Little Island Books has been publishing books for children and teenagers since 2010. It is Ireland's only English-language publisher that publishes exclusively for young people. Little Island specialises in new Irish writers and illustrators, and also has a commitment to publishing books in translation.

www.littleisland.ie

Little
Island